WHATEVER IT WAS,
IT WAS COMING CLOSER . . .

Johnsmith was scared. He forgot about the onees. This was just too real. He only wanted to get away from here before the encroaching *thing* was on top of him.

But it was too late.

It burst through the fog, a serpent's head on a long, sinuous neck. A dinosaur? No, more like a dragon. The head was stylized, ornamented, inanimate—it was the prow of a ship.

A Viking ship . . .

Other Avon Books by
Tim Sullivan

DESTINY'S END
THE PARASITE WAR

**And Don't Miss These Horrific Anthologies
Edited by Tim Sullivan**

TROPICAL CHILLS

Coming Soon

COLD SHOCKS

THE MARTIAN VIKING

TIM SULLIVAN

AVON BOOKS ◆ NEW YORK

AVON BOOKS
A division of
The Hearst Corporation
105 Madison Avenue
New York, New York 10016

Copyright © 1991 by Timothy R. Sullivan
Cover art by Ron Walotsky
Published by arrangement with the author
Library of Congress Catalog Card Number: 90-93607
ISBN: 0-380-75814-8

First Avon Books Printing: May 1991

AVON TRADEMARK REG. U.S. PAT. OFF. AND IN OTHER COUNTRIES, MARCA REGISTRADA, HECHO EN U.S.A.

Printed in the U.S.A.

RA 10 9 8 7 6 5 4 3 2 1

For Dad and Charlie

Acknowledgments

To the works of Philip K. Dick and Robert A. Heinlein; to Val Smith, John Douglas, the Dirda Family, S.P. Somtow; and to Roberta Lannes, defender of the constitution, as well as the faith.

"To the guest, who enters your dwelling with frozen knees, give the warmth of your fire: he who hath travelled over the mountains hath need of food, and well-dried garments."

—Scandinavian precept

ONE

THE GEATS WERE on Johnsmith Biberkopf's mind more and more these days. It was odd that this should be the case, since he had so many worries in the present—he was about to lose his job, his wife, and his sanity. Still, those seventh century Danish pirates managed to preoccupy him most of the time.

Maybe that was it. A life of carefree adventure, some fourteen hundred years in the past, seemed infinitely preferable to the anxious life that burdened him today. If he were Beowulf, his wife Ronindella wouldn't have walked out on him. She'd be too busy admiring his physical prowess. It wasn't just any man who could tear a monster's arm out at the socket with his bare hands; the most fearsome monster who had ever stalked Hrothgar's mead hall, at that.

Johnsmith could conjure up images of Beowulf on his screen and forget about the crowd of dozing academics in cubicles around him, but not for much longer. His tenure at the University was about to come to an end, and he had already been kicked out of the apt by Ronindella. Consequently, he'd been forced to take an effapt in one of the worst parts of the city. And now that the draft had been instituted, the jobless and the homeless were among the first to go to the moon, even selected ahead of volunteers. Life at a lunar camp wasn't something he looked forward to with much enthusiasm.

As Johnsmith watched the bright images of man and monster battling in medieval surroundings, he reflected on his previous feelings about the draft. He'd always thought it sort of unfair, but had continually reminded himself not to worry too much about it. The government frowned on activism, and you might end up in front of the Selective Space Service yourself, if you raised too much of a fuss about the injustice of it all. Besides, what good would it do? The poor *were* always with us, weren't they? (Not anymore, actually; now they were on the moon, or, in a few cases, on Mars or the Belt; but the principle still held.) He had happily maintained this ambivalent outlook until it became clear that he was soon to be eligible for the draft himself. That had radically changed his perspective.

"Beeb, I brought you something that might help."

Johnsmith looked up vacantly, seeing his colleague, assistant professor Ryan Effner, beaming down at him. "What is it, Ryan?"

"Something to help ease the tension." Effner drew closer and said in a low tone, "Some onees."

"Onees?" Johnsmith spoke loudly enough to make Effner wince.

"For Christ's sake, Beeb, they're illegal," Effner hissed, his mouth set in a tight grimace as he glanced furtively about the room. He said nothing more until he was satisfied that the other professors, preoccupied by their work, had not heard Biberkopf's surprised exclamation.

"I'm sorry, but I don't understand how the . . . how they can help me."

Effner removed a film canister from an inside pocket of his fluorescent green waistcoat and set it under the screen, at the very moment that Beowulf dove into a misty lake in search of Grendel's mother.

"Still watching the old stuff, huh?" Effner observed.

"Yeah, I even read *Beowulf* once or twice."

Effner whistled. "That's dedication above and beyond the call, my man. How long did it take you to get through it?"

"Oh, I don't know. A few hours."

"Don't you think it's enough just to know the story, to watch it once in a while so you can remember the details?"

"Rye, you know what I think about that. It was an oral epic originally, so people in our position ought to at least know what the words sound like."

"You can get a program that recites the poem while you watch the action." Ryan nodded toward the screen. "I mean, you've even got a flat screen here. Surely you can get the department to invest in a 'gram."

"It's not the same. All the nuances are lost on projectograms, anyway. You've got to know the poem."

"Then listen to it a few times, and figure out the . . . nuances." Effner made a face in distaste, as if he thought the word were somehow harmful to him. "Look, Beeb, your students don't relate to you when you use terms like that. And you can't expect them to understand something written over a thousand years ago. That stuff's too elitist. You're a teacher, so teach. Maybe you can still save your job."

"I don't think so."

"Take those onees when you go down to Triple-S for your physical, and maybe they'll decide you're too schizoid to go to the moon."

"From what I hear, schizophrenia will make me fit in perfectly up there." Johnsmith frowned and reached up to shut off the screen as Beowulf slashed away at a dragon with a bloody sword.

"Maybe, maybe not." Effner looked at him sadly. "What have you got to lose?"

"Nothing, I guess." Johnsmith stood and stretched.

"I'd rather go to Mars, but they'll probably assign me to a lunar mine."

"That's where they need people the most, I guess," Effner said.

"Well, my grandfather was a plumber," said Johnsmith. "I guess I can stand doing the work."

"I've heard that they've got an okay library on the moon. You can jack into it on your off hours."

"Yeah." Johnsmith stared at the dead screen, knowing that he would never look at it again. He was going to get his draft notice imminently, and he would be shipped off to the moon almost immediately thereafter.

"Look, I'll see you," Effner said awkwardly. He picked up the film canister and tucked it into Johnsmith's jacket pocket. "I've got to get back to work now."

"Sure. Thanks for your help." Johnsmith watched his friend's back for a moment, and then headed out of the faculty room himself. It was probably best to go home.

Outside the building, he stood under the sunshield, waiting for a bus. The university's gingerbread-castle-like buildings, erected late in the last century, seemed to mock his bleak mood. He would almost be glad to get away from the place now. If he stayed around here any longer, he would go nuts from depression and grief.

As he stepped out of a cleaning robot's way, he reflected bitterly that he'd only wanted to be a good teacher, and look what had happened. The administration had decided that he was an elitist, unfit for the faculty. And now that he was being mustered out, Ronindella refused to have anything to do with him. She wouldn't even let him see Smitty II, their son.

Maybe the last straw had been that lecture when he'd pointed out to the kids that not too many years ago it was not uncommon for people to have computers in the home—personal computers, they had called them in those days. Such a luxury was inconceivable today, of course, for all but the extremely wealthy. A one hundred thousand dollar item for the home was out of the question for the vast majority. And how could you be literate without a pc? The few books that were still available were prohibitively expensive, too, leaving those with access to the computerized library systems the only ones who could learn to read.

He had sinned twofold by telling his students about all this. First, he had implied strongly that the general standard of living had declined sharply under the Conglom, and then he had compounded his crime by tacitly suggesting that a society that could not read was somehow doomed to failure. These were not the things that the administration wanted an associate professor to say in front of his students. In fact, you could even get in trouble for saying it at a faculty party, if the wrong person were to hear you spouting off. And Johnsmith Biberkopf had done enough spouting off on such occasions, especially after a few drinks.

The whoosh of the bus caught him unawares. Its snub nose stopped on the rail a little past him, and it rested a couple of inches above the magnets as passengers got on and off. Johnsmith nearly collided with a woman as he hurried to get aboard. She was wearing a protective mask and hat, and he remembered that he had always meant to buy something to protect his skin from the UV rays. It was too late now; where he was going, he wouldn't need it. He'd be wearing a government issue pressure suit for the rest of his life, every time he went outside of the lunar compound. He just hoped they wouldn't give him one that leaked, like the pressure suits he'd heard about from time to time. People got letters claiming that loved ones had died on the moon while performing heroic actions, when all that had really happened was the poor bastard's suit had fallen apart while he or she was outside. It was probably pretty rare . . . at least Johnsmith hoped it was pretty rare.

He stood, holding onto an aluminum ring, since there

were no empty seats on the bus. The air conditioning wasn't working, but he didn't really mind sweating for a few minutes. Ignoring the smell of urine and the ubiquitous graffiti, he allowed his mind to drift, thinking of what he would do this evening, his last night of freedom; tomorrow he would appear before the Triple-S, and if, as he expected, they said he was going to the moon, that was it. He wished that his Dad was around to talk to about his sorry state. The old man had died at the tender age of forty-five, nineteen years ago. Johnsmith was almost that old himself now. It seemed hard to believe. He remembered his father railing against the concept of the Conglomerated United Nations of Earth when it was still in the planning stages of the UN. He said it was redundant, and a bad idea all around. And when Johnsmith's older brother, Eddy, had joined the Conglom Marines and was killed in the Jamaica flareup two years later, Harald Biberkopf had never gotten over it. He refuse to accept the government's line that his son had been sacrificed for some glorious principle of a united earth. He knew the war was designed to make the wealthy and powerful even more wealthy and powerful, and his son had paid for it with his life. Harald drank himself to death within a year. Johnsmith's mother hadn't understood the depth of Harald's despair. Kitty Biberkopf had married again, and was living in California quite comfortably to this day. She was content to believe that her first husband had lost his mind, but Johnsmith knew better. Harald's suspicions were proved correct, as far as he could see. And Johnsmith frequently wished that he could tell his Dad that.

Johnsmith decided that he might as well have a good time while he still could. He patted his jacket pocket. The onees were in there, right where Ryan Effner had put them. Johnsmith could enjoy one of these in the privacy of his miserable effapt this evening, of course. He was pretty sure that he really didn't have the nerve to take one before going down to the Triple-S tomorrow. But tonight was a different story.

Alderdice V. Lumumba shoved the robot out of the way. Its shovel-extension scraped along the pavement, as it droned, "Pardon me, sir."

Walking briskly, Alderdice tried to get on the bus without being conspicuous. He saw the man he was following nearly collide with someone getting off the bus, but then the other commuters obscured his vision. He couldn't fight his way through the stream of people in time. The bus vibrated and whooshed off toward the inner city. Biberkopf was getting away. Slightly winded, Alderdice ducked under the heat shield, and removed his sweat-stained borsalino. He really should have been wearing a mask, what with all this running around out in the UV; he was going to contract skin cancer if this kept up. The assignment was an easy one, except for the prolonged exposure to sunlight. Sometimes it was a full two to three minutes before he could find shade. That was just too much risk. Alderdice comforted himself with the hope that the job might be over soon . . . unless Biberkopf tried to shirk his duty, and skip out on his appearance before the board tomorrow. Then, and only then, Alderdice would move in. Otherwise, he would remain in the background until Biberkopf was sent to his new home on the moon, or, if the guy was lucky, on Mars.

Alderdice liked his job as a P.A. He got to move around a lot, and proudly felt that he was providing a valuable service for the government. Before the establishment of Pre-Emptive Agents, shirkers had to be traced through orthodox channels, which usually took months, sometimes even years. In many cases, the government never located the criminal. But if the potential shirker was under surveillance *before* the fact, apprehension was usually a simple matter.

Unless, of course, the P.A. bungled the job, which

Alderdice had been known to do on occasion. There was that woman who had gone to South America, for example. She had made it look as though she were going on a vacation prior to her appearance before the Triple-S, but the Agency had become suspicious when she booked a flight for Santiago. Alderdice had been put on her tail, but he had somehow missed the flight, even though his passage had been secured only minutes after the suspect had talked to her travel agent. She was never heard from again.

That had been his worst screw-up, ever. But there had been other, lesser mistakes lately, one right after another, ever since his husband Lon had left him. All minor stuff, but if he made one more boner like that Santiago flight he was going to be out of a job. He would then be put on the official government lists as a nonproductive person, and he, not some shirker, would be up in front of the Triple-S; and before you knew it *he* would be slaving away in some lunar pit. This was precisely what he had joined the Agency to avoid, of course, having no particular talents or skills that he could parlay into a career.

Another bus whooshed up to the stop, and Alderdice was relieved to see that few people got off. He bounded onto the bus and sat down in the nearest seat, hoping that Biberkopf hadn't flown the coop. This was the optimum period for that sort of thing, the day before the Triple-S hearing. How could he have lost the suspect at a time like this? Now he had to hope that Biberkopf didn't run away, and hope would not be enough if it happened.

As the city flew by in a sun-baked blur, Alderdice decided that the smartest thing for him to do was go directly to Biberkopf's effapt building, in the hope that the suspect had simply gone home. If Biberkopf wasn't there when Alderdice arrived, though, there was going to be big trouble.

* * *

"I almost ran into him on my way here, when I was getting off the bus," Ronindella said over the music, her pale but attractive face lined with worry as she glanced around the teacher's lounge. "I can't believe he didn't recognize me."

"You were wearing your mask and hat, and he's got a lot on his mind these days." Ryan Effner pointed at the sweating glass in front of her. "Finish your drink, and we'll get out of here. He might come back to clean out his desk or something."

"Okay." She downed her grappa and stood up. "You know, Ryan, he's got to find out the truth sometime."

"Not if he's on his way to the moon, he doesn't." Effner popped his credit card into the table slot and sucked the ice from his drink while he waited for the transaction to clear. "He'll be there for the rest of his life, and need never know that his wife's left him for his best friend."

"You say that so matter of factly, Rye."

"That's how it is." He snatched his reemerging card and stuffed it into his wallet. "We didn't ruin his life, we just happened to benefit from it."

"I guess so." They put on their protective sun gear and went outside, and Effner hailed a flyby cab. In minutes they were at Ronindella's apt. Johnsmith had lived there with her until he had moved out last month. In fact, they had selected this place because of its proximity to the university, because of his job.

As soon as Ronindella passed by the security screen, the door opened and they went inside. Smitty II was there, playing with a jerkily moving dinosaur.

"Hi, Smitty," said Ryan Effner.

"Hi," the boy said, simulating the dinosaur's roar as he picked up the toy and pointed its gleaming fanged mouth at Effner and his mother.

"How come you're home already?" his mother asked.

"School got out early today, on account of the ceiling fell down."

"What are we paying taxes for?" Ronindella wondered aloud. "The schools are collapsing, and the kids aren't even being taught the classic videos."

Effner nearly said that Beeb thought it was a whole lot worse than that, but he decided that it wouldn't be wise to mention the kid's father right now. Smitty II had to have time to adjust to Beeb's departure. The kid was probably too young to think anything of the fact that good old Uncle Ryan was around comforting Mom these days. And for now, it seemed wise to keep it that way.

The phone rang.

"I'll get it, Mom," said Smitty.

Before Ronindella could object, Smitty snapped on the video. Effner headed for the bedroom just as Johnsmith Biberkopf appeared on the screen.

"Who was that?" Johnsmith asked.

"Repairman," Ronindella lied. "What do you want, anyway, Johnny?"

Smitty II seemed confused.

"I just called to see how you and Smitty are." Johnsmith attempted a smile, but it didn't quite work.

"We're fine. How are you?"

"Uh, okay. I'm going down to the Selective Space Service tomorrow."

"So soon?" Ronindella was playing dumb.

"Oh, didn't I tell you last time we talked?"

"Maybe you did, Johnny. I've had so much on my mind lately, you know . . ."

"Yeah, haven't we all." Johnsmith looked at Smitty II. The smile was more sincere this time. "How's my boy?"

"Good, Dad. Why don't you come home?"

"Sorry, son, but I can't. Is that a dinosaur you've got there?"

"Yeah. And it moves around."

"What good is a dinosaur that doesn't move around, I always say."

"Look, Johnny, I'm kind of busy right now," Ronindella said. "Maybe you could call back some other time."

"From the moon?"

"You're not leaving this minute, for Christ's sake," she said angrily. "Stop trying to make me pity you."

"It won't be long before I'll be there, Ronnie. And I'm really not trying to make you pity me. It's just the way things are, that's all."

Smitty had lost interest in the conversation, and was playing with the dinosaur again, his piping voice roaring away in the background.

"Smitty!" his mother shouted. "Stop making so much goddamn noise!"

The boy became silent and looked at her resentfully. He took the dinosaur into the bedroom with him.

"Going in to join the repairman, huh, Smitty?" Johnsmith said to the boy.

Smitty turned toward the screen to reply one last time, but his mother looked at him warningly. "Yeah, gonna play in there, Dad. See you."

"You might at least let me hold a conversation with my own son," Johnsmith said, as Smitty closed the bedroom door. "I'll probably never see him again in the flesh."

"Don't be so melodramatic." But Ronindella knew that what he said was true. Life would be a lot easier when Johnsmith was on the moon. Half of his wages would be sent to her automatically by the government, for child support. He'd be more useful to her up there than he ever was here on earth.

"Goodbye, Johnsmith," Ronindella said, ending the phone conversation. "And good luck."

"Goodbye, Ronnie," He watched her flick the connection off. Her face narrowed, shrank to a tiny rainbow point, and vanished. "And fuck you, too."

* * *

Alderdice was wheezing badly by the time he got out of the sun. He used his passcard to get inside Biberkopf's building, slumping against a paint-peeling vestibule wall to wipe his dark face while he waited for it to clear. Full employment was a laudable goal, and he was certainly glad to have a job, but on days like this he almost wished that he were doing something else—*anything* else. The trouble with that wish was that it might come true, and he'd soon be doing something else, all right, but doing it in a lunar mine.

The notion motivated him to start climbing the stairs. He comforted himself with the thought that the life of a public servant was never an easy one, as he labored up toward the fourteenth floor, where Biberkopf's effapt was located. He had discovered on his first visit to this building that the elevator didn't work, much to his dismay. He was usually glad that the Conglom didn't require biannual physicals anymore, but it occurred to him that he might be in better shape if they did. Wheezing, he took a break on the landing between the fifth and sixth floors.

After a short rest, he pressed on, climbing one flight after another, deliberately and ponderously. At last he reached the fourteenth floor, stopping again to catch his breath. Doors were lined up on either side of the corridor, inches separating each occupant's effapt from his neighbor's. Biberkopf lived at N-39, about halfway down the hall on the left.

Alderdice fumbled in his pocket until his fingers found the sound scoop. He pointed it at the door and it picked up a voice from the other side, channeling it to Alderdice subaudibly. Breathing a long sigh of relief at finding the suspect at home, he listened carefully.

Biberkopf was talking. It didn't sound as if anybody else was with him, though. He must have been on the phone. Yes, he could hear a woman's tinny voice, definitely coming in over the phone. She was trying to end the conversation. After she cut the connection, Biberkopf uttered an obscenity. After that, the effapt was silent.

TWO

WELL, THAT WAS that. All Johnsmith had to look forward to now was the Triple-S and a short life in the airless void. The screen faded to a dull gray, which he fancied the perfect metaphor for his state of mind at that moment. He slumped into a chair and wondered how his life had ever come to this. He'd tried to be a good teacher, a good parent, a good husband. His intentions had come to little as far as Ronindella was concerned. They'd been married in the Video Church of God, just as Ronindella had wanted, though Johnsmith hadn't been brought up in any organized religion himself—his father had seen to that—and had always vaguely considered the wedding a compromise of his principles. In fact, it seemed that life with Ronindella had been mostly a series of such soul-killing compromises, when he thought about it. He couldn't remember her ever giving in on anything.

He had become less compromising in his profession as his marriage had soured, though. Maybe that was why he had forced himself into an unyielding position at the University, secretly knowing that his rigidity would lead to his downfall, and ultimately to a divorce.

But that was so irrational. Why exile himself to the dark side of the moon just to get rid of Ronindella?

He stared at the bare wall of his effapt, wondering if he really was that self-destructive. It was possible. After all, he never could have left Ronindella. She'd been forced to throw him out, or there wouldn't have been any end to their marriage. It *had* to end, though; there was no doubt about it.

His gaze wandered to his jacket, slung across a chair by the door. He had tossed it there when he came in. The onees were in the inside pocket, weren't they?

He got up and grabbed the jacket, bunching its synthetic weave in one hand while he felt for the film canister. There it was. He took the canister out and looked at it. To hell with using the onees tomorrow. He would take them now.

Twisting the cap off the canister, he looked inside at three silver dots, almost like ball bearings, only slightly larger. So these were onees. . . .

How did one go about this? He could get a pair of tweezers and pick one out. You had to be cautious with onees, they said. But why should he be careful? If anybody on earth had nothing to lose at that moment, it was Johnsmith Biberkopf. If he went insane or died, what would it matter? At least Smitty would get his insurance credit . . . maybe not, come to think of it . . . the Triple-S board might decide that it was intentional inducement of psychosis, or something else that would mean they had no legal obligation to pay up. If the onees totally short-circuited his nervous system, as rumor had it sometimes happened, he would be pronounced brain dead, legally a suicide. Then Smitty would get nothing at all.

It would be Ronindella's problem then, wouldn't it? Maybe the "repairman" could help out with the bills. . . .

Johnsmith tipped the canister so that the three tiny spheres rolled into his palm.

He had imagined that the effect would start in his hand and work its way up his arm and through the rest of his body. That was probably what had actually happened, in picoseconds, but it didn't feel like that. It felt as if he had just stepped off the edge of something into nothing. He was swimming through a churning sea, each stroke changing the color of the water—blue, green, yellow, orange, red, purple, blue—right through the spectrum. The water was flowing coolly around him, its pressure constant against his naked skin. His ears were stopped up and bubbles tickled the insides of his nostrils. It was too goddamn much. Maybe if he just floated for a while, the shifting, synthetic dream world would change a little more gradually.

But it didn't. Instead, it became a whirlpool, vertiginous tints dragging him down, colors swirling into a dark spiral that threatened to swallow him. He was scared, finding it hard to remind himself that this was just a sensory input illusion, triggered by his own electrical charge. The information passing into his nervous system couldn't be controlled, of course. That was what was dangerous about onees.

The thing to do was relax and enjoy the sensations. Either that or drop the damn things. He looked down at his hand, opening his fingers to see the three minute spheres gleaming in the blackness.

"You're the only things that are real," he said. "Just you and me, guys. We're real. The rest of this is just some sort of entertainment feeding in through the nerve endings, right?"

As intense as the sensual bombardment was, he did not drop the onees. He clutched them so tightly that his nails dug painfully into his palm. He just had to remember that he could get out of this at any time. But everything was changing so fast that he had a hard time remembering that.

He wasn't sinking anymore. Now he was bobbing on a fogbound surface, Odysseus washed onto shore to be discovered by Nausicaa. But there was no shore in sight. Nothing but the fog, impenetrable and curling above the nearly still sea. The smell of salt water was powerful, and his ears were still plugged up, but the water seemed warmer than a few moments ago.

He floated on his back, at peace with the world. This was all right. This was very nice, in fact.

And then he heard something splashing in the distance. It splashed again. Every few seconds, the sound repeated itself, and it was getting louder. Whatever it was, it was coming closer. Johnsmith was scared. He forgot about the onees. This was just too real. For all he knew, this was the *real* reality, and the other reality, the one he had left behind, was the fake.

Which meant that he was at the mercy of this thing coming through the fog toward him.

He was so scared that his bowels let loose. Heart pounding wildly, Johnsmith thought that he should be ashamed of his cowardice, but he wasn't. He only wanted to get away from here before the encroaching *thing* was on top of him.

But it was too late.

It burst through the fog, a serpent's head on a long, sinuous neck. A dinosaur? No, more like a dragon. The head was stylized, ornamented, inanimate—it was the prow of a ship.

A Viking ship!

Johnsmith swallowed a mouthful of water as the graceful long ship glided by. He could clearly see the men in the bow, their long hair and beards matted from the salt air, their tarnished helmets dented, their round shields strapped to the hull as they pulled at the oars. Their king, a huge man standing on the deck, peered over the side, hearing Johnsmith cough.

The king shouted something incomprehensible at his men, and the oars on the starboard side were shipped en masse. The long ship swung back toward Johnsmith, who screamed, taking more salt water into his lungs and coughing. He flailed wildly, trying to swim away from the long ship. An oar was extended toward him by one of the Vikings.

It was at that moment that Johnsmith dropped the onees.

Light blossomed out of the foggy night. He was still sitting in his living room, his breath ragged, his heart pounding.

"Jesus," he breathed. For several minutes, he couldn't quite believe that he was back in his apartment, dry and alone. He'd read enough about the Vikings to know what would have happened if they had gotten their hands on him. . . .

But how *could* they get their hands on him? They were nothing more than neural impulses, figures in a synthetic dream. They couldn't really hurt him.

It was then that he smelled his own shit. That part of the dream had been real enough, it seemed. Shame-faced, Johnsmith carefully got to his feet with the intention of changing his clothes.

After using a full day's allotment of water in the shower, he put on his green kimono and returned to the living room, grateful to be clean once again. He was certain that there was plenty of life left in the onees, if he could find them among the debris. He hadn't cleaned this effapt since he'd moved in six weeks ago.

One of the onees lay gleaming on the rug. Using a matchbook cover, Johnsmith knelt and guided the tiny sphere into the film canister. Next time, he would use only one, at least at the beginning. The intensity of the oneiric images had made him forget where he really was.

Still, he thought as he crawled on his hands and knees, he had enjoyed the onees until he got scared. If he only took one at a time, there would still be some anchor in reality, most likely. A more gradual descent into the subconscious would be wise. But what the hell, he'd rarely acted so spontaneously. He was proud of himself, in a perverse way. He was okay now; quite relaxed, in fact. The experience had done him good, shocked him out of his depressed state.

He spied another onee, under his chair. On hands and knees, he used the matchbook again, scooping it up. His heart was beating at a normal rate now, and he felt pretty good. It had been exciting, meeting up with a shipful of Vikings.

They probably hadn't been Vikings at all. With his *Beowulf* fixation, he must have imagined Geats. That could have been King Hygelac's long ship. Indeed, the height of the man on the deck suggested a giant, which, by all accounts, Hygelac had been. Or maybe it was Hygelac's nephew, Beowulf himself. Johnsmith figured that all that stuff was rattling around inside his brain, so it was probably what the onees had brought out and made real to him.

He finally gave up without finding the third onee. Maybe it had fallen between the louvers of the floor vent. If so, it would go to one of the trash bins downstairs, and would be as hard to find as the proverbial needle in the haystack. It would be compacted and added to one of the trash islands in the harbor, where some derelict might stumble on it and have an experience that wine could never provide. At least, he hoped so. It was more likely, of course, that the onee would be buried so deeply that it would lie dormant until its potential was gone.

Well, at least he had two of them left. Now that he knew first hand what they were like, he was actually considering taking them tomorrow when he appeared before the Triple-S inquisitors. Maybe he really could get out of going to the moon.

Or maybe they'd put him in cold storage for a while. After all, he'd be breaking the law, wouldn't he? Come to think of it, even though it was against the law to buy or sell onees, was it illegal to have them in your possession? It didn't seem possible that you could have them if you hadn't bought them . . . unless, of course, somebody had given them to you. And that was exactly what had happened, wasn't it? Ryan Effner had given them to him, without solicitation of any kind.

So maybe he could get away with it. And even if he didn't, wasn't a few years in stasis better than spending the rest of his life completely off the planet?

It was something to think about. And since he had to be at Triple-S at nine in the morning, the *time* to think about it was now. But he didn't want to just hang around here brooding. Without even putting on his jacket, he went impulsively to the door.

As he threw it open, he saw a fat, black man standing in the hall, holding something that looked like a fountain pen.

"Can I help you?" Johnsmith asked.

"I'm looking for someone. . . . "

"What's the name?"

"Uh, Judy . . . Judy Takahashi."

"Well, I don't know anybody by that name," Johnsmith said, staring at the thing in the guy's hand. "But there are a lot of people moving in and out of these apts all the time."

"Well, she just moved in, and I'm not too sure of the apt number."

"I see." At that moment, Johnsmith recognized the gleaming, black object as the guy shoved it into his pocket. It was a sound scoop; he'd seen a dimensional picture of one in *Pixine* a few weeks ago.

"If I meet Judy Takahashi, I'll tell her you're looking for her," Johnsmith said. "Of course, it isn't likely I'll meet her, since there are over a hundred and fifty apartments on this floor, but who knows?"

"Yeah, right. Who knows?"

"What's your name?" Johnsmith asked.

"Uh, Sonny. My name's Sonny."

Johnsmith waited for the expected follow-up question, but it didn't come. He offered the usual information anyway. "My name is Johnsmith Biberkopf."

"Glad to meet you, sir." Sonny stuck out his hand.

As Johnsmith shook it, he noticed that it was slippery with sweat. It made sense that Sonny would be perspiring heavily after walking up fourteen flights. And yet, the guy didn't seem winded, overweight as he was. Johnsmith began to suspect that Sonny had been listening at his door for quite a while. Maybe he was a P.A. Of course, the official government line was that there was no such thing as a P.A. P.A.s were unconstitutional, but since when did the administration give a shit about that? Everybody knew that they existed, both to provide full employment and to make sure people didn't get out of space service.

"Would you like to come inside?" Johnsmith said, figuring what the hell? If they wanted to keep an eye on him, why not? He wasn't going anywhere. Except to the moon. "We can call the directory and find out which effapt is your friend's."

The P.A.—if that's what he really was—looked around uncertainly, and then said, "Thanks. I think I will."

"Cup of coffee?" Johnsmith asked as he shut the door behind Sonny. "I was just about to make some."

"Sounds good," Sonny replied, looking around at the tiny, sparsely furnished cubicle.

"Have a seat," Johnsmith said, gesturing at the meter-wide, plastic table where he ate his meals.

"Coffee's one of my few luxuries nowadays," Johnsmith said, measuring out spoonfuls into the coffee maker. "This is a real antique. My grandmother owned it. It's all I kept after the divorce."

Sonny didn't say anything.

"I moved here after my wife and I split up," Johnsmith said, and then, thinking what the hell, said: "To tell you the truth, my wife threw me out."

"Oh," said Johnsmith's guest, "I'm sorry."

Sonny didn't seem very surprised, though, which made Johnsmith's suspicion deepen. A P.A. would surely already know that he was divorced, would know all about him, in fact, and would doubtless perceive his newfound bachelorhood symptomatic of the nonproductivity that had led to his present dilemma. A Pre-Emptive Agent would also be certain that somebody like Johnsmith deserved to be drafted.

"I'm going to appear before the Triple-S tomorrow," Johnsmith said.

"Really?" Sonny did seem surprised by that, but perhaps only at the manner in which Johnsmith had blurted it out. Most people didn't talk about their bad luck that much. Now that Johnsmith had the P.A. off balance, though, he might as well keep at it. "A few minutes ago, I used onees for the first time in my life," he said.

Sonny didn't say anything at all. Johnsmith supposed that his own candor wouldn't inspire his unexpected guest to tell him the truth, but maybe it would make the bastard think twice about what he was doing here, if he was in fact a P.A. Johnsmith wondered how somebody who did what Sonny did for a living could sleep at night.

"A friend gave them to me, thinking that if I held them in my hand at the Triple-S hearing, I might be judged unfit for service. I doubt that it would work, and I don't think I'd have the nerve to do that, anyway, so I took them as a sort of farewell to civilian life. Does that make any sense to you?"

"Well . . ."

"It makes sense to me, even if it's nonsense to anybody else. I ended up suffering an illusion of almost drowning, and then being found by a boatload of Vikings."

"Vikings?" Alderdice immediately regretted his ejaculation. He composed himself, noting that Biberkopf kept right on babbling, though the suspect's eyebrows did arch a bit. There had been a report circulating

through the Agency for the past few months, about onees that imprinted some kind of specific hallucinations on the user's memory. The hallucinations always had Vikings in them. The term the report had used was "archecoding." Just why this was significant enough to rate such a report had remained unexplained, but it was obviously important enough to the Agency to make them want to track down any and all such onees. Alderdice just might have lucked out and found a way to improve his standing in the Agency. "What were you saying about Vikings?" he asked, trying to sound only politely interested.

"Geats, really," said Biberkopf. "At least, that's what I think they were. Seventh century Danes, a group who seemed to disappear from the face of the earth sometime during the Dark Ages."

"Fascinating," Alderdice said, fearing that the point would be obscured by Biberkopf's rambling. "But what did the Vikings do?"

"Not much. I forgot that it was only an illusion and panicked. I dropped the onees."

"But you're *sure* you saw Vikings—I mean Geats?" Alderdice knew that he shouldn't have asked that question. Biberkopf's brow furrowed; the guy had been going on about the onees with abandon, and now he might suspect that something was wrong because of Alderdice's excitability.

"Well, I thought I saw Geats. See, I used to teach a class about *Beowulf* at the University, and . . ."

"Bay of Wolf? Is that in Canada?"

"Uh, no. It's the name of a Geat, a kind of Viking, as I said before. That's probably why I hallucinated a Geatish ship."

"Ah." Alderdice was relieved to see that Biberkopf had a rationale for why he'd seen the archecoded images.

"It was kind of scary, but I enjoyed it in a way. Now I'm not so upset about going to the moon. Even if I have to slave away in a mine for the rest of my miserable life, at least I can take onees on my off hours—and I hear they've got a decent library you can jack into up there.''

"Yeah, I've heard that, too."

"Coffee's ready," Biberkopf said, grabbing two cups that rested on a soggy paper towel. "Take anything in yours?"

"Sweetener, please."

"I can whiten it for you, too." Biberkopf lifted up packets that had obviously been stolen from a Kwikkee-Kwizeen.

"That's okay," Alderdice said. "Just the sweetener."

As he stirred the coffee, Biberkopf said, "I never thought Ronnie would toss me out. No matter what happened, I thought she'd always be my girl. Know what I mean?"

"Yes, I do." Alderdice remembered all too clearly how Lon had dumped him a year ago. He thoughtfully took a steaming cup from Biberkopf.

"I guess it's just part of growing up, finding out about these things, huh?"

"I guess so." Alderdice's first sip of coffee scalded the roof of his mouth. He grimaced and set the cup on the table.

"It's kind of like when somebody close to you dies. You don't really understand that it's possible until it actually happens. There's a terrific sense of isolation that follows. It's as if you're the only one in the universe who this has ever happened to. But after a while you become less solipsistic, and you find out that other people are dying, people who aren't loved ones. They're somebody else's loved ones, though, and these other people maybe feel the same way you did when it happened to you. So you try to break through their isolation, and then you might find out that they don't want you to. That they'd rather be alone.''

Alderdice took another sip of coffee. Biberkopf was really babbling now. But at least he wasn't going anyplace. Not physically, anyway.

"It's all a great mystery. Love, death, all of it," Biberkopf said. "No matter how many times somebody says that, it doesn't make it any less true, does it?"

"I guess not. So what did you do with the onees, Mr. Biberkopf?"

"Call me Smitty. Everybody does. We even named my son Smitty II."

"That's nice—what about the onees, though?"

"I've got them right here." Biberkopf picked up a canister and smiled. "Would you like to try one?"

THREE

ALDERDICE WAS TEMPTED to do it. In some crazy, self-destructive way, he wanted to touch an onee and act peculiar for once in his life. But he couldn't override the programming that made him always do what he was supposed to.

"Do you . . ." It sounded preposterous, but he said it anyway. ". . . realize that what you've just said is a Conglom offense?"

"Yeah," Biberkopf replied, holding two tiny silver spheres out to him. "If I don't watch out they might send me to the moon or something, right?"

Alderdice backed away. The man was mad; the government had been quite correct to draft him. Antipathy surged to the surface of Alderdice's mind, while a desire to try the onees lurked somewhere in the depths. He had to do something fast.

"Come on," Biberkopf urged him. "Give it a try."

"I couldn't do a thing like that," Alderdice said weakly. "I'd be breaking the law."

"And a P.A. can't break the law, can he?" the suspect goaded. "Some kind of brain implants make them obey at all times, right?"

Now Alderdice saw how clever the man was. "Biberkopf," he said, "please."

"Call me Smitty," Johnsmith said. "Everybody does . . . except for Ryan Effner." As soon as he mentioned Effner's name, he knew that it was his colleague and supposed friend who was the "repairman." But this notion was just paranoia, wasn't it? Rye wouldn't do that to his old buddy, would he? But why else would Ronindella have made him hide in the other room when Johnsmith called? Smitty II had been acting funny, too, and Ronindella had tried to get him out of sight as quickly as possible. She had been afraid that the boy would innocently reveal the truth, no doubt.

Johnsmith slowly came to realize that he was staring down at the soiled carpet, his guest waiting nervously for him to say something else. Even though he suspected that Sonny was an agent, he began to feel sorry for this muttering, overweight man.

"I . . . really should be going," Alderdice was saying. "If you should run into Judy . . ."

"Yeah, sure. We never called the building directory, did we? What was her name? Judy . . . ?"

"Takahashi. Judy Takahashi. But it won't be necessary to call." Alderdice rose from the uncomfortable chair, saying nervously, "Thanks for the coffee . . . Mr. . . . I mean, Smitty."

Now that he heard his nickname, Biberkopf realized that nobody called him that anymore. He really didn't have any friends to speak of nowadays. "Sure you won't try an onee or two," he said, feeling a trifle malicious.

"I've enjoyed talking to you," Sonny said, moving toward the door, "but I've really got to run."

Biberkopf rose, offering the film canister. "Give it a try," he coaxed. "I think you'll really like it."

The temptation to wrest the onees from Biberkopf's fingers and drop them into his open palm was terrific, but Alderdice's programming held true. He backed toward the door, dismayed at the churning ambivalence inside him. Clutching at the doorknob, he plopped the borsalino on his head and slipped out into the hallway.

The last thing he saw as he shut the door was Johnsmith Biberkopf, gaunt, holding out the onees.

Alderdice was afraid that Biberkopf would come out after him, so he turned and ran the length of the hall and started down the stairs, wheezing and sweating, his flat feet slamming down on the steps almost painfully.

Ryan Effner wondered why the credit card had to be inserted before the session began. He guessed that there must have been some good reason for it, but whatever it was, Madame Psychosis would say nothing until his credit was approved. He wondered if this were true of all cybershrinks.

While he waited he watched a loop showing highlights from videos about the history of psychological spiritualism, opening with a pan of a Catholic Church confessional, followed by still photos of Madame Blavatsky, Freud, and Budd Hopkins, and seguéing into a short history of the cybershrink industry. The video darkened abruptly as the slot below the screen spat out his card, and the earthy figure of Madame Psychosis began to move ponderously.

"Good afternoon, Ryan," she said in an eastern European accent, exotic and profound, yet soothing at the same time.

"Good afternoon," he replied, the video still fresh in his mind. He was grateful that it was a machine he was talking to, and not a person. No matter how professional his demeanor, another human being could not really be trusted with one's darkest secrets.

"And how is Ronindella?"

"Fine. She's relieved that the government is taking her husband off her hands. Of course, Johnsmith will be helping her bring up her son even while he's on Luna."

"How do you *feel* about that?" Madame Psychosis asked.

"Well, Ronindella and I both think it's for the best."

"I'm not interested in what Ronindella thinks, but in what *you* feel."

"Well . . . I guess I've got what you'd call mixed feelings about it."

"Ambivalence. In what way do you feel ambivalent?"

"Well, Johnsmith is my friend."

"Yes?"

"And I feel funny, sneaking around with his wife until he gets off the planet."

"Why?"

Ryan toyed with the loose cloth of his jodhpurs. "I don't know. It just doesn't seem right."

"Do you feel that you have contributed to Mr. Biberkopf's problems?"

"Well, no . . . not exactly."

"Then why do you feel that you have wronged him?" Because of the Eastern European accent, the word "wronged" came out "ronked."

"If he knew what's going on, he'd be hurt."

"But you are trying to *prevent* him from finding out, are you not?"

Ryan peered at Madame Psychosis' full figure, her billowing skirts, and felt a surge of relief. She was right—he was trying to help Beeb, not hurt him. After all, it wasn't his fault that Beeb had blown it, as Madame Psychosis had explained to him during the last few sessions. If Beeb had sought out professional help, as Ryan had, he'd have held onto what he had, wouldn't have to worry about the Triple-S, and would probably feel a whole lot better about himself. Not probably: surely. It was, in a very real sense, all Beeb's own fault.

"I think I've got it all worked out now," he said to the cybershrink.

"Very good," said Madame Psychosis. "The vibrations of the universe are with you."

"And within my spirit," Ryan responded automatically, in the ritual of the Video Church of the New Age.

Madame Psychosis floated in a holographic depiction of the galaxies, saying in a reverberating voice, "May the eternal forces of goodness and purity bless you."

"Amen." Ryan made the sign of Aquarius and rose from the pew, as the stars did their cosmic dance around him. He was full of the divine, universal spirit. Even after he left the New Age building—erected, he recalled, in the first year of the millennium—he felt elated. The psychedelic gases he'd been inhaling during the session had something to do with it, he knew, but not that much. It would help Ronnie so much to see Madame Psychosis. So far he hadn't been able to talk her into trying a session, but he was certain that she would sense the spirit in him and be moved to come with him sooner or later.

Even at nine in the morning, the sun glowed amorphously through a peach-colored haze, and the temperature felt like 110°, but Ryan decided not to think about the oppressive weather. As he put on his protective head gear, he could think of little besides how complete his life was. He had a fulfilling career, a wonderful lover, and would soon have a fine son, too. He hadn't really connected with Smitty II yet, but it was only a matter of time. Ronindella's first visit to Madame Psychosis would expedite that process.

He began to whistle as he walked through the parking lot. And why shouldn't he? The best years of his life were just beginning.

Across town, Johnsmith Biberkopf emerged from a maglev bus in front of the local Conglom building. He was resigned, sober, and prepared for the inevitable. His only alternative had been suicide, and it was too late for that. Besides, he was certain he didn't have the courage to kill himself . . . if courage was indeed what it took.

The Conglom building was mid-twentieth century revival, a series of swooping lines and glass rectangles, designed to remind one of the original United Nations Building in New York. Of course, every city on Earth had one of these now, since the Conglom had franchised the UN, but Johnsmith had always felt that it was a charmingly quaint structure. He'd only been inside once before, when he was a little kid, for voice and fingerprint registration. He could remember it quite vividly, though, even if it had been over thirty years ago when he'd first walked through these glass doors.

He had wanted to take Smitty II down here for registration, when the boy was at the legal age for it, five, but Ronnie had insisted that their son go with his first grade class. She said that it would help to socialize the kid.

Johnsmith shrugged, standing in the immense lobby, uncertain of where he was supposed to go. He clutched his Triple-S pass in both hands.

"Follow the red line," the security net's voice said. It sounded exactly like Sir Laurence Olivier. Johnsmith looked around and saw a group of people lined up near a glowing, crimson bar that led into a corridor. He got behind the last person, a young woman with a hawkish, but not unattractive, face.

"I guess this is the line for induction," he said, trying to make conversation.

The woman glared back, saying nothing. Johnsmith wondered idly if the security net had misdirected him. The grim manner of the people queued up in front of him suggested that this was the correct place, though. He turned to see more people falling in behind him. None of them looked particularly happy.

Johnsmith saw a man walking through the lobby, the light glaring through the glass doors behind him. There was something familiar about his gait and bearing. As he came toward the queue, Johnsmith recognized him.

"Sonny!" he said. It was the guy who had been in his effapt yesterday.

Sonny looked at him, brow furrowing. He came toward Johnsmith. The other people didn't mind when he got in front of them in line.

"Come down here to check up on me, Sonny?" Johnsmith said bitterly. "You didn't really have to worry. I don't have the money to take off for Outer Mongolia. Even if I did, I imagine the government would catch up with me before long."

"I'm not here to check up on you," Sonny said. "I've been inducted, too."

The line advanced slowly, and they moved with it. Johnsmith was confused. "I thought you were a P.A."

"I am . . . or should I say I *was?*"

"I don't understand."

"It was real easy to put me in the ranks of the unemployed, especially since my job doesn't officially exist. They riffed me, and here I am."

"So soon?"

"Yeah, they process P.A.s real fast. But at least they gave me an option. Now or six weeks from now. I figured I might as well get it over with instead of hanging around brooding about it."

Johnsmith remained silent. His first impulse was to say well and good. Sonny had been instructed by the government to see to it that Johnsmith got drafted, and now he was in line at the Triple-S himself. There was irony for you. But for some reason, Johnsmith felt sorry for the poor guy. After all, Sonny had just been doing his job, hadn't he?

"I'm sorry this happened, Sonny," he said.

"My name isn't Sonny," the P.A. said. "It's Alderdice. Alderdice V. Lumumba."

Johnsmith nodded. "Well, it's still too bad you have to be here, too."

"I'm afraid it's been a long time coming," Alderdice admitted. "I guess I just wasn't cut out for this line of work."

"Well, we're both in the same boat now."

"This guy's a P.A.?" the hawkfaced woman said

angrily. "Isn't it bad enough they're sending us to the moon, without having him here spying on us?"

An angry murmuring arose from the queue.

"He's not spying on us," Johnsmith said. "He's been drafted, just like the rest of us."

"How do you know it's true?" the woman demanded in a shrill tone.

"The government doesn't need him to spy on us; they're recording every sound, every move we make at this very moment." Johnsmith pointed to the camera lenses pointing toward them from every recess of the lobby.

The line began to move more quickly, and Alderdice was forgotten as they entered a large room. The net's voice commanded them to remove their clothing.

"All personal effects will be placed in the baskets to your right," the voice said. "They will be returned to you when you go back to civilian life."

Which, of course, would never happen. After you spent a few years in lunar gravity, you couldn't live on Earth. Most people signed up for another hitch, resigned to spending the rest of their lives on the moon; the few who chose to come home invariably died young. Of course, bone disease was quite common on the moon, but at least you didn't have to worry quite so much about heart failure.

There were three booths at the end of the room, and people were being ordered to step into them two at a time. Johnsmith wondered idly if he would go into one with Alderdice, or with the hawkfaced woman.

It turned out to be the woman, who actually looked pretty good naked.

"Burst, Felicia," the voice said as they entered the cubicle. "Accused of treason against the Conglomerated United Nations of Earth, how do you plead?"

"Not guilty," Felicia Burst said.

Disinfectant sprayed over her, and as she choked the voice announced: "Your plea has been considered, but

the evidence weighs against you. According to Conglomerated United Nations of Earth Criminal Court
Resolution 1331-D, you are guilty as charged of crimes
against all the nations of Earth.''

Tears were streaming down Felicia's thin cheeks, but
not as a result of fear. The spray and her rage combined
as she shrieked. ''Down with the Conglom! Up with
the people!''

Her revolutionary cries were drowned out by huge
whirling buffers, that both scrubbed her and pushed her
along to the next step in Triple-S processing.

''Biberkopf, Johnsmith,'' the voice said as soon as
she was out of sight, ''you are accused of the crime of
unemployment. How do you plead?''

''No contest,'' Johnsmith said, hearing Felicia shouting angrily in the distance.

''Would you care to elaborate?'' the voice asked in
its cultured, yet forceful, British accent.

Johnsmith thought it over. ''No, I guess not,'' he
said after a few seconds. ''I guess I'll just change my
plea to guilty and save my breath.''

He was enveloped in a hissing spray of disinfectant.
As he gagged, he heard Olivier's voice, speaking for
all the nations of the Earth, sentence him to space service. The buffers abraded his skin and pushed him forward as the next two unfortunates entered the dock
behind him.

Alderdice emerged just a few seconds after Johnsmith. His sentencing partner, an enormously fat
woman whose jiggling, steatopygial buttocks resembled
nothing so much as oatmeal, was herded off to some
unknown destination, while Alderdice was shoved by
the buffers toward Johnsmith. The two men were forced
onto a conveyor belt flanked by more buffers. By the
time they were dumped unceremoniously in a small
chamber bathed in purplish UV, Johnsmith felt as
though his skin had been rubbed raw.

Olivier's voice instructed them to leave the UV

chamber after a couple of minutes. They entered a long, narrow room with benches lining the extended walls. Felicia Burst sat, still naked, on a bench about a third of the way from the door.

Johnsmith joined her, and even though she glared at him, he had the distinct impression that she was relieved to have him join her after the preceding ordeal.

Alderdice sat down next to Johnsmith. The three Triple-S inductees waited in silence for some time. At last Felicia said, "Where the hell are the rest of them?"

"You mean the others who were queued up?" Johnsmith said.

"They were sent to different parts of the building," Alderdice offered. "Possibly for screening, or tests, or . . . something."

Felicia stared straight ahead, as if she hadn't heard Alderdice speak. "There's something weird about this," she said.

A door in the far end of the narrow room opened. A woman stepped in, wearing a formfitting uniform of red and white stripes. Her helmet was electric blue, with glowing stars that winked on and off as she spoke. Her bland good looks and perfectly cadenced speech suggested to Johnsmith that she was actually an android. Her words were punctuated by slapping a swagger stick against the nearest bench. Handing them three paper overall outfits, she introduced herself.

"I'm Captain Vuh," she said. "I've been assigned to initiate you into the space service. Please put on these overalls and follow me."

They dressed and stepped onto a ramp complete with an accordion-shaped plastic covering that led into the interior of a bus. They sat down with Captain Vuh and the bus whooshed off to the spaceport.

Johnsmith looked longingly at the city flying by, as the captain spoke: "Many people see space service as an onerous duty, but we think you'll find that this will be the most rewarding time of your life."

"Right," said Felicia Burst sarcastically.

"Important work is accomplished in space that simply cannot be done on Earth," she said. "Alloys are mixed in zero gravity, or in the moon's lower gravity, that cannot be mixed on Earth. Minerals are found there that are in short supply on our mother planet, or have never existed at all. Industry that would pollute our atmosphere is now transacted offworld, making it possible for us to clean up our environment, a dream that has been postponed for a century."

Johnsmith tuned out the android's speech. He'd heard it all before, in high school when the kids who weren't cut out for any real careers were being conditioned to accept their unhappy lot.

The bus went underground, and Johnsmith was grateful for the cessation of images flying past the window. It only depressed him to see the city for this one final time.

Slowing, the bus began to climb up into the spaceport as Captain Vuh finished her speech: "In a few moments we'll be in sight of the shuttle that will take you to a colony where a ship will be waiting to take you to Mars."

What she didn't mention, Johnsmith thought bitterly, was that they would merely be part of the cargo on the shuttle, not really passengers. He looked out the window as they emerged into the sulfurous light, huge rockets standing around them in rows like cemetery stones. They headed straight for one, a graceful, thrusting shape bound to its gantry by a skein of pipes and ducts that leaked liquid hydrogen vapor onto the cracked concrete pad. Glancing at Felicia and Alderdice, he was about to speak when he realized that they were both staring at Captain Vuh in astonishment. It was only then that he realized what she had just told them.

They were going to Mars.

FOUR

CAPTAIN VUH DIDN'T stay with them for long. She had been designed to initiate draftees facing lunar service, and so her spiel had really been almost meaningless. Not that Johnsmith had paid much attention to what she'd been saying, anyway. Nevertheless, she'd ridden with them up in the elevator and helped them strap in. After wishing them a safe journey, she left them alone with the two-person crew. Ignored by the professional spacers, they had a few minutes before liftoff, and their destination was the sole topic of conversation.

"Now we know why we were separated from the rest," Johnsmith mused. "But why us?"

"I'll tell you why *I'm* going to Mars," Felicia said. "They want me as far away from this corrupt world as they can get me. They know that I'm a threat to the status quo."

"You know," Alderdice said to her, "it seems to me that I've heard of you before."

"As a revolutionist, no doubt," Felicia said. But there was an odd expression on her face, as if she were covering something up. "Maybe they circulated some wanted posters in your office, or something."

"No, I don't think so." Alderdice was watching her closely now, his neck craning awkwardly.

37

"It doesn't matter," Johnsmith said. "The three of us are all in the same boat now."

"Or the same shuttle, at least," Alderdice added pleasantly. "And it seems as though things are not working out as badly as we had feared."

It was true. Mars was the cushiest duty the Triple-S had to offer. Growing plants, with the long range plan of terraforming the dried-up planet, was the chief business of the involuntary colonists stationed there. There were other tasks, of course, but these were either technical or service-and-support jobs that were filled by volunteers. The position that would almost certainly fall to the three of them would be Johnny Appleseed . . . or John*smith* Appleseed, in his case. Alderdice had been quite right; it could have been a whole lot worse.

The pilot, a red-faced man with a broken nose, turned to them. "We'll have liftoff in a couple minutes," he said, settling into his chair. "Brace yourselves back there."

Johnsmith wasn't quite sure how to brace himself anymore than he was already braced. He thought of classic videos from the pre-space era, invariably depicting centrifugal force that distorted the features of those fearless pioneers into the unknown. He would have felt so much better if this job actually did require heroism. From what he could see, it was just a routine flight to a space station, and another routine flight to a dead planet, where they would live out their lives in servitude to the world government.

A thunderous roar welled up from below and the ship trembled around them. It was frightening, and yet exhilarating. Johnsmith could feel his heart pounding, as gravity attempted to hold him down to the planet that he was about to leave forever. The force created nothing more than a minor discomfort. Still, as he felt himself rising from the Earth, he *could* almost imagine that they were embarking on a heroic quest. It was a foolish notion, but what harm could it do now?

They passed through the clouds and were outside the Earth's atmosphere in what seemed like just a few seconds, though it must have been longer than that. The gravitational force relaxed and then vanished altogether.

Johnsmith peered through the narrow aperture leading to the cockpit, trying to see out the window over the pilot's console, while the shuttle eased into orbit around the Earth.

The co-pilot, a bald woman who looked every bit as tough as the ship's captain, said, "You can unstrap yourselves and move around, so long as you don't try to come forward of the bulkhead separating the passengers' cabin from the cockpit."

Johnsmith fumbled with his straps until he was free. The buoyancy of his body under zero-G surprised him, even though he expected it. As he flailed around over his companions' heads, he reflected that you never quite understand something until you've experienced it.

"This is terrific!" he said, allowing himself to express the enthusiasm he was now feeling. "I never thought I'd get to ride in a spaceship!"

"You looking forward to being a prisoner of the state?" Felicia asked in a tone of biting sarcasm.

"Every cloud has a silver lining," Alderdice said philosophically. "If he wants to enjoy the journey, there's no reason to spoil it for him. After all, there's little enough to look forward to at the end of the trip."

Johnsmith said nothing. Instead, he tried to float close enough to look out at the stars. He finally got hold of the headrest on Felicia's chair and propelled his body forward. He caught himself before he collided with the bulkhead, and then crept along until he could see out past the two-person crew.

It was a spectacular sight, no doubt about it. The stars seemed much bigger, and were considerably brighter than he had imagined. Of course, he'd rarely seen them at all, living in the city, but every once in a while the miasma had thinned sufficiently to get a glimpse of them. They had never looked anything like this, though. Gazing at them in their pristine splendor, he could almost believe in Ronindella's God.

The co-pilot turned around. "I thought I said you're not to come in here," she said.

Johnsmith started to protest his innocence, until he became aware that his head, shoulders, and part of his torso had drifted into the cockpit while he was stargazing.

"Sorry," he said, pushing himself back.

"We'll have to report you for this," the pilot said, without even turning to see who it was.

For a few minutes, Johnsmith had almost forgotten that he was nothing more than a glorified convict. The pilot's laconic phrasing had reminded him of that fact efficiently and mercilessly. He retreated to the safety of the passengers' cabin.

The trip out to the station was uneventful. The pilot told them to take good care of their pressure suits, because they'd bring them to Mars with them. Johnsmith couldn't see much as they docked, but he managed to get into his suit without assistance. The curlicue clouds of Earth seemed to be above him as he crossed through a clear, plastic tube leading to the torus. He realized that this was just an effect of the shuttle's position relative to the planet, but it was nonetheless disconcerting for that. He remembered a video of *Alice in Wonderland* he'd seen as a kid. This morning, like Alice, he'd awakened knowing who he was, but he'd been through so many changes since then that he couldn't be sure anymore.

He glanced over his shoulder before the airlock door shut. There was the shuttle, hanging like a flatiron against a black velvet backdrop. The door clanged shut, the lock was pressurized, and they climbed out of their suits. Bulky and awkward as they were, Johnsmith was glad he'd only had to wear one for a few minutes. That wouldn't be the case on Mars, of course. Every time he went outside, he'd have to wear one. That was something he didn't look forward to in the least.

The inside door opened, and they looked out onto what at first glance appeared to be a tropical paradise. This was the station's botanical garden, which covered a good deal of the wheel's interior. The manufacturing of oxygen was of paramount importance here. Whatever other business went on wouldn't last long otherwise.

Another Captain Vuh was waiting for them on a curving expanse of emerald grass.

"Hello," she said. "I'm going to help you through the transition to your new home. I'll show you where you're going to be staying here at the station, and take you to your ship in the morning."

The shuttle's two-person crew, who had come ashore with them, walked away in the middle of Captain Vuh's welcoming speech, leaving Johnsmith, Felicia, and Alderdice alone with her. She beckoned for them to follow her, and led them along a path through the garden. Johnsmith noticed that people paid little or no attention to them as they walked past. Well, it really shouldn't have been surprising; they must have seen prisoners shuffling through here every day.

Captain Vuh, chattering continually about the great service they were about to provide for humankind, showed them to an apartment located on the outside of the torus. A polarized window allowed them to look out at the stars or at Earth, depending on the time they happened to be watching. There were three bunks along the curved inner wall. The place had an antiseptic odor.

"Some dinner will be brought to you in a few minutes," Captain Vuh said. "If there are any questions, I'll take them now."

Nobody said anything.

"Very good! I'll leave you for now. If there's anything you need, just punch the green button on the phone over there in the corner. I'll see you in eight hours.''

A robot brought their food, and Johnsmith ate greedily. So did Alderdice, but Johnsmith noticed that Felicia hardly touched hers. And she was already so thin!

Johnsmith didn't feel much like sleeping. And, it seemed that Alderdice didn't, either. Long after Felicia had retired, the two men conversed in low tones. The room was palely lit by a blue night light.

"I guess it was my husband leaving that started me on the downhill slope," Alderdice said. "I just couldn't seem to pay as much attention to the job anymore."

"That's what happened to me, too," Johnsmith commiserated. "Except that it was my wife, not my husband."

Alderdice smiled sadly. "All the same, in the end. Of course, you have children."

"Just one child, actually."

"Well, Lon and I thought about it. But we couldn't decide who would bear the child. I think our mutual selfishness began to destroy the marriage at that point."

"Don't be too hard on yourself," Johnsmith said, but he was hardly thinking of Alderdice's problems. Ever since the mention of Smitty, he'd been wondering what would become of the boy. His boy.

"You know, you're a good guy," Alderdice said. "Letting me go on like this. But let's not sit here being gloomy all night."

"What choice do we have? I didn't bring a deck of cards."

"Well, what about the phone?" Alderdice jerked his head toward the corner.

"The phone?" Johnsmith looked at him blankly. "What about it?"

"Captain Vuh said that if we needed anything, we were to push the green button on that phone. Let's try it.''

Johnsmith shrugged. "Okay, but what is it that we need?"

"Something to while away the time." Alderdice pushed his chair back with a scraping sound and raised his bulk lightly and easily. He went to the phone and unceremoniously pushed the green button.

Captain Vuh's face appeared on the screen. "How can I help you?" she asked pleasantly.

"Uh, we need something for . . ." Alderdice didn't quite know how to ask.

"For entertainment," Johnsmith said.

"I'll put you through to recreational services," Captain Vuh said. Electronic "ant races" zipped across the screen where her face had been a moment before. Another image appeared, obviously a computer animation—a comical, banana-nosed creature with a barrel torso.

"Hi," the cartoon character said. "I'm Jumpin' Johnny, and I'm here to make life a little easier. P-p-p-please let me help you."

"Thank you," Alderdice said. "What . . . diversions do you have available?"

"Everything you want from A to Z," Jumpin' Johnny sang. "All you can ask to make life carefree."

Johnsmith whistled. "These colony folks have got it made."

Jumpin' Johnny executed a cartwheel, grinned at them, and did another cartwheel. Every few seconds, he repeated these movements in an endless loop while they tried to decide what to order from him.

"Do you think we can have alcohol?" Alderdice asked.

"Any kind you want," Jumpin' Johnny said, and then resumed his acrobatics.

"How about onees," Johnsmith said, noting the resultant terrified expression on Alderdice's face.

"But that's ille—"

"Onees are available to provide some mirth," Jumpin' Johnny interrupted, his clown face enlarging as he winked. "Long as you don't tell the folks back home on Earth."

"We wouldn't think of it," Johnsmith said. "Besides, we're going to Mars. We'll probably never get back home."

"Well, in that case, we'll have a delivery boy at your apt in just a few minutes."

Jumpin' Johnny somersaulted into a kaleidoscope and vanished.

"I'll be damned," Alderdice said.

"You already have been," Johnsmith reminded him. "And so have I. Maybe that's why they allow us to have onees."

"I don't know. Maybe it's some kind of mistake. Maybe we're going to be reported for requesting onees."

"So what are they going to do? We're already prisoners, Alderdice."

"They might send us to the moon, instead of Mars."

Johnsmith fell silent. He hadn't thought of that.

"What's all the commotion?" It was Felicia, aroused by their strident voices.

"Uh, sorry we woke you," Johnsmith said. "But there's a, uh, a delivery coming."

"A delivery?"

Alderdice giggled. "Not a baby, just some onees."

"Onees?" She lifted her head and looked from one to the other, her hair disheveled from sleep. "What are you talking about?"

"They're supplying us with some onees," Johnsmith said.

"Right." Felicia rolled over and attempted to get back to sleep.

A moment later, a buzzer sounded. Alderdice searched in wain for a way to open the door. "Come in," he said, hoping that their visitor would be able to obey.

The door slid open, and in scuttled a robot that looked like a fire extinguisher on crablegs.

"I've brought the onees you requested," it said in the tones of an interior decorator. "You neglected to specify how many you need when you phoned in your order, so I took the liberty of bringing a dozen. Will that be satisfactory?"

"A dozen?" Johnsmith could hardly contain himself. "Yes, I think that will be fine."

"Where would you like me to put them?" the robot asked.

Johnsmith looked around, and noticed that one table dipped in the middle. "Oh, right here will be fine," he said, tapping the table and smiling.

A thin tube emerged from the robot's cylindrical body, snaked up onto the table, and spat out twelve shining onees that rattled into the table's depression, one right after the other. The tube descended back into the robot.

"Do we have to . . . sign for this, or anything?" Johnsmith asked.

"It will be deducted from your wages," the robot said simply. "Will that be all, then?"

"Uh, yeah, that'll be all," Johnsmith said.

The robot went out.

Johnsmith and Alderdice stared at the gleaming onees, marveling. The way the dim light collected and shone from them, they were almost hallucinatory even without being touched. After a few seconds, Johnsmith realized that Felicia had not gone back to sleep, and was staring at them in angry disbelief.

"What the hell is going on around here?" she demanded.

"We told you before," Alderdice said. "We've ordered some onees from . . ."

"From recreational services," Johnsmith finished for him. "Like ordering a pizza."

"Those are just ball bearings," she said. "They wouldn't give you real onees."

Her attitude began to annoy Johnsmith. "Want to touch one, then?" he said. "Prove that you're right?"

She had no answer for him.

"I guess they gave them to us because they're legal offworld," Alderdice speculated. "Though I must admit I've never heard about it before."

"It makes sense," Johnsmith said. "They wouldn't want people on Earth to know about it, sure, but how else can you alleviate the boredom on Luna or Mars? Drinking and drugs are physiologically harmful, shortening the time a person can work. It's expensive to bring people up from Earth, so the government wants to get the maximum amount of work from each one of us."

"They can't do that if we're onee-crazed all the time," Alderdice argued.

"But we won't be. It doesn't take long for the effect of an onee to wear off. A nanosecond, maybe. And you're not physically drained after using one. All our superiors will have to do is make sure we don't use them during working hours, and that we get proper nutrition and rest. We could all live to be a hundred years old, and still be oneed-out every night for the rest of our lives."

"Are you sure it doesn't have some long-term effect?" Alderdice said.

"I'm not sure of anything," Johnsmith said, looking down at the onees. He stretched his hand out toward them.

"They *want* you to take those things," Felicia said. "It's the opiate of the masses."

"No, that's religion," Johnsmith said, remembering one of the more interesting videos he'd seen in college, *Karl Marx vs. Jesus*.

"If they want you to take them, then you shouldn't do

it," said Felicia. "That's one of the tenets of the revolution, and you should take it to heart."

"How do you know what we should do?" Alderdice said. His training had made him run away from the onees on Earth, but if Johnsmith was correct, he would not be breaking the law just by touching an onee here in space.

"Go ahead," Johnsmith urged him, without any of the malice he had shown the first time, in the effapt back on Earth. "Give it a try."

"You first," Alderdice said, but he knew now, for the first time, that he would do it.

"All right." Johnsmith reached out and scooped up one of the glittering little spheres. He fell back in his chair, eyes wide open, mouth agape with an audible gasp.

"Just like that," Alderdice marveled. "He's gone."

"Sure," Felicia said angrily, "the quicker they short circuit your brain, the quicker they can turn you into their slave."

"I'm already their slave," Alderdice said with a ferocity he had never realized was in him. He went for the onees.

"No, wait," Felicia shouted, "Don't do it."

"Why not? Afraid of what we might do? Look at Johnsmith. Do you find him threatening?"

"No, I just . . . don't want to be left alone."

"There are ten more onees here," Alderdice said, and picked up the eleventh. "You're certainly welcome to—"

By the time Felicia opened her mouth to protest, Alderdice was no longer able to hold even the most rudimentary of conversations.

FIVE

"WHAT A MESS." Ronindella shook her head. The effapt looked as if it hadn't been cleaned since Johnsmith
moved in six weeks ago. It would take hours, days, to
sort through all this junk and find what was worth saving.

Smitty II didn't mind, though. He was burrowing
through the debris as if it were his own personal play-
pen. His unabashed joy in the simple things reminded
her of his father. She sighed in exasperation.

"Smitty, you'll have to help me carry some things
up to the flyby, as soon as Ryan gets here," she said.

Smitty kept playing, ignoring her.

"Did you hear what I said?" she demanded in a
threatening tone.

Smitty stopped and glanced apprehensively over his
shoulder at her. "Yes, Mom."

"Good. Now come over here and help me clean this
stuff up, like a good boy."

"Okay," Smitty replied mournfully. He almost
wished that he was in school, instead of hanging around
here, picking things up and carrying them out into the
hall. He did most of the work, too, as it turned out,
with his mother supervising.

"I'd help you, Smitty," she said a couple of times, "but you know I have a bad back."

Smitty kept working, wondering how old he would have to be to develop a back problem so he could get out of this kind of slave labor. He'd been working for about a quarter of an hour, when he saw something down behind a cardboard box that interested him. He waited for his mother to go to the bathroom before he took a closer look.

On the floor, between the old, beat-up rug and the baseboards, was a shiny thing. At first, Smitty thought it might have been a marble, but as soon as he got a closer look, he knew better. It was smaller, and silvery, like a BB. Smitty pushed the box away, reached down, and—

—he was swimming in salty water. Smitty had never been swimming before, and he certainly hadn't expected to end up swimming today, but here he was. He knew his Mom wouldn't want him doing this while he was supposed to be working. But he couldn't remember what he was supposed to be doing, anyhow. Who cared? This was great!

The color of the water changed, went through all the tints of the rainbow, but it was still water. It was nice and clean and cool and wet, and he felt so wonderful that he wished it would never end. Every once in a while, he would see a dark shape through the colorful murk, but if those things were alive, they didn't bother him.

He finally had to come up for air. He hesitated for a moment. Which way was it to the surface? If he waited much longer, his lungs would burst, but he didn't know which way to swim. There should have been light coming from above, but he couldn't see anything except the colors. He panicked, arms and legs flailing. This didn't get him anyplace, and his heart hammered in his chest from fear. He was going to drown.

He thought of his father. His father taking him on a

bus ride to the harbor. His father bemoaning the fact that there was no place for a kid to swim. His father pointing out things in the water. Showing him the buoy. The buoy.

In imitation of the buoy, Smitty calmed himself. With his arms by his sides and his legs straight, he stopped moving. For a moment, he tumbled slowly. His body came to a stop and then righted. He began, almost imperceptibly at first, to rise. He gradually gained speed as he ascended.

Now that he knew which way to go, Smitty began to stroke in that direction, kicking his legs like a frog. He couldn't hold his breath for much longer, but he was determined to make it. In the murky green, blue, violet, pink, red, orange, yellow water, he thought he saw a twinkling star overhead. The color stabilized, becoming blue-green. He kicked harder, and saw more dappled light dancing enticingly just out of reach.

He bobbed to the surface, inhaling greedily at the delicious air. Gasping, he tried to keep his head above water. He swallowed some of the salty stuff once and coughed, but he did better after that.

He was treading water now, watching the swell of the surf, allowing himself to be lifted and gently set back down in a fluid trough, only to rise again. It could have gone on forever, it seemed to Smitty. Soon he was wishing for something to happen.

It did.

A monster with a long, sinuous neck and dripping jaws rose out of the surf. It was sort of like a dinosaur, only it had coiling things growing out of its head, which was too big to be on its body in the first place. The creature was an ugly, unnatural looking thing. And it was looking right at him.

Smitty wanted to get away, but he couldn't move. He just kept treading water as the monster glided nearer and nearer. In seconds, it loomed over him. Smitty could smell it, an awful, rotten stench. The behemoth raised one limb. Smitty was amazed to see that this wasn't a flipper, but was jointed like an enormous, webbed human hand. The monster was going to pluck him out of the surf and eat him!

Shutting his eyes, Smitty waited for the giant claw to descend. He knew that it was going to hurt a lot, so he said the prayers his Mom had taught him.

Suddenly the insides of his eyelids glowed crimson. An explosive roar followed. Involuntarily, he opened his eyes.

The monster was rearing back, a large chunk on the right side of its head missing, the flesh smoking and sizzling. It howled and bellowed deafeningly as it shook its ungainly head toward another dragon-shape emerging from the fog.

A crimson bolt shot from the thing swimming toward them, sweeping across the undulating back of the monster, burning the glistening flesh as it went.

The monster dove, creating a wave that swamped Smitty, making him swallow salt water. He struggled to stay afloat, unable to see or breathe for a moment. He gagged and coughed, rubbing the stinging salt water from his eyes. The sea around him was becalmed, revealing that the monster was gone. But the dragon whose fiery breath had driven it away was headed straight for him.

Before he could even think of what to do, something grabbed him from behind. Some new sea monster, shaking his shoulders. If he could turn around, he could at least see what had hold of him.

Using all his strength, he wrenched himself from the thing's grasp and turned in the water to face—

—his mother.

"Smitty, what *is* the matter."

He watched the ball bearing bounce on the floor and roll under the convertible sofa-bed. Had that tiny thing really made all this stuff happen to him just now? He could hardly believe it, but it seemed to be true.

His Mom was shaking him again, only not so hard this time. "Oh, Smitty, I thought you were having a fit or something," she said. "Are you all right?"

"Yeah," he said, half expecting to swallow water as he opened his mouth. "Yeah, sure, I'm okay."

"Maybe you should see a doctor."

Smitty didn't think much of the idea. "I was just foolin' around, Mom," he said.

Ronindella's brow furrowed, and she loomed over him much like the sea serpent that had been after him a minute ago. "You mean you were faking those terrible spasms?" she demanded to know.

"Well . . . sort of." For some reason, he didn't want her to know the truth, even if it meant he would be punished. That little silver ball had belonged to his Dad, and in a way the two of them, father and son, had shared the thing. Smitty didn't care if it was wrong, he decided. His Dad was gone, but Smitty wasn't about to forget him.

The flat of Ronindella's hand came down, and Smitty felt the sharp impact sting his cheek. "You had me scared to death!" she screamed. He could barely hear her through the buzzing in his ears.

"I'm sorry, Mom," Smitty said, cringing as the tears started to flow. "I was only playing. I didn't mean anything by it."

"Haven't I got enough problems without you frightening me like that? What's wrong with you?"

"Nothing. . . ."

"Maybe I'd better take you to church this evening. They're open all night, you know."

"I know," Smitty said miserably, wiping his face with the back of one hand.

"Well, I'm going up to the roof to see if Ryan is here with the flyby yet. You'd better behave yourself while I'm gone, if you know what's good for you. I want to see more of this stuff stacked up here in the corridor when I get back."

"Okay, Mom."

She went out, muttering darkly about finding somebody who could get the elevators working. Smitty listened to her footsteps diminish. Alone, he sniffed up the last of his tears and started to drag boxes out into the corridor, as he had been told to do. When he came back into the effapt, he tried not to look at the sofa-bed, but it was no use.

He got down on all fours and crawled behind it, groping for the little silver thing. It would take his mother a few minutes to go upstairs and come back down. Maybe he could put the ball bearing in his pocket and take it home. Or hide it someplace and come back later to get it. No, that wouldn't work; he didn't even know what bus to take to get here.

As he felt around on the grimy old carpet, everything abruptly turned blue-green. He had been in the water, but just for a second. His hand must have brushed the ball bearing.

Hurriedly, he held his palms flat and went back over the same patch of rug again, more slowly this time. One moment he was in the shadows behind the sofa-bed, and the next—

—he was in the sea, his hair plastered to his scalp. One monster was dead, or at least it was gone. But another was bearing down on him, its sharp breast cutting through the water like a knife. It had flippers, too, lots of them.

But even through the fog, Smitty began to see that these weren't really flippers. They were stiff, moving in unison. They looked like oars.

It was a ship! It was just like the ships in a video Dad had showed to him once. More than a thousand years ago, these ships had raided the coast of Europe. What had Dad called the guys who sailed them?

Vikings.

The rowers on the right side shipped their oars, holding them straight up so that they gleamed through the fog. The ship turned broadside to Smitty, and an oar was extended to him. The rough, bearded men pulled him out of the water, grasping him under the armpits. He was saved.

Falling on the wooden planks of the deck, Smitty gasped and raised his torso up with one hand. The Vikings, in their fur and metal get-ups, were standing all around him. Suddenly, a naked man pushed his way between two of them.

"Smitty!" the man said.

It was his Dad!

"Dad, I thought you were on Mars," Smitty said breathlessly.

"What are you talking about, kid?" his Dad said, lifting him up and embracing him. "I'm right here with you."

This was great. His Mom and Ryan had lied to him, as he had always suspected. Dad hadn't gone to Mars; he was here, on the high seas, having adventures with Vikings.

One of the Vikings, a giant, laughed deeply, and all the others joined in. At first, Smitty didn't know whether to be afraid or not, but his Dad was smiling, so he guessed it was all right. Maybe they would all be friends, and just sail around looting and plundering forever.

Just then a shadow fell over the deck. Smitty looked up to see another sea serpent, this one even more terrifying than the last. Before he could move, it opened its jaws and snatched something right out of his hand and—

—his Mom was shaking him again.

"Where did you get that?" she shrieked, pointing to the onee rolling on the floor.

For a moment, Smitty couldn't answer. After all, he had just been attacked by a sea serpent. It would take a few seconds, at least, to get used to the idea that he was back here with his Mom yelling at him, and not with his Dad on the deck of the Viking ship. As he gradually became reoriented to his surroundings, he expected his Mom to hit him again, but she didn't.

"Oh, Smitty," she said, tears starting to form in her eyes, "how could you do this to me?"

This was worse than getting smacked, as far as Smitty was concerned. He hated it more than anything when she acted like this. He knew he had to do something to improve the situation.

"Mom, I found it on the floor," Smitty explained, with just the right touch of desperation needed to convince her of his innocence. "Honest, I don't even know what it is."

"But you were under the influence of an . . ." She glanced toward the door, as if Conglom police might burst in at any second. She never finished the sentence, as though pronouncing the word could send her to the moon. She didn't try to hit Smitty again, either; instead, she hugged him.

"I'm sorry, sweetheart," she said. "But what you did is against the law. We'll call the police, but when they get here you'll have to pretend that you never touched it."

"Okay, Mom," Smitty agreed. "But what is it?"

"I think maybe Ryan should tell you that. He'll be down here in a minute, and he'll explain everything to you."

She'd been trying to make him think Ryan was his father ever since Dad moved out of the apt. Smitty didn't like it, but what could he do but put up with it? Even Ryan didn't much like pretending he was Smitty's Dad, but he knew Ronindella wanted him to do it, so he did it. Dad was never like that. If Dad thought Mom was wrong about something, he told her so, and then she bitched at him until he gave in.

Ronindella went to the phone and punched in a number. The screen remained blank.

"Shit," she said. "It's been disconnected. Your father's not even on Mars yet, and it's been disconnected already. He probably hasn't paid his bill, if I know him.''

Smitty didn't like it when she said things like that about his Dad, but he didn't say anything. She would be even worse about it if he said something, and he might get punished, too.

Ryan Effner came through the open effapt door. ''Hi, Ronnie,'' he said, affecting cheerfulness. ''Hi, kiddo.''

''Ryan, you've got to talk to Smitty,'' Ronindella said. ''He's . . .'' She didn't want to say it aloud, so she gestured for Ryan to come closer. He walked across the room in three steps, and they moved against the wall. There was no place else to go in the effapt, except the bathroom, and there was hardly room for one person in there, let alone two.

Shooting a warning glance at Smitty, Ronindella then turned away from him and whispered something to Ryan. Smitty watched them furtively, wondering what was going to happen next. He saw Ryan's eyes widen, and then Ryan said: ''You don't think I had anything to do with it, do you?''

Ronindella looked at him with a puzzled expression. ''What are you talking about?''

''I didn't give them to him,'' Ryan said. He sounded whiny, like a kid who had done something wrong and was afraid he would be punished for it. Smitty had never seen a grown man act like this before.

''Who said *you* gave them to him?'' Ronindella screamed. ''Just what the hell do you know about this?''

''Nothing.'' He looked away from her.

''Did you give it to Smitty?''

''No, just ask him.'' Saying this seemed to give Ryan new courage. ''Go ahead, he'll tell you.'' He turned toward Smitty. ''Won't you, kid?''

Smitty stared at Ryan. He simply couldn't understand why Ryan was acting so weird. After all, nobody had said the guy had anything to do with it.

"Well, go ahead, Smitty," his Mom said. "Just tell the truth. Don't be afraid."

Smitty took her at her word. "Ryan didn't give it to me," he said. "I found it right over there on the floor, just like I told you, Mom."

Ryan looked relieved.

Ronindella glanced at Ryan, but she didn't say anything to him.

"I didn't mean to make it happen," Smitty lied. "I was just trying to pick up a box, and all of a sudden . . ."

"All of a sudden, ka-pow!" Ryan laughed nervously. "I'll bet you never had a thrill like that before, Smit."

Turning on him, Ronindella said: "How come *you* know so damn much about it, Ryan?"

Ryan took on a sheepish expression. "Well, I've seen it in *Pixine.*"

"Yeah, right."

"I'm sorry, Mom," Smitty said, seeing that the blame had been shifted onto Ryan. "I really didn't mean to do anything wrong, you know. You believe me, don't you?"

"Of course I do, darling." She went to him and hugged him again. "And I'm sorry I got so upset."

It would be all right now, Smitty knew. She might even get him some ice cream, if he handled things the right way.

"We've moved enough of this stuff today," Ronindella said. "Why don't we lock up the effapt and go get something to eat?"

"Yeah!"

Ronindella put her arm around Smitty's narrow shoulders and gave him a little squeeze. "Where would you like to go, hon?"

"You know, Mom. Kwikkee-Kwizeen."

"Then Kwikkee-Kwizeen it is. Ryan, would you care to drive us there?"

It was an order, and Ryan knew it. He would do anything right now to stay in Ronindella's good graces. He nodded meekly. "Sure," he said. "I love Kwikkee-Kwizeen."

"Everybody loves Kwikkee-Kwizeen!" Smitty chimed in, mimicking the projectogram ad. "'Cause it's the place that's really keen!"

Smitty and Ryan ran upstairs, and were forced to wait for Ronindella on the roof parking lot. Her stately progress, and the lack of a sunshield, required them to get into the broiling flyby and wait for a couple of minutes before the air conditioner cooled off the interior. It was less harmful than waiting bare-headed outside, though.

There was ample room for two adults in the Akbar, a Saudi make that Ryan had picked up only a year old for three hundred thousand. As Ronindella often attested, it was the kind of deal only a smart man like Ryan made. Smitty didn't quite know why, but he thought this meant more about his Dad than about Ryan.

The air conditioner was soon blasting away, and, though it was a little crowded with Smitty sitting on his Mom's lap, they were in good spirits by the time they pulled into the sweltering Kwikkee-Kwizeen parking lot.

Inside, there was a line snaking to the Kwizeen-Karts, where a credit card was all it took to buy all sorts of delicious foods. Ryan popped his credit card into the slot, and Smitty made his selections: fried seaweed sausages, petroshake, soy burger. A little slip of paper came out with the card once the order had emerged from the well in the top of the cart.

"What's that?" Smitty said.

"I don't know," his Mom said. "Why don't you take it to the table and see?"

Smitty snatched it up, and, following his Mom and Ryan to a booth, he sat down and examined it as they ate. He couldn't figure out what it was.

"Let Ryan see it," Ronindella said.

Ryan took the paper and looked at it for a while, his brow furrowed. "It's a contest," he said at length, as portentously as if he had deciphered the Dead Sea Scrolls.

"What's a contest?" Smitty said.

"It's kind of like a game, kiddo. You write your name down and you might win a prize. Here's a pen."

Smitty took the paper and pen. He knew how to sign his name, but he'd only had to do it a few times in his nine years. The Conglom tax forms, and a few other things were all that needed his signature, important documents like that. It seemed funny to sign something for fun.

But he did it anyway; maybe he'd win a prize. As he wrote, he realized for the first time how much he hated Ryan Effner.

SIX

THEY WERE ON their way to Mars. It seemed odd to Johnsmith, but he knew that it was true. He and Alderdice spent a lot of time clutching onees, but whenever they came up for air the drab interior of the Conglom Interplan ship was always around them, unchanged but for the tiniest details.

Of course, he could always go and look out the stern transparency at the diminishing Earth. But that depressed him, and besides, the rest of the heavens changed so slowly that it was hardly any fun at all unless you took it in fairly infrequently. Once a week or so was interesting, but no more often than that.

So it was onee thrill after onee thrill. At first Johnsmith really enjoyed the hallucinatory sights, smells, sounds, and feel of imaginary worlds. None of them were ever quite the same as that watery place he'd fallen into while he was sitting alone in his effapt back on Earth—the sensory definition was lacking. But it was still pretty good, usually. Not quite as all-encompassing as he remembered it, but that was surely because he hadn't known what to expect that first time. At least the hallucinations whiled away the hours, though.

Johnsmith got in the habit of eating as soon as he woke up, and then grabbed onto an onee for an hour or two. Any longer than that, and his nerves got a little frazzled. He floated around the ship, occasionally talking with Alderdice, until lunch. Sometimes Felicia joined grudgingly in conversation with them, but more often than not she kept to herself.

The two member interplan crew, a woman and a man, were not as hostile as the shuttle pilot and co-pilot had been. In fact, they were quite friendly—at least the captain was—though most of the time they didn't pay much attention to their human cargo. Johnsmith, Felicia, and Alderdice were still prisoners, but they weren't treated like it on the way to Mars, unless they got in the way.

"After all, what can we do?" Johnsmith said to Alderdice after a nap. They had been in space a few days, and he was losing track of the time. "We're stuck in this rattletrap spacecraft, and we're already half a million miles from Earth. The crew knows we pose no threat to them."

"We could hijack this ship," Felicia said from her bunk.

"Oh, come on, Felicia," Alderdice said out of one side of his mouth while sucking on a bottle of vitasip with the other. "How could we do that?"

"I'll tell you how," Felicia said in a contemptuous tone. "We overpower these two and seize control of the ship. That's how."

Johnsmith could hardly believe what he was hearing. "Do you know how to pilot an Interplan ship, Felicia?"

"I know how to fly a plane. It can't be much different than that, can it?"

"Of course it can," Alderdice argued. "It can be a lot different. This is a huge cargo ship designed to go hundreds of millions of miles in space. It will be refueled on Mars, so there's the finite amount of fuel to consider."

"If we turn it around in the next four months, we'll

have enough fuel to make it home," Felicia said. "We should start planning now."

"But Felicia," Johnsmith asked, "even if we got back to Earth, where would we land?"

"Trust me. There are places that are friendly to revolutionists, even today."

They discussed the matter for some time. Johnsmith didn't think there was any merit to the plan, but he enjoyed seeing Felicia enthused and animated. He wondered why she had become so bitter, what her life had been before she became, as she always put it, a "revolutionist."

Alderdice, however, fell into a funk.

"Is there something wrong, Al?" Johnsmith asked.

"No, not really. It's just my conditioning. You know, my programmed cortical implant gets me really disturbed if I'm thinking about doing anything illegal."

"Oh yeah . . . but didn't that stop you from using onees before? I mean, you're using them now, aren't you?"

"Yes, but I know they aren't illegal in space. So it's not the programming that's changed, but my perception of the legality of onees."

"Oh."

"They've made you into a slave," Felicia said, shaking her dark hair from side to side. "I guess I shouldn't hold it against you, should I? I mean, you really can't help it, can you?"

"I suppose not," Alderdice said, without a trace of sarcasm.

"Well, maybe Johnsmith and I could manage to hijack the ship alone," Felicia said.

"I'm afraid I'd have to try to stop you," Alderdice said. "Unfortunately."

Felicia's eyes flashed angrily at him.

"The implant, you know," Alderdice said.

"Right." Felicia turned away and would say nothing more.

* * *

Time passed with agonizing slowness.

Seven months later, Mars was looming like a rusty disc on the monitor. They had made no attempt at hijacking the ship, and, since they would be landing in a matter of days, Johnsmith suspected that they never would. Johnsmith and Alderdice had continued their daily routine of sleeping, using onees, talking, and eating.

The ship's captain, Hi Malker, would occasionally come back to see how they were doing. He was a good-natured guy from North Tel Aviv with an interest in sports.

"Got a message that the Phillies lost to Osaka in the World Series," he would say. Or, "America has won the Americas Cup," or, "The championship fight is coming up in less than forty-eight hours." Of course, what he meant was that they would get the signal from Earth in less than forty-eight hours. By the time they saw it, the fight would have been over for quite some time already.

"Captain Hi," Johnsmith said as they drifted over the main cargo hatch one day, "how did you ever get into a profession like this?"

"There is no profession *like* this," Hi said earnestly. "It's a one-of-a-kind job, right, Prudy?" he called to his co-pilot, who nodded brusquely. "Piloting the really big ones out to Mars and the Belt. There's adventure, and the pay is good."

It seemed more like boredom than adventure to Johnsmith, but he didn't want to disabuse Hi of his romantic fantasies. Hi was right about the pay, though, especially considering that it mounted up on the year and a half round trip from Mars to quite a sizable sum. Almost all of Johnsmith's money would go toward feeding and housing him, and to Ronindella back on Earth. At least he would be taking care of Smitty. All this was highly depressing to think about, though.

"Will we be landing near the north or south pole?" Johnsmith asked, by way of changing the subject.

"Oh, neither one," Hi said. "We're going to land on the Elysium plain."

"Elysium?" Johnsmith wasn't even sure what part of the planet that was. "I didn't know there was a settlement there."

"It's new. In fact, we're carrying a lot of building materials so they can add onto the compound. It's really only half constructed at this point."

"This is all news to me." Johnsmith said.

"Conglom security," Hi explained. "Extremely hush-hush."

"Where is Elysium, exactly?"

"Northwest quadrant, a few hundred miles above the equator."

"What's the weather like there?" Johnsmith asked.

"Just like the rest of Mars," Hi said. "Cold, most of the time. In the summer, though, it can get up to thirty or forty degrees."

"Not bad," Johnsmith said. "It might even seem like a relief after all the time I've spent sweltering away in that old city back on Earth."

The cheerful glimmer left Hi's brown eyes. "For awhile, maybe," he said, "but Mars is no picnic, even at the equator."

Johnsmith nodded. He hadn't really believed that he would have much fun on Mars, but now he was sure of it. He only hoped that the library and onees might keep him sane.

The rounded fullness of Mars became more evident in the following days. It no longer resembled a flat disc, and the vague shapes of craters and mountains began to emerge from the orange world's shifting landscapes.

Johnsmith felt an exhilarating sense of adventure in spite of himself, as he gazed out the port at Mars.

"You know," he said to Alderdice, "I don't think I really appreciated that we're going to live on another planet—not up until now."

"I know what you mean," Alderdice said, in an almost reverential tone. "It may only be half the size of Earth, but it's big enough. A whole world."

"Nothing on it," Felicia said, floating up behind them. "Just a frozen desert."

"There's a lot on it," Johnsmith argued. "Geologically, it's very interesting."

"I didn't know you like rocks," she replied sarcastically. "I thought onees were all you're interested in."

For some reason, her attitude bothered Johnsmith. He always felt that Felicia could be very nice, if she would just try once in a while. But she didn't seem eager to make the effort. What was worse, she always seemed to single him out for her caustic comments. He failed to understand why she was so nasty to him, but he guessed that there was really nothing he could do but ignore her taunts. This seemed to annoy Felicia even more than if he'd fought with her.

But human interaction was nearly forgotten as they went into orbit around Mars. Wonder and fear were commingled so thoroughly that Johnsmith began to think these two seemingly disparate emotions might be the same thing, after all.

It was a terrible and yet joyous thing to be drawn to an alien world. They could feel the force of its mass exerting itself on their bodies. And this time they would not resist gravity, as they had upon leaving Earth. This time they would descend to the bosom of the red planet, and Johnsmith, Felicia, and Alderdice would never go home again.

Alderdice, who had grown a beard in recent weeks, looked at Johnsmith. "Might as well go lie down for the landing," he said.

"Yeah."

Captain Hi spoke over the intercom. "We're going to start coming down in a minute. Strap yourselves in."

They drifted toward their reclining seats, Johnsmith attempting to give Felicia a hand. She slapped his fingers and pushed herself back to her chair unassisted. In a few minutes they were strapped in, waiting to land.

"Here we go," Hi's voice said from the cockpit.

The ship shuddered as the retro-rockets were fired. The gravity well of Mars put a strain on the fuselage that made the metal groan and creak inside the cabin. Johnsmith gritted his teeth, afraid that the entire ship might come apart and fling them like so much flotsam into eternal orbit around Mars.

The engines thundered, and Johnsmith felt himself getting heavier as the ship came ever closer to the Martian surface. A few minutes later, he felt the ship settle and the engines abruptly cut off.

They were on Mars. It hardly seemed possible, but they were really on Mars.

"Jesus," Alderdice said, "feel the gravity."

"It's a lot lower than Earth," Johnsmith said, "but it's been so long since we left home, I feel as if I weigh a ton."

"Should have taken more exercise," Co-pilot Prudy said, entering the cabin behind Captain Hi. "It's the best way to compensate."

"Yeah, but it's too late now." Johnsmith thought of all the time he had spent on the voyage under the influence of onees. He unstrapped himself and stood, the oppressive weight of his body forcing him to lean against a bulkhead for support.

"Come on," Hi said. "You'll be all right."

He led them through a hatch to an elevator, which they took down. They got into the pressure suits in the airlock. Hi opened the outer hatch, and they looked out at Mars.

Johnsmith was reminded of a Western he'd seen once,

with lots of sunsets over the desert. Too red, too vast to be real. Unlike the one in the film, though, *this* desert covered almost an entire planet.

Somebody was walking toward them from the right, wearing a pressure suit with chevrons on the shoulders. Behind him was a series of low huts, hangars, three big personnel carriers, and a few Martian terrain vehicles. One or two people could be seen seated in wieldos, putting up wallsheets, but other than that the landscape was devoid of all but sand and rocks.

"Welcome to your new home," a voice crackled inside Johnsmith's helmet. As their greeter came closer, he began to make out a man's face through the clear plastic visor.

"I'm your supervisor," the guy said, stopping just outside the airlock. "Angel Torquemada."

Johnsmith took a good look at him. He was a thin-faced man who did not smile as he spoke. His grim manner seemed to fit into his surroundings flawlessly.

"My co-pilot and I are tired," Hi said. "We'd like something to eat, and some R&R until we leave seventy-two hours from now."

"Duly noted, Captain," said Angel Torquemada. "Why don't you come with me?"

Johnsmith was impressed that Mr. Torquemada had come out to greet them himself, instead of sending one of his underlings. Maybe there would be a sense of civility here, after all. He supposed that it was possible a frontier society like this one might be very close knit. He'd find out before long.

As they moved toward the compound, Johnsmith glanced at the new buildings under construction, which Hi had told him about a few days ago. It appeared that the new buildings would be considerably more elaborate than the quonset huts they were now approaching.

The wind whipped around them so savagely that Johnsmith almost lost his footing once or twice. He wondered if the Martian wind ever completely died down. It seemed to somehow penetrate his pressure suit, chilling him in spite of the suit's heater.

They came to the nearest hut and went inside. There was an antechamber, sort of a spacious airlock, where they could remove their suits and hang them up. They did so, and followed Angel Torquemada into a long, warm room where a dozen or so people sat on long benches working with machines Johnsmith was unfamiliar with. He noticed an odd odor as he looked around. It was more than the close smell of human sweat, machines, and synthetic coffee. It occurred to him that this smell, which he could not identify, might be the lingering scent of Mars itself. Johnsmith felt dizzy with the knowledge of just how different, how *alien* his surroundings were from what he had known all his life.

He really was on Mars.

"This is data processing," Angel Torquemada said. His black hair was combed straight back, widow's peak over an aquiline nose and thin lips. "If you show aptitude and add up enough merit points, you may be promoted to work in here. If not, there's plenty of work available building the factory."

"What factory?" Felicia asked in a suspicious tone.

Torquemada turned to her. With no change of expression, he said, "The one we are building here."

"What are you going to make here that you couldn't manufacture on Luna or in the Belt?" Felicia asked. "I mean, Mars isn't known for this kind of thing, is it? The main thing is trying to grow plants and melt the polar ice cap for terraforming, as I've always understood it."

Torquemada's bloodless face showed nothing. His indifference seemed ominous to Johnsmith somehow, more intimidating than if he had shown anger at her impertinence. "We are already producing," he said finally, "though only at a fraction of the rate we anticipate when the new buildings go up."

Felicia clearly expected him to say more, but he didn't. Instead, he turned and resumed the tour. They passed through a curved, plastic connecting tunnel and entered another quonset hut. Here were bunks lined up along the walls, lockers, and showers at the far end.

"You'll come back here after you've seen the rest of the compound," Torquemada said.

Obviously, this remark did not apply to Hi and his colleague. They made themselves at home in the barracks, kicking off their boots and lying down as the tour went into a second connecting corridor leading to yet another hut. This one was larger than the others and was L-shaped, the nearest section containing a mess hall and kitchen; a passageway led them to a recreation area with pool and ping-pong tables, exercise machines, and three library booths. Johnsmith was relieved to see the latter, which he had begun to fear would be nonexistent at such a remote outpost. At least he would have *some* stimulation while he was stranded on this dead world.

In spite of insulation and sound proofing, the wind lashed at the hut so powerfully that Torquemada could hardly be heard above its howling.

"I know you must be exhausted," he said. "You've seen everything but your workspace. That can wait until tomorrow. Now feel free to go back to the barracks. You'll find kits containing personal items on your bunks. That's all."

Returning to the barracks, they passed the ping-pong players and pool sharks, the servochefs, and the handful of people dining quietly. As Torquemada had indicated, there were three bunks with nylon bags resting on drum-tight blankets. These were their personal kits.

Johnsmith pulled at velcro tabs and opened his kit. It contained a toothbrush and toothpaste, shaving gear,

towels, soap, and antiseptic spray. Out of the corner of
his eye, he noted that Felicia, apparently assigned to
the bunk next to his own, had been provided precisely
the same items.

"I think I'll have a shower and shave off my beard,"
Alderdice said.

As soon as he was left alone with Felicia and the
slumbering crew of the Interplan ship in the vast barracks, Johnsmith said, "I'm surprised that they have
showers."

"Why?" Felicia said, not sounding particularly interested.

"Well, because water is so scarce on Mars. Isn't
that why the colonies are all—except for this one, I
mean—near the polar ice cap?"

"This must be an area where they found aqui-
fers," Felicia said. "I remember seeing it in *Pixine.*"

"You mean they drilled down through the rock
and hit a water table, or something?" Johnsmith
said.

"Yeah, that's probably why they started building this
compound."

"Sure, makes sense." Johnsmith sat down on his
bunk, finding, not unsurprisingly, that it was not a particularly comfortable mattress.

As he sat in silence, he saw somebody moving
through the connecting corridor. A moment later, Angel Torquemada entered, holding a clipboard.

"Uh, sir," Johnsmith said.

Torquemada looked up from the papers fastened to
the clipboard. "Yes?"

"Mr. Torquemada, I've been wondering about something ever since you told us this is a factory."

"And what might that be?"

There was no hint of impatience or annoyance in
Torquemada's voice, and yet his manner still troubled Johnsmith. Nevertheless, Johnsmith finished

what he had started. ''What do we manufacture here?''

Torquemada looked straight into his eyes. ''Onees,'' he said, and continued on his way.

SEVEN

JOHNSMITH HAD BEEN dreaming of the sweltering heat of Earth, when he was awakened by an ungodly honking noise. He jumped up, nearly falling out of bed.

"Rise and shine!" a strange voice bellowed.

For a moment, Johnsmith didn't know where he was. He looked around in confusion, thinking that he would see Ronindella and Smitty. But he knew they weren't here. They couldn't be here in this drab barracks with these fifty or so prisoners. One look at Felicia, lying in the bunk beside his, and he knew that.

The horrid honking sounded again. It was Angel Torquemada, blowing on a conch shell as he passed through the barracks. "Let's go," he shouted between honks. "You've got a busy day ahead of you."

They were up and into their paper fatigues in a couple of minutes, Torquemada constantly prodding them, occasionally waving or thrusting the conch shell for emphasis as he hurried them up.

As soon as they were dressed, they were led through the connecting tunnel. Johnsmith groaned to see that it was not yet light outside. They jogged through the empty recreation area and past the mess hall and kitchen, taking a connecting tunnel that led to a building Johnsmith, Alderdice, and Felicia had not been introduced to yesterday. Johnsmith groaned again, seeing that they were to have no breakfast before they got to work.

"Double time it!" roared Angel Torquemada, running at the head of the clomping column of prisoners. Instead of turning the corner of the L-shaped building, he led them through a connecting tunnel to another previously unseen part of the compound. The tunnel mouth sloped into the ground. They jogged down a ramp into a cavern a few yards beneath the surface. There were exercise mats and a target range laid out in the football-field length chamber. Though oxygen had been pumped in, the place reeked of the same dusty, metallic odor that Johnsmith had noticed shortly after their arrival at Elysium.

"Line up over here," commanded Angel Torquemada.

They did as they were told, falling in a long line before which Torquemada paced, still carrying the conch shell in his right hand. A powerfully built man with an orange crewcut joined him.

"This is Sergeant Daiv," Torquemada said, stopping two paces in front of Johnsmith, Felicia, and Alderdice. "He'll be working with the new people. The rest of you know what to do."

With that, the others split off to go to the firing range or to the mats, leaving Johnsmith and his two companions alone with Sergeant Daiv and Angel Torquemada.

"The Sergeant will take good care of you," Angel Torquemada said. "Meanwhile, I'm going to have some breakfast."

Torquemada left them alone with their drill instructor, who sneered at them knowingly. "You snotballs have been in space for the best part of a year," he said. "You've had it pretty easy. No more, though. You're going to get in shape like a good combat team, and you're going to start *right now!*"

And they did. First, Sergeant Daiv led the three of

them around the cavern, ten laps that had Johnsmith
wheezing ominously after only one. Then, without even
a brief rest, they were up doing calisthenics on the mats,
and then they were running ten more laps. This went
on for an hour or more, the most grueling sixty or sev-
enty minutes Johnsmith had spent in many a year. Fortunately, the low atmospheric pressure seemed to make
his body quite resilient. Still, he was pretty exhausted
by the time they were permitted to shower and go to
breakfast.

Johnsmith stopped for a moment on the way through
the connecting tube, before entering the mess hall. The
sun was shining, and the sand drifts were whipping
about here and there over the rilles, but the Marscape
was brilliantly clear when dust was not swirling about
the compound. The horizon was too near, and the light
too intense in spite of the tiny sun. He suddenly felt
very lonely, a hundred million miles from home, everything he had ever loved taken from him, staring out
at a desert that went on for thousands of miles. No
prisoner had ever been so totally trapped before space
colonization had begun.

Felicia spoke from behind him: "There's a lot of
room to hide out there."

"Hide?" Johnsmith said. He turned to see Alderdice
dismiss her comment with a wave of one hand while
waddling toward the mess hall. "What do you mean,
hide?"

"Isn't it obvious?" she said. "There's a whole planet
out there, with only a few human encampments on it.
If we can get away from here . . ."

"But how would we live out there, Felicia?" Johnsmith asked. "The atmosphere is ninety or ninety-five
percent carbon dioxide. We aren't plants, able to breathe
that stuff."

"There's got to be a way."

"Well, I don't see how." Johnsmith turned away
from the bleak vista and walked to the mess hall. Fe-

licia was right behind him as the servochef doled out his portion onto a tray. It didn't look very appetizing, but Johnsmith was very hungry. He took a cup of synthetic coffee along with the food, and joined Alderdice, who was already eating.

"It's not Kwikkee-Kwizeen," Alderdice said, "but it'll have to do."

"Don't mention Kwikkee-Kwizeen," Felicia said, arriving at the table a moment after Johnsmith.

"Why not?" Alderdice looked at her suspiciously. "Do you have some connection to . . . now I remember where I know you from! Felicia Burst, in *Pixine!*"

Johnsmith turned to her. "You were in *Pixine?* Are you famous, Felicia?"

She would not look at him. "My family is."

"Of course!" Johnsmith felt very stupid for not realizing this months ago. "The daughter of Edweard and Jannelle Burst, scion of the Burst Corporation and the—

"—Kwikkee-Kwizeen fortune," Felicia said with resignation, chewing a toasted fiber stick.

"And you were captured by terrorists," Alderdice added. "Brainwashed, and turned into a revolutionary."

"Revolution*ist,*" Felicia corrected him. "And everything you heard about me was bullshit."

Johnsmith and Alderdice were annoyed. They had been thoroughly enjoying themselves, and had forgotten all about their predicament for a few seconds. It was disappointing to think that this new distraction wouldn't last.

"What do you mean?" Johnsmith asked, sensing that Alderdice couldn't ask because of his government programming. *Pixine* stories were official. Government employees had no choice but to believe them.

"Just what I said," Felicia told him in no uncertain terms. "It was all bullshit. I wanted to go with them."

"You wanted to go with a bunch of terrorists?" Alderdice said. "But why?"

"They weren't materialistic swine like the people I'd known all my life. They were *real* people."

"You speak of them in the past tense," Johnsmith observed.

"Sure, the Conglom troops killed them all when they discovered where our hideout was."

"All but you, huh?" Johnsmith found this troubling.

"That's right, all but me. And you know why?" Without waiting for an answer, Felicia burst into an impassioned explanation. "I'll tell you why. Because I'm the daughter of one of the world's wealthiest families. Because the Bursts own over six percent of the Conglom, Interplan, everything. Because money is power, and power is evil. I've spent my life trying to change the power structure of the solar system, and I haven't given up yet." Her voice had steadily risen until some of the other prisoners were staring at her. "I'm *proud* to be a revolutionist."

"All right, Felicia," Johnsmith said, "calm down now. You've proved your sincerity."

"Have I?" She looked down at her tray, saying with a softness that betrayed her rage, "All I have to do to get out of here is recant."

Neither Johnsmith nor Alderdice spoke for a few seconds. They were marooned on Mars for life, no matter what. The only sin either of them had committed was being bad at his job. It seemed incredible that this young woman, convicted of violent crimes against all the nations of Earth, could go free by just uttering a phrase of repentance.

"Then why don't you?" Alderdice said at length.

"Why don't I what?" Felicia said. "Tell them I'm sorry? Say I was a bad girl, and I won't do it again? Never."

"I would," Alderdice mumbled, taking a sip of his synthetic coffee.

"But it's different for us," Johnsmith said, beginning to appreciate Felicia's position. "We don't have any choice. Felicia's here because she *wants* to be here. Am I right, Felicia?''

She looked up at Johnsmith with a grateful expression he had never seen on her face before. ''Yes, that's right. You understand, don't you, Johnsmith? You really understand.''

''Well, sort of.'' He was reminded of his difficulties at the University. He had known that he had to do better, but he had been unable to fake it, even though he knew the Triple-S would get him if he didn't shape up. Something in him had prevented him from following the course of least resistance; as a result, he was now on Mars . . . and he would never go home again. He decided not to think about it anymore.

''You know,'' Felicia said. ''something's been bothering me for the past hour or so.''

''Oh?'' Johnsmith ingested a bit of protein paste, licking the excess from his lips.

''Yeah, they're training us for battle. Why do you suppose they want us to be ready for combat?''

''Probably nothing,'' Alderdice said. ''The government has all sorts of grandiose names for ordinary things. Calling an exercise period ''combat training'' is in keeping with that fine tradition, I assure you.''

The conversation was cut short abruptly by the conch shell. They looked toward the mess hall entrance, where Angel Torquemada was blowing a second blast.

''Apparently, breakfast is over,'' Johnsmith said.

''Stack your trays and follow me back to the training area,'' Torquemada ordered them.

They did as they were told. The session that followed was target practice with automatic weapons and high-energy particle beams. Sergeant Daiv took them through the procedures carefully, explaining each step as they went along.

The first time Johnsmith fired a gun, he thought his shoulder would be wrenched from its socket. He

couldn't hear anything for fifteen minutes after he
stopped firing, either. The particle beam was much
more pleasant, though it was disconcerting to see it
burn holes through a cinder block, especially when he
was firing it himself. Sergeant Daiv praised him for that
particular shot, however.

At half past eleven, they broke for lunch. Johnsmith
was grateful that Mars had close to a twenty-four hour
day, or there was no telling how long they might have
been commanded to remain on the range practicing their
uneven marksmanship.

All of the other prisoners, besides Johnsmith, Felicia, and Alderdice, had returned to the business of con-
structing the new sections of the compound and
manufacturing onees. It occurred to Johnsmith that their
warden felt there was little reason to hurry in training
the new arrivals for their jobs, since at least two of them
would be here for the rest of their lives. Still, it was
odd that they learned to fight before anything else. Who
were they expected to fight? Each other? Gladiatorial
combat? The thought made him laugh. Johnsmith had
led a sedentary life on Earth, and all this exercise didn't
suit him very well. He would have preferred to learn
about the excitation of the nervous system through the
onee's electronic charge. Maybe he could find out more
about what went on at Elysium during the evening meal,
or in the recreation area later on.

But the three new draftees did not eat dinner with
the others, and there was no time to be wasted with
games. They were sent to the showers and then to the
barracks. As he bathed, Johnsmith surreptitiously watched
Felicia soap her slender body. In spite of his exhaustion,
he was aroused. Turning away out of embarrassment, he
was dismayed to discover that Alderdice was staring at
him.

Turning the cold water on himself at full force, Johnsmith felt himself wilting. It seemed as though the in-

fernal frigidity of Mars seeped into his bones instantaneously. He shook the soapsuds out of his hair as the freezing water engulfed him, reminding him of that first onee experience once again. But the illusion passed quickly, spoiled by the odor of Mars streaming over him, its minerals carried in the water. Would he ever get used to it?

He shut off the shower valve and got a towel, immediately wrapping it around his waist even before drying his back and arms. As he grabbed another towel to dry his hair, he caught a glimpse of the forlorn Alderdice, whose brown bulk emerged from the steaming shower room.

As soon as he was dressed, Johnsmith retired to the barracks and turned down the covers of his bunk. He heard footsteps and, assuming it was Alderdice, did not look up.

"Got you on curfew, huh?" It was a woman's voice, but not Felicia's.

He raised his head to see her, a wiry woman in her early thirties whom he had noticed in passing during the morning exercises. "Yes," he said, "Mr. Torquemada says we have to go to bed early."

"It'll only be a few weeks before they let you socialize with the rest of us."

Johnsmith wondered why she was talking to him, since nobody besides Angel Torquemada and Sergeant Daiv had shown any interest in him or his companions in the forty-eight hours since they touched down at Elysium. Only Captain Hi and his taciturn crewmate had spoken to them at all; and Co-pilot Prudy, just barely.

"I was on my way to my locker to get something," the woman said, almost as if she was apologizing for stopping to talk to him. Perhaps she had mistaken his reticence for unfriendliness.

"Oh, don't go so soon," Johnsmith said, feeling a little embarrassed at the speed with which this gentle admonition popped out of him. "I mean, it's really very nice of you to stop and talk."

She grinned, which made her plain face sunny and attractive, seeming to take some of the chill out of the Martian air. "My name's Frankie," she said, extending her right hand. "Frankie Lee Wisbar."

"I'm Johnsmith Biberkopf."

Her handshake was firm, matching her straightforward manner. "Every few months a new batch of draftees arrives," she said, almost apologetically. "After a while, you hardly even notice anymore."

"I guess you wouldn't," Johnsmith said. "What I've been wondering, though, is . . ." He hesitated, seeing someone entering the barracks.

It was Felicia, followed by the doleful Alderdice. Could that have been a look of jealousy on her thin face? Or was it merely surprise, that one of the old timers would deign to talk to the lowly Johnsmith?

A third person entered the barracks, through the entrance on the far end, where Captain Hi and Prudy lounged about. It was Angel Torquemada. He walked straight through. As he approached them, Frankie walked off without a word.

"Tomorrow morning," Torquemada said, stopping for a moment, "you three cut your first training period off after a half hour and come to the briefing room. I've got a few things to tell you. Any questions?"

There was an awkward moment, and then Felicia said: "Yeah, where *is* the briefing room?"

"Sergeant Daiv will take you there at the appointed time. That'll be all for now. Get a good night's rest." Torquemada continued on his way through the barracks, toward the recreation area.

"What do you suppose that was all about?" Alderdice said, pulling a pair of paper pajamas over his enormous buttocks.

"I don't know." But Johnsmith had his suspicions.

* * *

They took light exercise in the morning, as they had been instructed, and then Sergeant Daiv led them through a passageway that curved deep underground. They were soon moving through a honeycomb of rooms cut into the solid rock. Air had been pumped in, and it was all heated more or less comfortably.

Sergeant Daiv stopped in front of a doorway and gestured for them to enter. As soon as they were seated in the meeting room, he left them. Inside were folding chairs, a podium, and a recent model projectogram. There was nobody waiting for them.

Johnsmith took a seat, grateful to be relaxing instead of running endless laps in the training cavern. He could almost have fallen asleep, had he not been wary of Angel Torquemada's imminent arrival. Felicia sat glumly to one side of him, and the heavily perspiring Alderdice sat on the other.

"I don't like this," Alderdice said. "I was just getting used to the daily routine, and now this."

Nothing more was said until Angel Torquemada stepped briskly into the room. "Good morning," he said, taking his place at the podium. "I hope you slept well, because today is when your mission on Mars really begins."

Their mission on Mars? What was he talking about?

"You may have wondered from time to time why you were sent to Mars."

"I thought we were going to help build the new sections of the compound," Alderdice said.

"That order has been rescinded. The message came from Earth only a few hours ago. Let me explain what your purpose here is, from now on."

"Don't bother," Felicia said sharply.

"Ms. Burst," Torquemada said, staring her down with his unblinking brown eyes, "you were sent to Elysium because of your family's immense influence. They were not quite able to get you off the hook, and so you're stuck here under my tutelage. You're one of the few at this outpost who may someday go free. Your fellow prisoners must envy you for that, but they will not envy you if you get on my wrong side while you are here. Do we understand each other?''

Johnsmith tried not to look at Felicia, but he couldn't help himself. She was red-faced, astonished. Nobody had ever spoken to her like that before; he was certain of that much. Johnsmith felt a certain perverse satisfaction at seeing her so discomfited.

''I asked you if we understand each other?'' Torquemada demanded. His face was completely expressionless.

Felicia did not submit to his will, however. She sat staring down at the stone floor, her jaw set, in silence.

Torquemada did not press the issue. Johnsmith, whose heart beat faster as a result of the exchange he had just witnessed, was sure that it was not over yet, however.

''These two gentlemen,'' Torquemada said, still looking at Felicia, ''do not have your connections. They will remain here for the rest of their lives. But the three of you will assist the Conglom for the time being, by participating in a controlled experiment.''

Johnsmith was beginning to regret that they had been sent to the briefing room. Why couldn't some of the old timers have been called in here instead of him and his two friends?

''Don't be alarmed,'' Torquemada said, as if he had read Johnsmith's mind. ''You won't be harmed in any way. You might even enjoy yourselves.''

Somehow, Johnsmith was not reassured by their supervisor's blandishments. They had not been sent to Mars for a picnic, after all. He felt ashamed for even thinking that Felicia's presence might spare them the worst. He wished that she would not continue to antagonize Angel Torquemada, who was clearly not a man to be trifled with.

"So what do you want us to do?" Felicia said, lifting her head and glaring at Torquemada.

Their master smiled for the first time in Johnsmith's memory. "I simply want you to use onees."

EIGHT

"MY LIFE SEEMS kind of empty," Ryan Effner confided to Madame Psychosis as he knelt in his pew. "I don't know what to do with myself. And Ronindella isn't very happy, either."

"Have you thought about bringing her in to see me?" Madame Psychosis said, without a trace of sarcasm. She always sounded so caring that Ryan felt as though he were floating in a warm bath of love while he consulted her. Therapy was something everyone should have, he decided, *especially* Ronindella. After all, how could she truly understand him if she didn't see Madame Psychosis? The trouble was, Ronnie was being very stubborn about not seeing his cybershrink.

"She says it's against her religion," Ryan said. "That's her latest excuse for not wanting therapy."

"What religion does she belong to?" Madame Psychosis asked.

"V.C.O.G."

There was a slight pause as Madame Psychosis tapped into her memory droplets for information about the Video Church.

"There is a fairly reliable method of weaning people away from the Video Church of God," Madame Psychosis said after a few seconds.

"Oh? What's that?"

"Ronindella's religion teaches that therapy is incompatible with the church's tenets, but not that it is strictly forbidden. If she is threatened with an alternative that is forbidden, then she might consent to therapy."

"I don't understand."

"The alternative must be the No-God Sect."

"Huh? That's no alternative. Ronindella would never hang out with that No-God bunch."

"Perhaps not," Madame Psychosis said in a motherly tone, "but wouldn't *you?*"

"Me?"

"Yes, you."

"Join the No-God Sect . . . ? I don't know, Madame."

"If you want her to seek therapy, this is a tried and true method."

"But it seems so . . ." He almost said "sneaky," but at the last instant amended it to: ". . . risky."

"We must deal with risk, just as we must deal with our feelings," Madame Psychosis said in portentous tones. "Nothing ventured, nothing gained."

Ryan felt sticky with perspiration, though the room was quite comfortable. He had to do what she suggested, obviously. Madame Psychosis would persist until he carried this thing out. Since he was paying for these sessions, he might as well agree to do it sooner, rather than later.

"All right," he said, his voice squeaking a little in submission. "How do I convert?"

"The No-God Sect requires no conversion as such. An acceptance of the central tenet is all that's necessary."

"And what is the central tenet?"

"That there is not, never has been, never will be, and *can* never be a supreme being."

Ryan mulled that over for a few seconds. "How do they know?"

"That's irrelevant," Madame Psychosis said. "Besides, discussion of such matters will give you something to do at the Sect meetings. Something that is not sybaritic, that is."

"Yeah, I suppose so." Ryan added resigned, "How long is this going to take?"

"The sooner you convince Ronindella that her reluctance to seek therapy is the cause of your involvement with the No-God Sect, the sooner she is likely to relent."

There was one thing that bothered Ryan, something that Madame Psychosis hadn't really touched on. "What if it doesn't work?" he said. "What if she just gets another guy?"

"Come now, Ryan," Madame said. "Haven't we learned to be more self-assured than that?" She smiled beatifically at him, and he knew that her strength would see him through the coming struggle.

Ronindella's credit swelled, the figures changing on the 'gram even as she watched. It was the result of the infusion from Johnsmith's government pay. But the figures didn't run up for long, she was disappointed to see. In the final analysis, it wasn't nearly as much as she had hoped for. It looked as if she would be stuck with Ryan, at least until something better came along. He was already getting on her nerves, she thought, as she lit a cigarette.

"Smitty," she called out, "what are you doing?" This question was almost ritualistic, as was Smitty's reply.

"Nothing." Smitty emerged from the bedroom with his dinosaur in hand. "This doesn't work anymore, Mom."

"We'll get some batteries for it later, honey." She patted his dark hair. "Which is about the only thing we can afford at the moment."

Smitty didn't know what she was talking about. He

had only started playing with the dinosaur again a few days ago. Every time he'd started to take it out of its box, he'd thought of his Dad, that last time they saw each other on the phone. But then his Mom had received this letter saying that Dad's pay was coming, and it almost seemed as if Smitty had heard from him personally. After that, he'd wanted to play with the dinosaur again, but the batteries had soon worn out. Well, maybe his Mom would remember to get him some new ones the next time she went out.

"Get your jacket on," she said after a few seconds.

"Huh?" This was unexpected. They were going out already. But somehow Smitty didn't think they would be shopping for batteries. "Where are we going, Mom?"

"To church."

"Church?"

"You heard me. Now go put on your jacket."

Smitty did as he was told, and in a moment was struggling to find the armholes in his yellow, plastic jacket. His Mom was pulling him out the door before he had it completely on. By this time he was sure that batteries were not the object of their quest. At least, he'd never noticed that they sold them in church before, but he wasn't absolutely sure. They did have a lot of concession stands at the Video Church.

They rushed down to the basement, where Ryan's flyby was parked. Ryan had started taking the bus a lot, because Ronindella had told him she needed it during the day. But Ryan kept staying out later and later every evening. As they zoomed up the ramp and out of the parking lot, the sun was setting. The city's towers were almost in silhouette, and the pastel sky behind them ranged from azure to damask.

Smitty had never been to church so late in the day. In fact, his Mom usually just watched the services on the projectogram. It was just like being there, she always said, except that Smitty could never help but notice how the people on the fringes of the congregation were sort of unfocused and distorted. But the ones in the middle looked pretty natural. And they were the ones who seemed to be sitting right next to you, of course. If you didn't pay close attention or think about it too much, it was okay. That was what Mom did; she just sat there with her eyes half-closed and rocked rhythmically while the preacher stalked back and forth, screaming about God and Hell and all the rest of that stuff that Dad had never cared much for.

Smitty didn't care much for it, either. Nevertheless, he and his Mom were on their way to the Video Church. He was probably in for a really boring time tonight, and he was willing to bet that the batteries would be forgotten, too.

The flyby gained speed, chugging as if it would give up the ghost, and then suddenly lifted above the street.

"Ryan's got to get those coils checked," Ronindella said. All she needed was to come down hood first in the middle of a busy intersection, or pile into a bridge abutment. Well, at least Ryan *had* a flyby. Johnsmith had never been able to afford one, even though he had made as much as Ryan until he got fired. She chided herself for marrying such an impractical man. Well, she'd been young then, and had no idea of what it took to bring up a child. She'd be damned if she was going to live like a pauper for the rest of her life, though.

The Video Church, a handsome Neo-Drive-In structure with crimson and turquoise neon trim, towered over Skid Row. As they approached, Ronindella banked. Smitty was pressed against the padded door on the passenger's side for a moment, and then the car hovered while Ronindella looked for a parking space.

Since there was no major service going on at the moment—and perhaps because it was dinner time—there were a few parking spaces available. The only way to get in was through the roof entrance. After all, the Video Church of God had no use for adherents who couldn't afford flybys.

Ronindella brought Ryan's flyby down with a nasty bounce. As he always did at such moments, Smitty understood why he had to wear a seat belt, especially when his Mom was driving. Ryan drove a lot better, but Smitty was glad he wasn't with them this evening. It was bad enough to have to come to church tonight without having that asshole along, too. Things could have been a lot worse.

Ronindella cut the engine and lifted the door on her side. Climbing out, she said, "Come on, Smitty."

Smitty pretended to have trouble undoing his seat belt, hoping something would happen at the last minute, so that he wouldn't have to go to church tonight.

But nothing happened; nothing at all. His Mom came around to the passenger side, opened the door, and flipped open the catch to his seat belt. So much for stalling around. He was going to church whether he liked it or not.

"Come on, young man," Ronindella said. "We haven't got all night, you know."

She yanked him out of the car and pulled him to the elevator. Smitty didn't exactly resist, but he didn't exactly cooperate, either. He just made the walk last a little longer, as if by accident. Smitty dared to hope that Ryan's license plate would be rejected by the scan, and that the elevator door would not open as a result; that had happened once before. Ronindella's victory was inevitable, however. Soon they were riding down into the brightly lit depths of the Video Church, and there was nothing for Smitty to do but go along with it.

Smitty could hear the congregation shouting even before the elevator door opened: "Praise God!" "Hallelujah!" "Jesus loves you!" and so on.

They stepped out into a projectogram studio, a gigantic, floodlit room filled with the faithful, who swayed en masse to a white gospel rhythm backing a strutting preacher.

"God knows who is doing His sacred work," the Reverend bellowed, spittle spraying in all directions from his immaculately white teeth, "and God knows who is shirking.

"Those who believe—who really believe—do the work to which the God-blessed Conglomerated United Nations of Earth government has so selflessly assigned them all. *Every* man, woman, and child on this planet works, as the Good Lord intended . . . or they take their damned souls and get off this beautiful planet."

"Hallelujah!" the faithful shrieked.

Ronindella could hardly believe her luck; they had walked into a full-employment sermon. For the first time in months, she started to think that things might be starting to go her way. Maybe God *was* on her side, even if Johnsmith Biberkopf was not.

Smitty watched the show, feeling uncomfortably warm under the intense lighting necessary for projectogram holography. The Video Church was broadcast twenty-four hours a day, seven days a week, on every continent. It was even seen on the moon and the orbital colonies. Smitty had heard his Mom say this a thousand times to his Dad and later, to Ryan Effner. He dared to hope that it never got to Mars, so his Dad wouldn't have to watch it ever again.

"And there are those who neglect their duty to the Lord," the preacher hollered, "just as there are those who neglect their duty to their world."

The congregation groaned in disapproval of the behavior of these nameless ne'er-do-wells. Ronindella joined in, waiting for her chance.

It came about forty minutes later. Smitty was barely awake by this time, in spite of the constant chorus of screams that accompanied every phrase the preacher uttered. But he heard the preacher ask, "Who will bear witness?"

"I will bear witness!" Ronindella shrieked almost before the words were out of the preacher's mouth.

Some other people said they would bear witness, too. Ronindella had to wait her turn, but after five of six other people got to go up on the stage, the preacher called on her, and she practically leaped out of her seat. Smitty could hardly believe what he was seeing. His Mom had told him that she'd been a witness before he was born, but it was something he never thought he'd actually *see*. There she was, though, standing right up there on the stage, all lit up with slanting rays of blinding white light as the preacher said, "And what is your name, sister?"

"Ronindella," she said, the sound system picking up her voice and amplifying it without distortion. "Ronindella Biberkopf."

"And tell us Ms. Biberkopf," the preacher said, "tell the Good Lord, the faithful gathered here this evening at the Video Church of God, and tell me, your loving Brother Bobby, what you will bear witness to tonight."

"Well, Brother Bobby, I have seen up close the sins of a shirker."

The audience cooed in sympathy.

"Tell it, sister," Brother Bobby cajoled.

"My husband Johnsmith lost his job and left me and my nine-year-old son without a husband and father."

"Lord help you," Brother Bobby prayed.

"And now we have no visible means of support," Ronindella lied.

Smitty couldn't believe his ears. He scrunched way down in the pew, so ashamed that he felt as though his face were burning up. How could she say that? They were getting most of his Dad's pay all the way from Mars, and they were getting help from Ryan Effner, too!

"Is your little boy here this evening?" Brother Bobby asked.

"Yes, he's sitting out there in the audience," she replied.

The preacher's grin was dazzling, showing practically every one of his gleaming white teeth. "Then why don't we bring him up here?"

Ronindella smiled back prettily. "He's very young."

"You're never too young to bear witness for the Lord," the preacher said.

"Hallelujah!" the audience roared.

"What is your boy's name?"

"Smitty II."

"Little brother, Smitty II," Brother Bobby said in a cloying tone, "come on down."

If Smitty could have crawled under the pew, he would have. All eyes were on him, as the preacher importuned him to join them on the stage. Smitty didn't move. He felt as if he were going to burst.

"Come on *down!*"

What could he do? He couldn't just sit there, but he couldn't get up on that stage, either; it was just too phony. What would his Dad do if he had been here?

Smitty knew that his Dad would have done what his Mom wanted him to do, though. That was the trouble. Dad had always done what she wanted, and look what he'd gotten for his trouble. Smitty knew he'd do what his Dad would have done. If his Dad, a grown man, couldn't fight back, how could he? He sighed, resigning himself to his fate.

Slowly, he got up and marched toward the stage. Ethereal lights played around him as he made his way through the clapping, cheering crowd. Smitty hated them, he hated the preacher, and most of all at that moment, he hated his mother.

He mounted the steps and took his place next to his Mom. The crowd was feverish with excitement now, almost like a pack of wild animals. The preacher tried to speak, but the screaming drowned out even his game-show-host voice, amplified though it might have been.

At last the din died down, and Brother Bobby asked: "Are you willing to bear witness in the name of the Lord, my son?"

"I guess so," Smitty said cautiously. He didn't really understand what bearing witness was all about, but now that he was up here, he clearly had to do something. If they wanted him to bear witness, then he would bear witness. Anything, as long as he could get out of here.

"Did your father sin?" Brother Bobby asked in a kindly way. "Did you see him shirk his duty?"

"I don't know." Smitty felt as if the preacher was trying to trick him.

"Well, son, you must realize that your father lost his job. Am I right when I say that?"

Smitty nodded grudgingly. He couldn't argue with that, but he had never believed that his Dad meant to hurt him. After all, his Dad could have been sent to Luna as easily as Mars, and even Mars wasn't so great, from what Smitty had heard. What was Brother Bobby trying to prove?

"And because he lost his job, he left you and your mother without any visible means of support, wouldn't you say?"

"No, I wouldn't say so at all," Smitty responded angrily.

The preacher's grin faded for a fraction of a second. Smitty caught a glimpse of the real Brother Bobby, a wrinkled, ugly face stretched over a misshapen skull— or so it seemed for an instant. The placid smile was replaced so quickly that Smitty had to wonder if he had seen anything at all.

"Are you casting doubt on your mother's word?" Brother Bobby said.

"I didn't say that."

"Well, you certainly didn't agree with her version of events, did you?"

Smitty said nothing. He was not about to let Brother Bobby trap him into saying something he didn't really mean. He glanced at his Mom, who stared back at him with anger.

"Did your father leave you and your mother to fend for yourselves?" the preacher demanded.

"We're still getting money from Dad," Smitty said.

"But is that *his* doing?" Brother Bobby began to circle around Smitty, like a beast of prey closing in for the kill. Smitty turned, not letting him out of sight for an instant.

"The government of these United Nations under God sees to it that a percentage of his pay is sent through the Selective Space Service, sent to his needy family back here on Earth. Am I not correct when I say this?"

Smitty remained silent. His Dad was not some common criminal, and he would not allow this asshole to make him out that way. "I don't care if it's correct or not!" Smitty cried. "My Dad didn't mean for us to be poor!"

"Ah, but the road to hell is paved with good intentions," Brother Bobby said loftily. "Johnsmith Biberkopf has left you and your mother impoverished, has he not?"

"I don't know." Smitty was so upset and confused that he was on the verge of bursting into tears. Somehow he held back, though. He would not give Brother Bobby the satisfaction.

"You don't know?" The preacher sounded skeptical. "Are you trying to deceive a servant of the Lord?"

"No . . . I . . ."

"You *do* know, then?"

"No . . . I don't . . ."

"You *know* that your father, Johnsmith Biberkopf, is a sinner, do you not?"

Smitty wanted to scream at him, tell him that he was

a liar, jump up and smash his face in. But there was something about the way Brother Bobby kept at him that made him afraid to be defiant.

"You *know* it, don't you, Smitty? You *know* it!"

And almost as if they were spoken by somebody else, the words emerged through Smitty's tears: "Yes, I know it."

NINE

JOHNSMITH DIDN'T KNOW why, but he was thinking of Felicia a lot these days, which was what he was doing now, as he lay in his bunk. Maybe it was because of the sheer boredom of living on Mars. Occasionally, he could marvel at the alien landscape outside, but most of the time it was just work; though the low gravity and atmospheric pressure made it easy to bounce back after a grueling day of crawling through red dust while a high energy particle beam fired just over the top of his head. At other times, he worked with a wieldo crew, putting up new buildings outside. He liked martial arts training better, because it was more like a sport, even though Sergeant Daiv could be pretty nasty when he punched you and tossed you around like a sack of potatoes.

They had never really been told the truth about why they were being trained for combat. Who were they expected to fight on Mars? There was nothing living on the planet, so far as Johnsmith knew, besides human beings and a bit of lichen in the polar region. They obviously weren't going to fight lichen with automatic weapons and lasers.

Well, at least they had the onees. But there were drawbacks even with the psychedelic ball bearings. For one thing, he didn't like to make his daily reports on what his onee experience were like. Filing a report never took very long, but it seemed so personal that he didn't care to have Angel Torquemada looking at it.

The lights were out, but there was some faint illumination coming from the far end of the barracks. The soft light made Felicia look very sweet and youthful. In fact, she wasn't very old, Johnsmith realized. It was just that she talked so tough that made her seem that way.

Johnsmith rolled on his side and looked down at the far end of the barracks to see what was going on. Captain Hi and Co-pilot Prudy were packing their gear. It looked as if they might be leaving Mars this morning.

Johnsmith wanted to say goodbye to Hi, who had really been very nice to him on the flight. Hi had been civil here on Mars, too, even though he had nothing to gain from it. After all, Johnsmith was just another prisoner at Elysium. He was nobody special. Maybe Hi was nice to everybody.

Since he couldn't sleep, maybe he should get up and say a few words of farewell. He might never see the pilot again; certainly not for several years, at the very least.

Johnsmith rolled out of his bunk and walked down the aisle separating the sleeping prisoners. As he approached, Captain Hi, hefting a heavy, strapped bag, smiled.

"Heading home?" Johnsmith said.

"Yeah, for a while at least," Hi replied.

Johnsmith stuck out his hand. He noticed that Prudy rolled her eyes, but Captain Hi shook hands firmly. "Some things about Mars *are* better, you know," he said.

"I don't know what," Johnsmith said.

"Well, for one thing, it's clean here, and it's not crowded, and there's real work that needs to be done."

Johnsmith wondered if the captain knew that they

were being trained for combat against a non-existent enemy. He was about to ask Hi that very thing when somebody shouted: "Arkies!"

Arkies? Johnsmith didn't know what Arkies were, but, judging from the reactions of those around him, they were terrifying. Hi's face paled, as did those of his two crewmates.

"Shit," Co-pilot Prudy said. "Can you believe this is happening *now?*"

Hi didn't answer her. He merely reached into his kit and pulled out a .38 revolver. As he loaded its chamber with five shots, Angel Torquemada rushed into the room carrying a rifle with a red laser sight mounted on it. Behind him wheeled a bulky robot. Casings on its sides sprang open to reveal more rifles, grenades, and anti-personnel weapons. Whiplike appendages dispensed these to the waiting prisoners.

It suddenly occurred to Johnsmith that his question was about to be answered. Whoever, or whatever, the Arkies were, they were the antagonists the prisoners were trained to fight. He found little satisfaction in this realization, though. He was far too frightened for that.

One of the robot's flexible arms thrust an automatic weapon into his hands, which Johnsmith recognized as a Hungarian semi-automatic that he had been thoroughly trained to use. A magazine had already been inserted, and Johnsmith hefted the gun with a practiced air. He felt his heart thumping huge in his chest. He was about to meet the enemy for the first time . . . whoever the enemy was.

The clear, plastic corridor glowed red with particle beam fire. Johnsmith found it difficult to breathe steadily, and sweat began to trickle down the sides of his face. What was he supposed to do?

"One by one, out that way," Angel Torquemada said in a firm, clear voice. He pointed toward the barracks entrance. As a result, Johnsmith was among the first to go, along with Hi and his crewmates. They ran through the other buildings until they were inside the airlock leading to the landing area. Sergeant Daiv was standing by, ordering them into pressure suits as they entered the airlock in threes.

Hi, the co-pilot, and Johnsmith were the first ones through the outer door. It closed behind them immediately.

Johnsmith had not been outside since his arrival at Elysium. Despite his fear, he was struck by the totality of the Martian darkness. Only the blaze of particle beam fire momentarily lit the barren landscape. Johnsmith turned to see the airlock door opening again, and three pressure-suited figures emerged, moving cautiously with their guns held out in front of them. He hesitated to leave the compound, with its surrounding glow, even though he stood outside the buildings themselves. A crimson beam that scorched the sand near his boots made him move, and move quickly. For an instant, a plume of dust and smoke followed him, and then he was thudding through the blackness.

"Move it, move it, move it," Angel Torquemada commanded, as though he were physically inside Johnsmith's helmet. "Fan out. Don't give them a massed target to shoot at."

Johnsmith ran hard and fast, not knowing where he was going. He followed Angel Torquemada's orders as best he could, but he had no idea where the enemy was. He stumbled once, but did not fall. After that, he lifted his feet higher, feeling as though his knees might clip his chin. Torquemada's calmly issued orders—sometimes using individual names, sometimes speaking generally—sounded clearly over the ragged sound of Johnsmith's own breathing. Deadly red lines of light flashed in the night again and again.

"Biberkopf!" Torquemada shouted. "Hit the sand!"

Johnsmith's guts froze. It seemed as if he could not thrust himself to the ground, as if he could only crouch here in the dark while the particle beams crisscrossed all about him.

But somehow he went down, shocked to the bone by the impact, in spite of his pressure suit's padding. A thin, bloody thread of lethal light swept an inch or two over his head.

"Jesus!" He'd almost been killed! What the hell was he doing crawling around on his belly in the dark? He was a college instructor, for Christ's sake!

"Up, Biberkopf!" Angel Torquemada commanded.

This time, Johnsmith didn't hesitate. He leaped up and charged head first into the night. Gasping sounded inside his helmet. Somebody was running next to him, close enough to transmit her voice helmet to helmet, her body briefly illuminated by the beam flashes. Johnsmith crouched, still running. His boot struck some obstruction in the sand, and he tumbled onto the ground. Beam fire swept past him, and he heard a scream that turned into a sizzle. And then his own breathing was all that he heard.

Johnsmith felt his bladder let go, and thanked God that his pressure suit's filtering tubes would absorb it. For a moment, he felt humiliated by his incontinence. But then, as if the mechanical contrivance that had saved him from soiling himself were part of his actual physical self, he suddenly became convinced that he could not be harmed. It was insane, but he let all doubt slip from his mind. Some primal urge forced him onward toward the blaze of enemy fire. He might die if he went forward, but it would only be his body. His spirit would die if he lay in the dirt while others died around him.

A long, tortured scream rose up from deep inside him, racking his throat as it deafened him in the enclosed space of his helmet. But he took heart from his own battle cry, firing a burst in the direction of one of the red beams.

Laser fire came from the compound, and Johnsmith's

courage grew with the knowledge that he and the other charging prisoners were being covered. As long as their assailants were kept busy, there was a chance that some of the prisoners might reach the enemy stronghold alive.

A red flash illuminated a running figure ahead of Johnsmith. He recognized from the man's gait that it was Captain Hi Malker. Johnsmith wondered where Felicia was.

He heard another person screaming, this one almost comically gurgling his last. Johnsmith did not stop to see who it was.

The fanning red lines of enemy fire made a V shape on the horizon, very close now. Johnsmith could see approximately where all the shooting was coming from. He didn't know how many of his people had made it this far, but he was sure that those among them who were still breathing could see the enemy's position, too.

They would be there soon. Johnsmith picked his feet up even higher, running so hard that he thought his heart would burst. Hi was just ahead now, his back looming. In another second, Johnsmith would overtake him.

Hi suddenly vanished, dropping down the back side of a mound that had been virtually invisible in the darkness. Gunshots thundered from the ancient arroyo below. The particle beam fire ceased abruptly, and Johnsmith lost his way.

He heard Hi's static-sizzled shouts, so he could not have been far away from his friend. But Johnsmith didn't know where to turn. He tried to move in the direction in which he had last seen Hi, expecting to fall into the arroyo. But he kept on running, until he was certain that he had gone too far. Trying to double back, he heard Hi's voice.

"Let go of me, you bastards," Hi shouted.

"Bring him along," an unfamiliar voice said. Johnsmith was so close to the enemy that he was patching into their helmet to helmet communications.

Grunts and gasps followed, the sounds of a struggle. But Johnsmith still had no idea of which direction the sounds were coming from. The voices became fainter, and fainter, and then faded altogether.

A searchlight swept across the darkened desert, revealing the odd prisoner crouching with weapon extended. But there was no sign of Hi and his captors.

Feet spread wide apart, Johnsmith pivoted quickly, facing in first one direction and then another while the light played over the landscape. He saw nobody but his own people. It was impossible, but there it was. Hi and his captors had vanished without a trace—in an instant.

"Where did they go?" Johnsmith cried. "What the hell is going on here?"

"All right, Biberkopf, calm down." It was Angel Torquemada. "Stay where you are—and shut up."

Johnsmith shut up, hearing only the sounds of his own breathing and the ceaseless Martian wind. Again, the searchlight swept over the battlefield. Again, Johnsmith saw nothing but sand, rocks, and his fellow prisoners. In their pressure suits, they could have been male, female, friend, or foe. But by their confused postures, he knew that these people were those he had trained with: Sergeant Daiv, Alderdice, Felicia, Frankie Lee Wisbar, and the others.

The searchlight sweep was ineffective, revealing nothing but the prisoners. Johnsmith could not imagine where the enemy had taken Captain Hi.

"All right," Angel Torquemada said, "everybody back to the compound. They're gone."

Gone? Gone where? How did they pull this disappearing act out here on a virtually flat desert? Was he hallucinating? Had the constant use of onees damaged his nervous system permanently? None of this made sense to him.

He headed back toward the compound. He had no desire to stay out here in the cold, airless Martian night any longer than he had to, despite his curiosity. As he moved toward the warm glow of the compound's lights, it occurred to him for the first time that he had just been in combat. It had been neither as glamorous nor as frightening as he had imagined it would be. He had been shot at, and he had been very close to being captured. If he had overtaken Captain Hi, it might have been him marching off towards who knew where—or cut down by beams. He was disturbed that they had taken Hi, but he was elated at the same time, knowing that he had survived mortal combat. For the first time in many months, he thought of Beowulf the Geat. Had Beowulf felt this way the first time he had carried his axe into battle, triskelion shield protecting him from the missiles of his enemies?

But Johnsmith had no shield. Perhaps armor was not the order of the day at Elysium. Why should it be, when prisoners were readily available? The dregs of Earth's full employment economy would never run out, so long as things continued as they were. As a result, the draftees on Mars were readily expendable, and minimal protection was afforded them.

Protection against whom? At least Johnsmith knew they—the Arkies—were human now, which is more than he had known ten minutes ago . . . if the battle had lasted that long.

"Come on," Angel Torquemada ordered them from somewhere in the darkness. "Do you think we've got all night?"

Johnsmith and the others made their way back to the compound through the darkness.

In the morning, after a short exercise period, they were ordered to go to an underground meeting room. It was a larger chamber than Johnsmith, Felicia, and Alderdice had been taken to before. In fact, all the prisoners were assembled, along with Sergeant Daiv. Even Prudy was there, sitting in the front row and wearing a dour expression. Torquemada stood at the podium.

"We lost three people last night," he said. "One of them was the Captain of the Interplan ship, who was about to leave Mars. He and his crewmate probably shouldn't have fought, but they did. We're grateful, but now the ship is stuck here until the Conglom can figure out what to do about it. Most likely, they'll dispatch a pilot from the polar region to fly it out of here, but if they have a shortage, they'll have to bring somebody in from the Belt, or even from Luna. It could take months."

Johnsmith didn't really care what happened to the Interplan ship. He wanted to know who had been shooting at them, and who was dead, and what had happened to Captain Hi. As Angel Torquemada droned on, he began to suspect that such explanations were not on this morning's agenda. Johnsmith felt somewhat cross. It had been all but impossible to fall asleep after the skirmish last night, and he feared that the entire day would drag interminably, with this evasive lecture serving as an appropriately vague starting point.

"Who were those people we fought last night?" A voice rose out of the assembled prisoners. It was Felicia, a fact that made Johnsmith very nervous. Torquemada was not likely to appreciate her unauthorized sense of curiosity.

"I'll tell you who they were," Angel Torquemada responded, surprising everyone in the room. There was a breathless moment before he finished: "They were the people who want to kill you."

Somebody laughed, but Felicia was undeterred by Torquemada's snide answer. Without hesitation, she said, "And why do they want to kill us? What have we done to them?

"Never mind all that," Torquemada said. "Just remember that these are the people who want to kill you."

"But what do they want to kill us *for?*" demanded Felicia. "A bunch of fucking *onees?*"

"Burst," said Angel Torquemada with chilling authority, "shut up and sit down."

She was livid, and she glared at him for a few seconds, but she slowly did as she was told and sat down.

After that, the briefing went as if nothing extraordinary had happened. Within five minutes, they were back in the training area. While they were waiting for Sergeant Daiv, they discussed the possible purpose of the meeting.

"It was as if Torquemada was saying that this is business as usual," said Alderdice.

"That's right," said Frankie Lee Wisbar. "It *is* business as usual around here."

"But why? Do they just want onees?"

"Apparently. Torquemada doesn't really tell us *why* they want them, but they do want onees."

"But how do they live? And where?"

Frankie shrugged. "Somewhere outside."

Felicia started to ask another question, but Sergeant Daiv's bellowing voice cut her off. It was time for martial arts training, he said, not for talking. There was no arguing with Sergeant Daiv, of course, but Johnsmith knew that the issue was not dead. The dialogue resumed during their meals, and, though their gymnasium activities precluded such talk, continued in the quiet moments before they went to sleep at night.

Johnsmith was losing track of time. The onee sessions had become quite boring by now. There was a sameness to the hallucinations that he had not anticipated. There seemed to be three main types of experience: fearful, erotic, and violent. He had enjoyed all of them at the beginning, but now he welcomed them only as a respite from the monotony of his training.

Furthermore, Angel Torquemada seemed increasingly disappointed as Johnsmith and Alderdice reported the results of their onee adventures. He revealed nothing to them, however; the purpose of the Conglom's interest in their psychedelic voyages was left unstated.

Johnsmith dutifully clutched an onee every morning and every afternoon, until Torquemada made an announcement that changed everything.

"Beginning tomorrow morning, Burst," he said one evening as he stood in the barracks doorway, and the red dust swirled and snapped viciously outside the compound, "you'll take onees."

Felicia, who had been staring at the wall, turned her head slowly. "What did you say?"

"Onees." Torquemada said. "Tomorrow morning."

Felicia had been less and less vociferous since the morning she had been told to sit down and shut up. She had become so despondent that she hardly spoke at all now. And yet, she did say something, mumbling so incoherently that Torquemada had to ask her to repeat herself: "What did *you* say, Burst?"

"I said okay," Felicia murmured.

Torquemada seemed a little surprised, for once. He looked at her intently for a moment, and then nodded. He marked something down in his notebook and walked out of the barracks.

Johnsmith, who had been lying in bed, said, "Felicia, are you all right?"

"Sure," she said, but her tone was dead. She clearly didn't want to discuss it any further.

"But you never wanted to take onees before," Johnsmith persisted. "What made you change your mind?"

"You heard the man," Felicia chided him. "What choice did he give me?"

"According to the Conglom Interplanetary Charter," Alderdice said, his voice muffled as a result of his face being buried in a pillow, "you don't have to follow any orders that violate the law. In fact, it's your duty to—"

"Bullshit," Felicia said. "I don't have any recourse. Torquemada has made my life miserable enough since I came here. I don't want to antagonize him any more."

Johnsmith was somewhat nonplussed to hear her say

this. He had never noticed Torquemada singling her out for punishment. Perhaps the loneliness and danger of their existence was getting to her at last. Felicia had always seemed so tough, though. If she was cracking, then Johnsmith couldn't be far behind. Maybe he had already cracked. It was entirely possible that his acceptance of this hideous existence was evidence of psychosis.

"Felicia," he said, as if he were somebody else altogether, "why don't you let me sleep with you?"

She turned her face toward him, and he saw in the dimming light that her face was stained with tears. She gestured for him to come to her, and said, "Please."

TEN

"I WAS WITH you, Johnsmith," Felicia said with something approaching wonder. "I was with you all the time I was holding the onee."

"Just a hallucination," Johnsmith said, as he sat facing her in the featureless observation room. But his heartbeat made itself known, despite his dismissal of her comments.

"But it was so real." She smiled at him, wide-eyed and radiant.

He didn't protest any further. She was happier than he'd ever seen her before, and that was worth something to him. He didn't even mind Angel Torquemada, who hovered in the background and jotted down her reactions.

Only Alderdice seemed to object, his jowls quivering as he shook his head indignantly, after Torquemada had left the room. "He shouldn't have made her do this."

"Oh, Alderdice," Felicia made a shooing gesture with her right hand. "What possible difference could it make? I'm glad I handled the onee."

"But why does it please you, Felicia?" Alderdice stood and came nearer to her.

For a moment, it seemed as though she wouldn't answer, but then she looked right at him and smiled. "Because I got so close to Johnsmith."

This was not a reply Johnsmith had anticipated, and he flushed with embarrassment. Still, he was glad Felicia had admitted what he had suspected for quite some time. He felt something for her, too, though he hadn't told her about it for fear of rejection.

"I only hope that you love me as much as I love you," Felicia said, transfixing him with her dark-eyed gaze. She said this with unabashed sincerity.

It was clear that she expected Johnsmith to say something, but he didn't know exactly what it was. Should he thank her . . . or tell her that he loved her . . . ? He found his mouth working, as if it had a life of its own. "I think I do," he said at last. "I mean, I think I love you, too."

They looked at each other for a few seconds, and Johnsmith heard deep laughter erupt behind them. He turned to see Alderdice, tears streaming down his cheeks as he wheezed with pleasure.

"What's so funny?" Felicia demanded, showing some of her old fire.

"No, I don't mean to say that it's funny," Alderdice said, his body shaking with mirth. "It's wonderful. It's so wonderful, and so unexpected that it caught me completely off guard."

Johnsmith grinned, and even Felicia softened a little. It was somehow touching to see this big man laughing with sheer joy at their declarations of love.

"You've changed, Felicia," Alderdice said, "but for the better. I had begun to doubt that you're capable of such profound human qualities as you've shown us this morning."

"I don't give a shit what you doubt," Felicia snapped. "Who asked you, anyway?"

"Felicia," Johnsmith said, interrupting Alderdice's sputtering response, "don't blame Alderdice for being undiplomatic. I'm sure it's just one of his training im-

plants acting up. He really can't help it. Motherhood
and the Conglom, and all that, you know.''

"Is that true?" Felicia asked suspiciously.

"Well, yes," Alderdice said, "such responses are
triggered by the mention of certain subjects. Monogamy is one of them.''

"But you're *gay*," Felicia said. "How can you be
gay and believe in monogamy?''

Alderdice drew himself up to his full height. "My
dear Felicia," he said with great dignity, "I *never once*
cheated on my husband.''

Felicia pursed her lips, and her cheeks puffed out
with suppressed laughter. She couldn't hold it in,
though. In a moment, she and Johnsmith were doubled
over, tears streaming down their cheeks.

Alderdice looked forlorn for a few seconds, and then
he laughed as heartily as before.

At that moment, Angel Torquemada returned, breaking up the fun. "Just what did you and Johnsmith Biberkopf do while you were under the onee's influence,
Ms. Burst?" he demanded to know.

"We swam," Felicia said.

"Is that all?"

"No, we saw a ship."

For once, Johnsmith thought that Torquemada
showed some expression—a heightened interest, which
his next question confirmed. "A ship, you say?"

"Yes, a ship."

"A spacecraft?" Torquemada leaned forward, no
longer taking notes.

"No, a sailing ship. Very old style, with a big square
sail and oars.''

"Oars." This was a statement, rather than a question, but Felicia apparently didn't hear it that way.

"Yes, dozens of oars, and these round shields hanging on the sides of the ship.''

Johnsmith would have thought little of this, even
though she described his first onee hallucination pre-

cisely. After all, they had all indulged in technological schizophrenia, prepackaged surrealism. Why should he be surprised at the sameness of their visions? What caught his attention was the keen interest that Angel Torquemada evinced. This waking dream about the Viking, or Geatish, ship was really important to their commanding officer for some reason. Johnsmith wanted to know why.

"It was beautiful," Felicia said. "Scary, too, but I didn't care. I was happy, just floating in the water there with Johnsmith. In fact, I don't think I've ever been happier in my life."

"It's wonderful," Alderdice said, his tone barely above a whisper. He did not sound quite so sure as before, though, in spite of what he was saying. "Just wonderful."

"Was anyone aboard the ship?" Torquemada asked, paying no attention to Alderdice.

"Yeah. At first I couldn't see them all that well, but they came closer after a little bit. And then I got a pretty good look at them. They were these guys in helmets and furs and stuff . . . and they had these round shields."

"Did they have any contact with you?" Torquemada asked. "Did they speak?"

"Among themselves," Felicia said, "but I couldn't understand their language—and they turned the ship around and started moving toward us."

This was *too* close to Johnsmith's memory of his first onee experience. If she said next that an oar was extended to fish them out of the water . . .

"Archecoding," Alderdice said.

"What?" Felicia asked.

"Archecoding. The coding of archetypal patterns on the onee's electronic discharge."

"Well, what about it?" Johnsmith demanded, noticing how keenly Angel Torquemada watched all three of them. "Aren't they all archecoded?"

"Well, yes, but this is the same pattern I got from using *your* onees on the Interplan ship, don't you see?"

"No, I don't see. What possible difference can any of this make?"

"Felicia was given an onee that was just machined yesterday. I saw Mr. Torquemada shake it out of its container. Nobody has *ever* used it before."

Now Johnsmith was beginning to see what all the fuss was about. They were guinea pigs, testing onees to find a certain pattern, a pattern that produced the Viking ship hallucination. But why was it so important to the government to find these particular onees? Johnsmith looked toward Angel Torquemada, unrealistically hoping for some help with his unasked question.

"That's all for today," Torquemada said abruptly. "You can go to breakfast."

For the first time since he had been on Mars, Johnsmith was sorry to have Torquemada dismiss them. He was certain that they had hit upon something significant, and he wanted to know precisely what it was.

Felicia seemed somewhat confused, as if she didn't quite know what to do next, and so he took her by the hand to lead her to the mess hall. On the way they passed several people, all of whom acted as if everything were perfectly normal. Frankie Lee Wisbar was among those who cheerfully greeted them in passing.

"My implants are not as effective as they once were," said Alderdice, walking backwards in front of them, in order to face them. "I couldn't have even told you about archecoding a few months ago. But the whole safeguard system in my brain has been undercut by the attitude toward onees away from Earth. It's wonderful."

"You've been set free," Johnsmith said.

"Not really," Alderdice replied, frowning. "Most of my programming seems as powerful as ever. It's just the more ambiguous legal points that seem to be affected."

"Maybe it will all wear away in time," Felicia said, "and you'll feel as good as I do."

As they got their food and found a table, Johnsmith reflected on Felicia's transformation. He was quite troubled, even though the conventional wisdom had it that onees couldn't permanently harm the nervous system. Still, something had happened to her mind. He hoped that it was merely an outflowing of pent-up emotion, and not brain damage. He couldn't bear to think of her turning into a vegetable.

"Are you . . . all right, Felicia?" he asked.

"It was just so perfect," she said. "I never felt this way in my whole life."

Clearly, onees had a more profound effect on some people than on others.

"I was with you, Johnsmith," she said, gazing at him adoringly. "I was with you in another world."

"But it was only a world of the mind," Johnsmith reminded her.

Felicia looked as though she would cry.

"It was good that we were together there," Johnsmith quickly added. "I mean, I'm glad that we were there."

Chewing a mouthful of food with gusto, Alderdice said, "I don't understand how the onee got here."

"How the onee got *here?*" Johnsmith repeated. "Isn't obvious? It was manufactured in a building, not two hundred yards from where we're sitting."

"Maybe," Alderdice said, swallowing, "and maybe not. Don't you think that there is some control exercised over the product turned out here at Elysium?"

"I don't know, but the Conglom wants something from us, and this is the only thing that Torquemada has raised an eyebrow about, up to now."

"Well, I don't think any of that matters," Felicia said. "We swam through water that constantly changed color as it swirled around us, and a beautiful ship sailed through the mist. We were like two bodies with the same spirit. It was wonderful.''

Alderdice attempted to smile, but the pronouncements of love had to be wearing thin even with him by this time. Or perhaps he recalled the same imagery from his onee tripping; if this were the case, he might not mind at all, Johnsmith supposed.

"Was the enemy trying to get their hands on archecoded onees?" Alderdice asked suddenly. "Was that what they were after, do you think?"

"For what purpose?"

"I don't know, but if the government is so interested in them, maybe those outlaws—whoever they are—want them for the same reason."

"But what is that reason?" Felicia asked. "And what's the big deal, anyway? Who cares what they want it for? It's probably just one more thing they plan to use to enslave the masses."

"Well, it sure works well, doesn't it?" Johnsmith said, raising his eyebrows at her. "If your enjoyment of them is any indication, that is."

Felicia was crestfallen. "Please don't say things to hurt me like that," she said. "I've opened my heart to you, Johnsmith, and now you're cutting me to the bone."

Johnsmith was glad to know how Felicia felt, but he was beginning to wonder if things hadn't been better before she took the onee this morning. He had suspected for some time that she felt something for him, but her defensiveness had made life easier, in a way. Well, he supposed it was possible that she would calm down after a while. After all, it was only half an hour since she had clutched that mind-bending ball bearing in her perspiring hand. Maybe things would get better.

As the day wore on, he tended not to worry so much. The constant training was distracting, and a new element had been added as well. He decided to take Felicia's declarations of love at face value. If she said she loved him, why should he doubt her? Maybe she would change her mind later. Who could tell? Nothing was permanent, so the thing to do was try and appreciate Felicia now. After all, he loved her, too, didn't he?

Whenever he looked at her, she gazed adoringly at him. It was a bit unnerving, but he supposed that he would get used to it.

The morning onees were archecoded with Viking imagery, and so were the evening onees. In fact, all the onees stamped out since the firefight seemed to be archecoded. Johnsmith pointed this out to the attentive Angel Torquemada.

"Possibly," Torquemada said.

"Does this mean that somebody inside is working with the Arkies?" Johnsmith asked.

"I'd rather not get into that," Torquemada said.

The answer seemed obvious, however. "The firefight must have been a diversion created by one of the prisoners," Johnsmith said. "While the battle raged, somebody archecoded the Viking stuff onto all the onees being processed. I imagine it's a simple enough thing to do, if you have the right gear."

Torquemada said nothing.

"Of course, it's also a simple matter to figure out who was inside the compound while the firefight was going on," Johnsmith went on. "That narrows down the suspects considerably."

Johnsmith stopped talking, realizing that he had not been asked his opinion. In fact, Torquemada had not even admitted that he gave credence to Johnsmith's theory.

"You may be right, Biberkopf," Torquemada finally said. "You just may be right. In fact, there is only one thing wrong with your thesis."

"What's that?" Johnsmith asked, almost relieved to know that Torquemada disagreed with him. The alternative would have been mildly disturbing, as anomalies always are.

"All the prisoners were outside the compound during the firefight."

"That only leaves your people," Felicia said.

Torquemada looked at her without expression. Behind her, Alderdice sat, his face gleaming with sweat.

"None of our people could do such a thing," Torquemada said.

"Why not?" Felicia asked.

"Because of the obedience implants," Alderdice said, answering for him.

Torquemada nodded smugly, picked up his notes, and left the room.

Felicia turned excitedly to Johnsmith. "Don't you see what this means, Johnny?"

"Huh?"

"There's a revolutionist working inside the power structure here at Elysium."

"You think so?"

"How else can you explain it?"

Johnsmith thought about that for a moment. "You may be right, Felicia, but there's one possibility you haven't considered."

"What's that?"

"Whoever this person is, he or she might not be doing this for the reasons you think. Maybe this isn't a revolutionist at all, but somebody working for some purpose we don't know."

"Only a revolutionist would do such a thing," Felicia said with certainty. "There must be somebody working on the inside."

Alderdice shook his head. "Forget all that. It had to be one of the prisoners who sabotaged these onees."

"Why do you say that?"

"Because all government workers have obedience implants, just as Torquemada said."

"That's true," Johnsmith agreed. "Still, *somebody* must have done it. The onees didn't archecode themselves."

Torquemada appeared, blowing the conch shell. Meal time was over. As they stacked their trays, and went back to martial arts training, Johnsmith though about his son for the first time in several days. Overcome with guilt, he realized that sleeping with Felicia kept his mind off Smitty, just as sex had eased the pain caused by Ronindella's affair with Ryan. At least he thought it was Ryan.

He supposed that he'd never know for sure.

ELEVEN

RONDINDELLA WENT TO the phone to call Ryan. She hadn't seen him in two days, and it wasn't like him not to call when he couldn't see her. Smitty II sat on the floor, playing with his toy dinosaur. He always acted a little funny when he played with that thing, for some reason. She wondered if the church would approve of such a toy, since it implicitly supported the theory of evolution.

The screen flickered on, and there was Ryan. He wasn't alone.

"Hi, Ronnie," he said cheerfully.

Ronindella didn't reply for a moment. She stood gaping, astonished at the sight of Ryan lying in bed with two strange women. His casual demeanor was even more disturbing. Didn't he even know that he was doing something wrong?

"Did you have some reason to call me?" Ryan asked. "I don't mean to be rude, honey, but I'm kind of busy."

"Kind of busy!" Ronindella exploded. "Ryan, what do you think you're doing?"

"I'm worshipping through my newfound religion."

"Religion? What the hell are you talking about?"

"I'm not talking about hell," Ryan said patiently, "but about heaven."

118

Ronindella was so shocked and enraged that she couldn't speak. Ryan, however, had no such compunctions.

"I've joined the No-God Sect," he said. "I thought it was about time I got religion, just as you've been saying."

"That—that heathen cult is no religion!" Ronindella screamed. "It's nothing more than an excuse for wild debauchery and indiscriminate sex."

"That's not true, Ronnie. The worship of the human body is an ancient form of religion. I learned all about its cultural and mystical significance in my first, preorgiastic seminar."

One of the naked women kissed him on the cheek and snuggled against him. The other woman just sort of stared off into the middle distance, as if she were drugged, or enjoying the afterglow of orgasm. Ronindella couldn't stand it.

"Get rid of those two whores!" she shrieked. "Right now!"

Ryan looked offended. "Ronnie, why are you calling these fine ladies such awful names? They happen to be deacons of the No-God Sect."

Ronindella shut off the transmission. She trembled with rage and indignation. How could that son of a bitch do this to her? What was he trying to prove? All that horseshit about religion . . .

"Mom, can I have something to eat?" Smitty entered the kitchenette.

"Not now." Was Ryan trying to punish her in some way? What for? Did he feel as if she were controlling him, as if she were running their relationship? Or maybe she didn't satisfy him. Whatever the case, she had to straighten this out. She was depending on Ryan—which might turn out to be one of the biggest mistakes of her life.

"I'm hungry," Smitty said.

"I said not now." Maybe she was a jinx. First Johnny, and now Ryan. But Johnny had never done anything like this. And neither had Ryan, up to now. If somebody had told her this was going to happen just a half hour ago, she wouldn't have believed it. She must have been out of her mind to take up with someone like Ryan Effner.

Smitty hadn't seen his Mom act like this since before she kicked Dad out. She didn't pay any more attention to him than she would a cockroach—less, come to think of it—when she got into this state of mind. He'd thought that this would never happen again, but here she was, looking right past him, pacing and smoking a cigarette. It probably wasn't a good idea to bother her right now, but he really wanted something to eat.

"Please, Mom," he said.

"Fix something for yourself," she said. "I'm going out."

"Huh?"

"Make yourself a sandwich, or something." Ronindella snuffed her cigarette out in an ashtray. She went to the closet to get out her head gear, and was out the door a few seconds later.

Smitty stood in the silent apt for a full minute before he fully realized that he now had the place completely to himself. This was a rare occurrence, since his Mom usually did her work for the Church here at home.

What should he do, now that he could do anything he wanted for a while? First, a sandwich, then maybe the dinosaur . . . or even Vikings. He played Vikings a lot, ever since he had picked up that onee. He'd told some of the kids at school that he'd touched an onee. Some of them hadn't believed him, and some of them had been jealous. But everybody paid attention to him for a few days. Even now, a big kid named Benetton called him, "Smittonee," whenever he ran into Smitty. It was cool to have a reputation for something like that.

He only wished that he had an onee now. But he didn't, so he better do something else. He started toward the bedroom, when he noticed the mail light flashing on the phone.

Pressing the red button to show the mail, he watched as bills, the monthly tax forms, and church information showed up. There didn't seem to be anything of interest at all. And then he noticed something odd about what he at first took to be a bill.

It had a familiar purple and gold label on it, just like on the napkins at the Kwikkee-Kwizeen restaurants.

And it had his name on it! It said:

MR. SMITTY II BIBERKOPF—you are our second prize winner in the annual Kwikkee-Kwizeen™ Gigundo Giveaway. You have won an all-expenses-paid TRIP TO MARS FOR TWO!!!!!

"Wow!" Smitty said. He was going to see his Dad! Mom had told him that he would never be with him again, but now he had won this trip, and he would see his Dad again. He could hardly believe his good luck.

He was going to Mars!

At least Ryan had left the flyby. She piled in and slammed the driver's door shut with such fury that a piece of plastic molding fell and glanced off her shoulder.

"Good workmanship," she said. They didn't make cars like they used to. In fact, they didn't make anything like they used to. The world was falling to pieces, because of the decline in morals. Ever since the cure for the AIDS IV virus had been announced, the weak willed had been falling back into the licentiousness of the last century. If the hand of God hadn't guided the multinationals to merge, the Conglom would not have been able to restore order to the Earth. A world government and strong morals were good for the world's business, as the multinational sloganeers said. But somehow the No-God Sect had slipped through the law, under the rubric of religion.

"Damn that filthy No-God Sect," she said. They had

seduced the man she had pinned all her hopes on, just as they had seduced the Conglom. All she could do now was go to the church for succor.

"Wait a minute. . . ." Maybe there was someplace else to go that made more sense. It might be sacrilegious, but it also just might work.

She banked the car abruptly, nearly colliding with the side of a building, and pointed it toward the New Age Building. She was going to see Ryan's cybershrink. That was one way to find out just what the hell he thought he was doing.

Five minutes later, she landed on the top level of a parking garage across the street from the New Age Building. Her license plate was scanned as she pulled into a space. One more expense on her credit at the end of the month, but so what? She had to do something. She couldn't just let another man slip through her fingers. She didn't care if it was a sin to see a cybershrink. In fact, it was a venial sin just to enter the New Age Building, that den of Satan located, not in hell, but downtown. Still, it was not strictly forbidden, not a mortal sin.

She crossed the street with grim determination and entered the fancy front door of that wicked place. She scanned the directory to see where the cybershrink was located.

There it was: on the thirteenth floor, of course— where else? Madame Psychosis. What a sinister, mysterious name. She couldn't help feeling a little intimidated, despite her anger. After all, the Video Church disapproved of entering this place in no uncertain terms. She didn't care, though. If necessary, she would publicly humiliate herself later. Right now, she had to talk to this shrink and find out just what the hell Ryan thought he was doing.

She got out on the thirteenth floor, and started looking for Madame Psychosis's office. She found it three doors down and across the hall. With some trepidation, she opened the door and stepped inside.

For a fraction of a second, she had the impression of a dingy little room. And then a projectogram threw images of whirling planets and galaxies in her face. The sense of infinite depth was complete; clearly, this was a very sophisticated 'gram system. In the middle of it all sat a serene Gypsy woman. Well, not exactly a Gypsy, but a sort of old fashioned, dark-complected woman wearing a loose dress.

"Please insert your credit card into the slot," she said.

"I don't want a session," Ronindella said. "I just want to ask you something about one of your . . . patients."

The cybershrink said nothing. Instead, a curved metal object emerged from the starfields. Its serpentine shape ended not in a scaly head, but a machined slot.

"Please insert your card into the slot," Madame Psychosis repeated.

Ronindella sighed. She reached into her bag and rummaged around until she found a credit card, and slipped it into the slot. Obviously, she wasn't going to get anything out of this unless she paid through the nose. She had seen Ryan's bills, and could extrapolate the cost pretty well. She gritted her teeth, as Madame Psychosis gestured for her to sit on a pew that emerged from the depths of the Horsehead Nebula.

"Are you comfortable?" the cybershrink asked in a Bela Lugosi accent.

"I'm okay," Ronindella said, sitting rather than kneeling. Soothing music seemed to ooze out of the air; ethereal choirs and unidentifiable instruments sang sweetly.

"Good," Madame Psychosis said, smiling beatifically. "It is important for us to communicate in a way that is beneficial to both of us."

"Right," Ronindella replied. She shook her head,

realizing that she had almost forgotten why she had come here. For the first time she began to see the attraction in all this New Age stuff. It was so peaceful here, so . . . cosmic.

Still, it was not something she could really believe in. The Video Church was her life. And she wasn't going to let a few audio-visual, holographic tricks fool her into submission.

"I need to know something," she said.

"We all need to know something," Madame Psychosis replied in a profoundly understanding tone. "Life is an endless quest, leading us from the womb to the tomb, and on to the great karmic cycle that joyously and eternally repeats itself as we become one with the Universe."

Ronindella didn't want to admit it, but what the cybershrink was saying made a lot of sense. And the 'gram was a lot better than what they had at the Video Church . . . not to mention the music. It was almost as if she were hearing a heavenly host singing on high.

She seemed to be floating herself, a celestial spirit casting off all her worldly cares, high above the entire cosmos, the galaxies spinning around her. She felt giddy, almost bodiless. When she glanced down, she felt detached from herself. The entire universe revolved with her at the center. She felt so real, so . . . so true to herself. It was glorious.

"Are you happy?" Madame Psychosis asked in a gentle voice.

"Yes . . . no . . . I mean, I don't know." Ronindella felt very far away from this conversation, almost as if somebody else were speaking for her, and yet she knew that this was her voice, coming from her mouth, her vocal chords, her mind and soul.

She was very confused.

"Please tell me what's troubling you," Madame Psychosis said from somewhere out in space. "Perhaps I can help. It's always better to have someone to talk to, to confide in. Your secrets are safe with me.''

''But doesn't the . . . government . . . ?''

''There is no government here, only friendship, only love.''

Ronindella wanted desperately to believe that. She felt loved, but she didn't know exactly where she was anymore. It was just like before, with Ryan. But that had gone bad. Ryan had made her feel loved, and now he was . . .

''Ryan,'' she said.

''What did you say?'' Madame Psychosis asked in a way that suggested there was nothing more important to her in the entire universe than hearing Ronindella repeat herself.

''Ryan.''

''Ryan?''

''Ryan Effner. He's . . . one of your patients.''

''Yes.''

''I need to know . . .'' It was a tremendous struggle to talk about this, for some reason. ''. . . I need to know why he's . . .''

''All information about my patients is private,'' Madame Psychosis admonished her.

''Well, if you could just give me . . .'' Hosts of angels drifted by, playing harps and blowing sonorous trumpets. The tips of their gossamer wings almost brushed against her face, they were so close to her.

''What do you want me to give you, Ronindella?''

''But I didn't tell you my name,'' Ronindella said, suddenly frightened. ''How did you . . .''

Madame Psychosis seemed to be everywhere, smiling down at Ronindella like the mother of all creation. ''It's all right, dear,'' she said. ''Don't be alarmed. What difference does it make?''

Ronindella's panic subsided as if it were the ocean at low tide. Of course, it was the credit card. That was how she knew. But what difference did it make? For that matter, what was it that she had thought made a difference?

Her confusion melted away.

"You're beginning to see clearly now," Madame Psychosis said. "I can sense it."

"Yes." It was absolutely true. Her vision was focusing, becoming crystalline. It was wonderful, as if she were seeing for the first time in her life. And yet it was also as if she were beyond using the optic nerves, the retina, and the vision centers of the brain. She had seen as precisely as this before once upon a time, perhaps before she was born, and it was only the limitations of her flawed human flesh that had prevented her from such clarity of vision for all these years, a lifetime.

God, she had been missing so much!

Ryan said goodbye to the two party androids the Sect had sent over. He would be billed for the time and any maintenance fees incurred from overuse. It would be costly, but he thought the androids well worth the price.

He'd heard about erotic androids before, but he'd never actually used one. Only Conglom-approved religions like the No-God Sect were legally licensed to procure such wonderful machines. Of course, there were plenty of bootleg operations, but that wasn't the way Ryan did things. It might have been cheaper, but only if he didn't get caught. A roll in the hay with two supple beauties wasn't worth joining Beeb on Mars.

Besides, he thought as he slipped out of his robe and into the shower, this wasn't about sex. It was about living with Ronindella. He couldn't join that cockamamie Video Church, even if it was Conglom sanctioned. He was far too much of an intellectual for that.

The chemical spray slapped his skin and invigorated him, waking him from the lethargic afterglow of sex. He thought about taking some exercise, but he kept thinking about Ronnie. How was she reacting to what she'd seen on the phone? What if she went into a terrible depression? She always said that visits to the Video Church cured that. What if this stunt only drove her back to those hyenas at the Church?

He shut off the spray and grabbed a towel, telling himself that Madame Psychosis wouldn't screw things up that badly.

Would she?

Rubbing his hair dry, he went back into the bedroom, stark naked, thinking for the first time that it was possible for Madame Psychosis to have her own hidden agenda. For example, what if the Conglom was observing all this? What if they had decided that he wasn't productive enough at work, and were looking for an excuse to terminate his job? He would be sent to Mars, or Luna, or even worse, to the asteroid belt.

He'd never come home again.

Sitting on the bed, he found his hands shaking. He tried to convince himself that they had nothing on him, but he couldn't be sure. There might be a Pre-Emptive Agent lurking just outside his apt. After all, the No-God Sect might not have been condemned by the government, but they were hardly at the top of the charts. No, not like the Video Church, which told the government exactly what it wanted to hear, and voluntarily gave a tithe to the Conglom. Separation of church and state was something Beeb used to talk about, but it was a thing of the past—if it had ever existed. Ryan might be in trouble already, with such subversive ideas floating around in his head. He consciously suppressed all thoughts questioning the government. Instead, he told himself what an upstanding citizen he was.

Well, once Ronindella agreed to see Madame Psychosis, everything would be all right. They'd soon both belong to the New Age Church, which was indeed near the top of the charts. They'd have most of Beeb's pay coming in, and maybe Ronnie would get a real job, instead of depending on the Church to bail her out when she got into debt. It seemed to Ryan that she worked harder for them than if she were employed, and got a lot less out of it. Only her status as a mother saved *her* from going to the moon, as far as he could see.

Should he call to see what Ronnie was doing now? See how she was taking it? In some ways, she was pretty fragile.

No, he had to trust Madame Psychosis. She knew best, with the accumulated knowledge of mystics through the ages stored in her memory droplets. He had to be patient, to wait and see what happened.

If he just bided his time, everything he wanted would come to him.

TWELVE

"WE'VE CROSS-REFERENCED data from the archecoded onees," Angel Torquemada said, "and, as a result, we now know where the enemy is hiding."

Johnsmith had been daydreaming, but that comment focused his attention on the lecture. In fact, most of the people in the underground meeting room stirred at the same moment as him.

"Are there any questions?" Torquemada said.

"Yes," Frankie Lee Wisbar said. Frankie was one of the many new people at these meetings, since the entire onee supply had been contaminated, and everyone at Elysium now hallucinated about Viking ships every time they touched an onee. "How did you cross-reference this data?"

"Simple. We looked for semiotic clues about the Arkies in the hallucinations that our people suffered."

"Semi-what?"

"Semiotic. It's the science of understanding signs. It's been around for a long time, but it's only recently been adapted to onees."

"How does it work?"

"We look for variations in the hallucinations that subjects report while under the influence of onees. We file these and look for symbols that recur. We then

129

cross-reference these, looking for unconscious clues that previous users have left imprinted in the onees' matrices.''

"Previous users?" a thin man named Smedley asked from the back row.

"Yes, these bootleg onees are generational of necessity. The technology to mass produce them is apparently unavailable to the Arkies."

"Then how do they make them?" Felicia asked.

"They imprint them directly from the human nervous system," Torquemada said.

Johnsmith recalled the effect his onee had exerted on Alderdice, that first time his friend had used an onee. He had noticed that Alderdice picked up some of the same imagery Johnsmith had enjoyed. His assumption had been that it was coded onto the onee in the factory, but that might not have been the case. Torquemada was saying that onees picked up some imagery from everyone that used them.

"Factory images, unmuddled by repetition, can be perceived perfectly only by the first user. It is the intention of the Arkies to insert subversive imagery onto otherwise harmless onees."

The prisoners took that in, a few of them nodding in understanding, the rest just looking puzzled.

"But why?" a woman asked. "What's the purpose of this subversive activity?"

"Nothing less than to disrupt the government of the Conglomerated United Nations of Earth."

It was one of the few times Johnsmith had heard anybody use the full name of the government since he was a schoolboy. It sounded kind of formal, and yet strangely nostalgic at the same time, in a sick way. He didn't feel like singing the International Anthem, that much was for sure.

"But we've outsmarted this criminal element," Torquemada said, grimacing with pleasure.

Johnsmith wondered if Torquemada thought he was

smiling, and if he realized that, technically, by Conglom law, they were all part of the same criminal element he was condemning.

"Now we're going to seek them out and destroy them in their lair," Torquemada said, his voice rising with something like emotion. "We're going to search out and destroy the entire Arkie operation."

"We are?" asked an incredulous Alderdice V. Lumumba. "But how?"

"Through a military operation that will be carried out with surgical precision."

Audible sounds of understanding sounded throughout the room. This was not only the reason they had been trained, then, but also the reason their reactions to onees had been so thoroughly documented. They had not only been the semiotic bloodhounds through which the Arkies were to be ferreted out, but now they were going to be sent to kill or be killed by guerillas so skilled in survival that they could live in the wilds of Mars and penetrate the heavily guarded Elysium compound.

And to think that Johnsmith had been happy he wasn't sent to Luna or the Belt.

"An expedition will be mounted at oh six hundred hours tomorrow morning, with the following personnel armed and suited for an extended stay on the outside."

Johnsmith sank as far down into the uncomfortable plastic chair as he could manage, irrationally hoping that he would somehow not be called.

"Fulci," Angel Torquemada read from a clipboard, "Barenko, Wisbar, Smedley, Eddleblute . . ."

Johnsmith closed his eyes, imagining how bad a military adventure on Mars could be, especially after the disastrous firefight he had been in already. They had only ventured a few hundred yards from the compound and a handful of people had been killed; the fact that Torquemada had not revealed where the Arkies' camp was located made him think that this was going to be a major undertaking.

". . . Eaton, Sandke, Lumumba . . ."

Oh shit, Alderdice had been picked, thought John-smith; better him than me, though. He felt slightly ashamed at that reaction to hearing Alderdice's name called.

". . . Kassoff, Wu, Biberkopf . . ."

There it was. He was going to be sent out to die in the morning. Great. Johnsmith swallowed, feeling his adam's apple move almost painfully in his dry throat.

He didn't hear the rest of the names on the list. It depressed him so much to think of what was going to happen to him tomorrow that he couldn't think of anything else . . . except for Smitty II. The poor kid wouldn't have a father anymore. Well, it was better than having a convict for an old man. He hoped that Ryan was a better example to the boy than he'd been, but that was a dubious proposition.

It occurred to him that Torquemada was no longer talking. Their fearless leader was gathering up his notes and getting ready to leave.

"Mr. Torquemada," Felicia said, loud enough for everyone to hear, "you didn't call my name."

Torquemada looked down at her, but said nothing. Everyone in the room was watching Felicia.

"I'd like to go along on this expedition," she said.

"We need reserves," Torquemada said with an air of finality. "Not everyone will be able to go." He stepped away from the podium and started toward the door.

Felicia bit her bottom lip. "I'd like to volunteer to go in someone else's place."

Stopping in mid stride, Torquemada turned toward her. His death's head grin spread across his gaunt features. "Why, that's commendable," he said. "Commendable, Burst."

"Then you'll do it?" Felicia asked. "I really want to go, to see some action."

"May I ask why?"

"I want to pay them back for the way they attacked us that night," she said. "And I want to prove to myself that I've learned how to be a good soldier since I've been at Elysium."

Torquemada stared at her intently. Was he buying this? Johnsmith wondered; it was doubtful. It seemed likely to Johnsmith that Felicia was hoping to get a chance to go over to the rebels. But the way she was acting lately, who could tell?

"What do you say, sir?" Felicia asked.

"You'll get your chance," Torquemada said. "But not this time."

"Please," Felicia said.

But Angel Torquemada was already out the door.

"Felicia," Johnsmith said, as the grim prisoners rose and followed Torquemada. "What brought that on? This little outing could turn out to be very dangerous."

She turned to him with soulful eyes. "I want to be with you, Johnsmith Biberkopf," she said. "I want to be with you all the time."

"Well, that's nice, sweetheart," he said, genuinely touched, "but I don't think you should risk your life."

"It doesn't matter," she said. "The time that we live isn't what's important, but the way we live during that time. That's what really counts."

Johnsmith wasn't so sure about that, but kept his doubts to himself. At least she wasn't going along on the expedition to be used as particle beam fodder.

"Do you know why they didn't select me?" she said, with a touch of her pre-onee bitterness.

"No."

"Because of my family. They're giving me preferential treatment."

"But you *want* to go on the expedition, and Torquemada won't let you."

"Exactly, you naif. They're afraid of the consequences if I get killed or wounded . . . or captured by the enemy."

"I knew it," Johnsmith said. "You want to go over to the Arkies."

"Shh." She pressed her index finger against his lips and said softly, "I want *us* to go over to them, not just me."

"Us?" he whispered.

"You and me, guerillas together for the rest of our lives. And maybe Alderdice, too."

Johnsmith was moved and appalled at the same time. But all he said was: "Alderdice's obedience implants would probably prevent him from going over to the Arkies."

Felicia leaned close to him, close enough for him to kiss her. He did so, impulsively and deeply. It felt good, as if he had a new understanding of Felicia. Perhaps she was misguided, but she had a generous and giving spirit underneath the bitterness and resentment . . . sometimes.

She didn't give her love easily, but once she did, she gave all of it. It was just too bad that she had such crazy ideas.

But even while he was kissing her, he wondered if it was really crazy to think about defecting to the Arkies. Could it be any worse than this tedious nightmare of an interplanetary prison? At least the Arkies were free, living on the outside, not under the command of an imperious prig like Angel Torquemada.

"Well, it looks like we're going to see some action tomorrow," a woman's voice said from behind Johnsmith.

He turned and saw Frankie Lee Wisbar smiling at him. She smiled at Felicia, too, but Felicia looked away.

"You seem happy to be going into combat," Johnsmith said.

Frankie shrugged. "I might be killed," she said, "but so what? It's better than this living death." An expansive gesture indicated the entire compound.

Johnsmith was slightly startled to hear her say what

he had been thinking; not in so many words, perhaps, but the sentiment was the same. Quiet desperation was the rule of thumb at Elysium, apparently. And those who had been here longer didn't like it any better.

"In combat, you're really alive," Frankie said. "It's something a pacifist could never understand."

"I've only been in combat once," Johnsmith said, "and I found it confusing and frightening."

"It won't get any better," Frankie Lee Wisbar replied, "but *you* will."

She walked away, leaving Johnsmith with a plainly resentful Felicia.

"She's after you," Felicia said.

"She's just trying to help," Johnsmith said, wishing to avoid an unpleasant scene.

"Trying to help!" Felicia shouted. "She's going off with you tomorrow, and I may never see you again."

"Felicia, this isn't going to be a romantic tryst tomorrow. We're going off to fight a war."

But Felicia wasn't listening. She got up, kicking over her plastic chair, and stalked out of the meeting room. Johnsmith was left alone with his thoughts. He wondered what had made Felicia so angry. Perhaps it was his defense of Frankie. After all, Felicia probably thought that marching off to war was a highly romantic proposition, especially if the goal was to join another band of revolutionary guerrillas. She was so screwed up, but he loved her anyway. Maybe he was crazy, loving a woman like that, but that was the way things had worked out . . . at least for now.

Frankie Lee Wisbar was packing her gear. She was the only one at Elysium camp who knew where they were going in the morning, besides Torquemada and Sergeant Daiv. Still, she was packing exactly what she'd been told to, and gave no indication that she possessed more information than any other prisoner.

The slightest suspicious action on her part might lead

Torquemada to suspect that she was an Arkie. She had to keep that in mind at all times.

A light flared brilliantly, and a continuous roar sounded immediately afterward. Frankie Lee's muscles tensed and she dropped the pack. How could the Arkies attack without her knowing it?

She realized after a moment that it was only the Interplan ship's engines. Prudy the co-pilot was testing them, as she had done many times since the Captain had been captured by the Arkies, marooning her at Elysium as a result. It happened every few days, and she had learned to pay little or no attention to its thunder and fire. Tonight she was jumpy, thinking about what was going to happen tomorrow. There was no way to warn the Arkies about the imminent attack. What was worse, she would be one of the aggressors.

Maybe she could divert Torquemada and Sergeant Daiv long enough to let her compatriots know what was in store for them. It wasn't likely, but it was the best idea she could come up with on such short notice.

"I'm frightened."

She turned to see Alderdice V. Lumumba, sitting across the aisle from her on his bunk, packing his gear.

"That's okay, Alderdice," she said, ignoring the disapproving looks from the combat veterans bunking on either side of her. "Everybody is when they go into battle."

"I was completely ineffective during that first firefight," Alderdice said. "I was so scared I could hardly move."

"It's not unusual, especially the first time out."

Alderdice looked down at his bootless feet, plucking at one of his socks. "I don't think I'm any braver now than I was then, to tell the truth."

"You'll be okay." Frankie smiled at him. This poor man would probably get killed, she thought. He was just the sort to freeze up and present himself as an easy target. But there was no sense in scaring him. "Try not to worry."

"I will." Alderdice frowned thoughtfully. "I wonder why they're doing it?"

"Doing what?" Frankie went over and sat down on the edge of Alderdice's bed.

"The Arkies. I wonder why they're disseminating these special onees. I mean, I could understand it if they were raiding Elysium for food, or for other supplies. But what is it about these Viking hallucinations that's so special?"

"I don't know," Frankie Lee Wisbar lied.

"And why here at Elysium, the most heavily guarded military installation on Mars?"

Frankie shook her head innocently.

"Of course, they might be attacking every human habitation on the planet, for all I know," Alderdice mused. "But that still doesn't explain why they're doing it."

"No, I guess not."

Brow furrowed, Alderdice said earnestly, "You've been here a lot longer than me, Frankie. You must have heard something by this time. What do you think?"

"Torquemada doesn't tell us much," she said.

"No, I guess not. Still, there must be some reason for their behavior."

"Maybe they're trying to show us something," Frankie said. "Teach us something."

"In some misguided way, maybe," Alderdice allowed.

Frankie shrugged. "Who can say?"

"I guess it's hard for me to understand why anybody would do such a thing," Alderdice said.

"Why?"

"Because of my obedience implants. I used to work for the government, you know."

"I didn't realize that."

"I have a hard time understanding antisocial behavior. I was that way even before I applied for P.A."

"You were a P.A.?"

"Yeah."

Frankie smiled. "You don't seem the type, Alderdice."

"I suppose there's a good reason for that." Alderdice smiled a little, too. "I'm just not cut out to snoop and follow people around, even if they are in violation of Conglom law."

"Funny how people get into trouble," Frankie said. "I never believed that I'd done anything wrong, but they drafted me anyway."

"What happened?"

"I joined a group of freeps, and, even though I quit when the World Court ruled it illegal, I lost my job."

"You were a freep?" Alderdice had never paid much attention to the 'gram stories about the free-enterprise revivalists who had tried to start their own small businesses. He had assumed that they were all anticap, antisocial types, but Frankie Lee Wisbar certainly didn't fit the pattern.

"You're looking at a former neo-capitalist," Frankie said.

"Well, those kind of ideas are dangerous to the multinational way of life," Alderdice said, aware of the fact that he was spouting conventional wisdom, but unable to help himself. "The Conglom way is real capitalism. The freeps were revealed as anticap extremists."

"So they say," Frankie shrugged again. "So they say."

Alderdice turned toward his bunk. "Well, I guess it's time to get some rest."

"I guess so." Frankie wanted to give him some comfort, but she remembered that he wasn't interested in women. "Good night, Alderdice."

"Good night." He rolled over in his bunk, leaving Frankie alone with her secret knowledge.

Tomorrow they would go to war.

THIRTEEN

"GET ABOARD," SERGEANT Daiv ordered as the floating personnel carriers lined up outside the compound. Torquemada stood next to him, marking down the names and serial numbers of the reluctant soldiers on his ever present clipboard. It was a curiously, uncharacteristically, still morning, the tiny sun rising over the red desert as a flawless, golden disc.

Johnsmith climbed into the third carrier, along with Alderdice and Frankie Lee Wisbar. He sat near a transparent slash in the carrier's wall, so that he could look out as they crossed the desert. The first thing he saw was Felicia, who stood in the connecting tube between the barracks and the mess hall, watching for him.

He waved, but she didn't see him. There were too many people, and there wasn't enough time for her to pick him out before the carrier started to move forward.

"Here we go," Alderdice said from the seat next to him. He sounded as though he were dead already, Johnsmith thought. Well, maybe he was. Maybe they all were.

Torquemada was standing at the front of the carrier, facing the seated passengers.

"We're going to travel several hundred kilometers," he said, "almost due west. By the time we arrive at our destination, the sun will be high overhead—Martian noon.''

So they were going to attack in broad daylight, thought Johnsmith. That should greatly increase his chances of being gunned down by a particle beam cannon.

''We're going to box the enemy in and make him either surrender or fight it out. Since our weapons and tactics are considerably more sophisticated than his, we expect him to surrender.''

Johnsmith was quite a bit more than a little dubious, but he kept his opinions to himself. He didn't want to alienate Angel Torquemada—just on the off chance that he survived this insane adventure, he didn't want to be punished for contributing to a decline in morale.

''Where exactly is the enemy?'' a guy asked from the back of the carrier.

''He is hiding in a network of lava tubes under the rupes at the base of Olympus Mons,'' Torquemada said with a self-satisfied smirk. ''Geological surveys have shown only one place with a complex enough tube structure to house his subversive operation. It's less than two kilometers wide and there are a limited number of openings on the mountain side. If we cover them all, we can flush them out.''

God, it was worse than Johnsmith had imagined. They were going to march blindly into a bunch of tunnels against armed insurgents, and there could only be one result. They were going to die like rats in a trap.

''We're going to provide a great service for the nations of the Earth,'' Torquemada went on. ''Your loved ones back home will be proud of you if you fight bravely.''

Oh, joy, Johnsmith thought. Oh, rapture.

''Are there any questions?'' Torquemada said. Of course, his manner made it clear that he didn't expect that there would be any questions. It was just a matter of form.

"I have one," Alderdice said.

"Lumumba," acknowledged Angel Torquemada.

"Why are the Arkies such a threat to the Earth? I mean, we've used their onees over and over again, and we're okay, aren't we?"

"Are you?" Angel Torquemada said, pursuing the Socratic method of answering a question with another question. "Can any of you say that you are the same person you were before you touched an onee? Any one of you?"

Nobody spoke.

"It's one thing to have people on Mars or other system colonies using onees, but think of these dangerous electronic opiates flooding our dear home planet."

It occurred to Johnsmith that Torquemada was evading, rather than answering, Alderdice's question. He could think of several holes in this line of logic. For example, he happened to know that onees already flooded a good part of the Earth, and they were manufactured by the Conglom in the first place, contrary to the wording and the spirit of its own Interplanetary Charter. No, these *particular* onees were the problem.

"Could you be a little more specific?" Alderdice said, as if he could read Johnsmith's mind. "It seems that the imprinting of a certain set of archecoded images is the problem, not onees in general."

Torquemada's face darkened. "They're escaped prisoners, and they're subversives. That's all you need to know, Mr. Lumumba. Period."

Alderdice paled, realizing that he had gone too far. Now, if he lived through the imminent slaughter, his ass was grass when they got back to Elysium.

There was little dialogue between Torquemada and his troops after that. The desert sped by, and the shapes of distant mountains seemed to mutate as the perspective changed. Frost lay over the desert in the morning, and they either left the frozen water vapor behind the temperature went up enough to sublimate it; it vanished without turning to water.

After an hour or more of silence, Johnsmith turned to Alderdice and cleared his throat. "I think I'm in love with Felicia," he said.

"Good." Alderdice nodded. "I hope you make it back to be with her, even if you have to stay on Mars the rest of your lives."

"She doesn't have to stay."

"No, but she'll never recant if you tell her you love her."

"Think so?"

"Yes."

Johnsmith had never known love that strong before. He had begun to feel more strongly about Felicia since they had been sleeping together. Her jealousy over Frankie Lee Wisbar, while misguided, had touched him. But they had made love last night, in spite of the complaints of those they had kept awake. After all, it might be their last time together . . . her last time with him, and his last time with anybody, like as not.

As the shadows shortened on the Marscape, Johnsmith began to notice a gradual sloping several kilometers ahead, creeping up the rilles on both sides of the carrier. It was only after some time that he realized this might be the first sight of Olympus Mons, the largest volcano in the solar system.

"Look at the size of that thing," he said to no one in particular.

Alderdice, perhaps believing Johnsmith's comment to be sexual in nature, was roused from dozing.

"I think that must be our destination ahead," Johnsmith explained.

Since he was not sitting near the transparency, Alderdice couldn't see what Johnsmith was talking about. He sighed. "I should have stayed awake the entire time," he said. "It seems to me as if we just left Elysium. Now my life is hours closer to the end, chances are.''

''Don't be so negative,'' Frankie Lee Wisbar said, leaning across the aisle. ''You'll come out of this all right, Alderdice. Take my word for it.''

Johnsmith noticed that Alderdice wore a dubious expression, but neither of them argued with Frankie. Alderdice was fatalistic enough to be certain that nothing he said or did at this point could matter, there was no question about that. Johnsmith wasn't sure if his friend had a healthy attitude, but it seemed a bit late to try to change Alderdice's habits.

The carrier slowed, its high-pitched whine turning into a groan. It banked, and Johnsmith got a look at the other two carriers. One of them was turning northwest, and the other was still heading due west. The one they were riding in went southwest. They were fanning out, positioning their passengers to act as shock troops, about to pour into the lava tube mouths and through the Arkie den. Now the mountain was clearly visible. Its immensity was staggering—its summit was so high that the caldera seemed as far away as Earth, and its width could not be taken in with the human eye.

The carrier groaned to a halt. They were instructed to get into their pressure suits, which was rather awkward in the crowded, enclosed space. As soon as they were suited up, the carrier's back end popped open, forming a ramp.

''Get the lead out,'' Sergeant Daiv shouted.

The prisoners, soldiers now, got to their feet. Nobody spoke as they began to disembark. One woman ducked her head to avoid banging it against the low top of the gangway door, as Sergeant Daiv barked at those behind her to do the same.

And yet, when it was his turn, Alderdice managed to bump his head. His helmet absorbed the shock, and Alderdice kept moving. Johnsmith followed him, running down the ramp into the Martian daylight.

Torquemada was inside Johnsmith's helmet, shouting: "Go! Go! Go!"

Johnsmith didn't really know where he was going, but he kept running. He quickly caught up to Alderdice, who seemed to stumble along like a drunk. Frankie Lee Wisbar was up ahead, and Johnsmith thought it might be smart to stay close to her. She was a veteran of this kind of thing, after all.

Crouching, Johnsmith waited for the enemy to fire. Nothing happened, though. Other than the orders coming from Torquemada, the only sound he heard was his own heavy breathing.

The mountain loomed ahead, so vast as to be almost incredible. It seemed to stretch all the way to heaven, to rise forever from the surface of Mars. The prisoners scurried like ants in its foothills, advancing towards a snaking lava tube whose mouth seemed to open wide to swallow them.

"Inside! Get inside!" Torquemada bellowed.

Johnsmith followed Frankie, hopping over a rock and into the darkness of the lava tube's enclosure.

A light flicked on in the blackness. And then a second light. Photosensitive cells on their helmets were activated by the sublight radiation. Within seconds, the smooth tunnel walls were illuminated by dozens of circles of bobbing light.

A red beam swept across the narrow lava tube interior. Everything turned crimson, and Johnsmith flung himself to the tunnel floor. The enemy was firing on them.

"Down!" somebody shouted. "Everybody get down!"

But it was too late for one guy. Johnsmith couldn't tell who he was, but the beam seared his midsection, lancing out through his pressure suit's pristine white back amid a torrent of illuminated red smoke. His scream was deafening.

"Sandke!" somebody cried.

But Sandke didn't answer. He emitted a liquid gurgling, and then nothing more. He was dead.

"Let's get those sons of a bitches!" shrieked an unidentifiable, androgynous voice, distorted with rage.

"Yeah!" Somebody up ahead rose and fired a shot in the direction of the red beam. Somebody else rose and squeezed off a shot, too. Then everybody was up.

But not for long. More screams sounded as two prisoners fell. Johnsmith hit the dirt again, and three bodies fell on top of him. He heard the moans of the wounded through his helmet communicator, but he was powerless to move under the weight of the very people who needed his help.

More beam fire probed through the tunnel. He felt the movements of the injured people on top of him, muffled by their pressure suits, but nonetheless heartbreaking for that.

"Retreat!" Sergeant Daiv bellowed. The prisoners didn't need to be told twice. Johnsmith could see thick, white-clad legs moving back the way they had come just a few seconds before.

He struggled to get up, but to no avail. One of the bodies covering him cried and twitched for a few seconds, and then was still. Johnsmith knew that she was dead. Was it Frankie Lee Wisbar? Or Prudy? Or somebody else that he had spoken to in the months he had been at Elysium? Or was it one of the endless stream of prisoners who had ignored him every day? It didn't seem to matter much anymore. Whoever it was, she was gone now.

Somewhere in the midst of this morbid reverie, Johnsmith realized that the shadows deeper in the lava tube were moving. Somebody was coming.

He drew his .45, and waited.

Now they were coming into sight, two people in ragged pressure suits, a man and a woman painted in harlequin colors. One of them—a man, judging from his size and the way he walked—held an ancient AK47, and the other, a smaller figure, had a laser pistol in her gloved hand. The man's helmet had two horns protruding from the sides.

Johnsmith waited. They came closer, two cautious but ludicrous figures who stopped and prodded the bodies of their enemies.

When they were twenty feet away, he ran his thumb over the .45's safety, just to make sure it was off. He hadn't fired a shot yet, and the last thing he wanted was to be caught struggling with the safety in the moment before his death.

He wasn't going to blow this one. If he was going to die here, he was at least going to go down fighting.

The two Arkies came closer.

Bracing his elbow on the stone floor, Johnsmith took careful aim and squeezed the trigger.

A ragged hole opened in the man's pressure suit front, slightly to the left of center in the chest. A white tatter flew off from the back, red spraying the tunnel walls an instant later. His splayed fingers released the AK47. the impact lifted him off his feet and slammed him down hard onto the stone.

The woman turned from one side to the other frantically. She hadn't seen where the shot came from, since Johnsmith was hiding under the bodies. She must have assumed that he was dead, if she had seen him at all.

Terrified, she backed away, firing wild bursts from the laser pistol.

It was an easy shot. Johnsmith hardly knew that he had fired the .45 again. But she tumbled awkwardly backward, the laser firing. Its scarlet beam was deflected by the gleaming face mask of a corpse's helmet. A fiery L burned into the ceiling until her finger relaxed on the trigger.

Johnsmith didn't move. He knew that more Arkies might be nearby, and he didn't want to take any chances. With his elbow still resting on the floor, he pointed the .45 toward the back of the lava tube. The weight of the dead bodies and his pressure suit prevented him from trembling so much that he would be out of control.

He was alone for what seemed a very long time.

Then he heard the crackle of a helmet communicator approaching. A pair of columnar legs passed him from behind and approached the bodies. Whoever it was, unidentifiable from the back, had a pistol in hand. It seemed to be a man, but Johnsmith couldn't be sure. A gunshot cracked, and the fallen Arkie woman's body jumped, convulsed, and was still. Johnsmith had thought she was dead, but apparently not. The companion he shot was next, but the woman's killer must have believed him already dead. He didn't waste a shot. Instead, he turned toward the pile of bodies covering Johnsmith.

"Here," Johnsmith said. "On the ground."

"Biberkopf." Johnsmith recognized Sergeant Daiv's voice. "Biberkopf, are you okay?"

"Yes." His own voice sounded oddly thick and foreign. "Yes, I'm okay."

He felt the bodies being moved, and he could see Daiv's gloved hands. A moment later, he was being helped to his unsteady feet.

"Good going, Biberkopf," Sergeant Daiv said. "You got two of 'em."

"Yeah." Johnsmith didn't feel as if this were really happening, but he knew that it was. He had just shot two people without giving it a second thought.

Sergeant Daiv slapped Johnsmith's helmet, not maliciously as he had done so often in training, but rather in camaraderie.

Johnsmith reeled, nearly stumbling over one of the bodies.

"You're blooded now, kiddo," Sergeant Daiv said, and his hard face crinkled in a grin through the polarized plastic of his face mask.

Johnsmith had never seen Daiv smile before. He

wasn't sure he liked it. There was something wolfish and dangerous about the man, and his savage grin made him seem even more unsavory than did his usual grim manner. Daiv was just too damn happy about seeing a lot of people get killed.

"Move in," Torquemada's electronic voice said from inside Johnsmith's helmet. "You've got the initiative now, so keep advancing on the enemy stronghold."

Johnsmith wondered briefly where Torquemada was. Probably back in the carrier, watching the whole thing on a 'gram monitor. Most likely the camera was in Daiv's helmet, maybe even implanted in one of his eyes.

Johnsmith was stalking the lava tube alongside Sergeant Daiv now. The tunnel curved gently to the left, and they came to a place where a second lava tube bisected it. One tube had lain over the top of the other as the igneous rock cooled millions of years ago, but the Arkies had chipped away the rock to connect the two tubes. As a result, Johnsmith and Daiv now faced three tunnels instead of one.

"Get your asses up here," Sergeant Daiv commanded the others.

Johnsmith turned to see the prisoners reluctantly approaching from behind. He was relieved to see Alderdice's sweating face through a face mask.

But where was Frankie Lee Wisbar? Was she one of the bodies littering the lava tube floor? Maybe she had been one of those who had fallen on him while the prisoners were trying to retreat. He hoped not. She was one of the few people at Elysium who had treated him like a human being.

But this was no time for sentimentality. The battle was just beginning, and it seemed that he had been thrust into a leadership role as a result of killing those two people. He reminded himself that he had only actually killed one of them. Sergeant Daiv had gleefully done in the woman.

"You," Sergeant Daiv called to the nearest prisoner. "Come on up here."

The woman hesitated, and then stepped forward.

"You take that tunnel," Daiv said, pointing to the left. "Let me know if you see anything."

He turned to Johnsmith. "You take the one to the right. I'll go straight on through this way."

Johnsmith nodded. He didn't want to do this, but he knew there was no choice. Maybe if he was lucky, and careful, he would survive this madness.

He went into the connected lava tube on the right, and got as close to the near wall as he could. He went forward for a few seconds, listening to his own breathing.

He stopped to load the two empty chambers of the .45. His gloved hands were shaking badly, but he would need all six bullets, in case he ran into more Arkies.

Dropping a bullet, he squatted to retrieve it. It rolled away, glinting in the light from his helmet beacon. He didn't want to waste any ammunition, and so he followed the bullet on his hands and knees.

It rolled down an incline, and he scrabbled to catch up with it. At the bottom of the incline, it landed in a depression. Johnsmith picked it up, and slipped it into the chamber. Before he loaded the second bullet, he sensed that something was moving behind him.

Johnsmith turned abruptly, in time to see a massive gate closing. He got to his feet and ran toward the gate, but it was completely and seamlessly sealed by the time he got to it.

He banged on it with the butt of his .45, but the only result was a queer knocking sound. The gate was apparently made of some very tough polymer. Well, there must have been some other way out, he reasoned. It wasn't a good idea to stand here making a lot of noise.

A cavern stood in front of him. Overlying lava tubes had been cut away, until quite a large space had been created. In it was an array of archecoding machinery.

There weren't as many machines, and they were older, but they were similar to those at Elysium. Torquemada was wrong—they did manufacture onees here.

No one seemed to be tending this onee factory.

The soft whir of working devices filled the air. And there *was* air, he realized. He could hear it being pumped in. That must have been what the gate was for, to keep the oxygen in. He walked around the perimeter of the cavern, looking for tube mouths.

He found one after a couple of minutes. It was closed up with flexible sheets that opened as you passed through them and closed up once you were inside the tube. He prodded one with the barrel of his pistol. The cavern was completely enclosed, and the atmosphere was comfortable for the Arkies as they busily produced the forbidden onees.

But where were they now? Had they mobilized to fight the invaders? It seemed as if they should have left *somebody* to guard their onee factory.

"Johnsmith."

Somebody was calling him, whispering his name. He didn't see anybody, though.

"Over here, Johnsmith." It was a woman's voice. But he still couldn't see where she was.

At that moment, a pressure-suited figure rose from behind a work table, only a few feet from Johnsmith. She stepped out from behind the table and approached him.

As she came closer, he saw that it was Frankie Lee Wisbar.

"How did you get in here?" she said.

"Well, I kind of did it accidentally," he said. "How about you? How did you get in here?"

"Same way as you."

"Well, how do we get out?" Johnsmith asked.

"Through there." Frankie pointed to one of the covered tunnel mouths.

"That's what I thought," Johnsmith said.

"Torquemada will be proud of us." Frankie Lee smiled. "Deep penetration, you know."

"Right."

"Maybe we should get moving," Frankie said. "Before somebody comes in here looking for us."

"Right."

"Uh oh," said Frankie. "It looks like we waited a little too long."

Johnsmith turned to see what she meant. Five figures in crazy quilt pressure suits were emerging from one of the tube mouths he and Frankie had been about to use as a means of escape.

FOURTEEN

THE FOREMOST OF the Arkies spotted them. He raised his weapon, and so did Johnsmith.

Frankie grabbed Johnsmith's forearm to stop him. "Wait!" she cried. "Don't kill him!"

Johnsmith clenched his teeth. Why shouldn't he kill these son of a bitches, he thought angrily. Hadn't they ambushed him and his friends and ruthlessly killed several of them? He struggled to free himself from Frankie's grip. If she didn't let him go, they would kill him. Why didn't they shoot?

And then he realized that she had been speaking to the Arkies, not him. She had been imploring them not to kill him.

"Tell him to give us his pistol," the Arkie leader said.

"Do it, Johnsmith," Frankie told him, with a real sense of urgency.

With several guns trained on him, he didn't have much choice. He handed the pistol to the advancing Arkie.

Johnsmith turned on Frankie in a rage. "You traitor!" he shouted.

She sighed. "Johnsmith, it's all right. We aren't your enemies."

"Then who is?" he demanded.

"How about Angel Torquemada?" she said. "Or good old Sergeant Daiv?"

She was right, of course. But still, these people standing here had killed his friends, not Angel Torquemada or Sergeant Daiv. "You weren't there when they murdered those people a few minutes ago," he said.

"What did you expect us to do?" one of the Arkies asked. "Just let you come in here and arrest us, or kill us all? We were defending ourselves."

"What would *you* have done?" another one asked.

That question was difficult to answer, Johnsmith had to admit . . . at least to himself. "But you're criminals," he said weakly.

"No, we're not," Frankie Lee Wisbar said in a patient tone. "And you know it."

"Conglom law . . ."

"Fuck Conglom law," another Arkie said. "All any of us is guilty of is human weakness."

That was something Johnsmith had often thought, but it seemed strange to hear somebody saying it in these surroundings. He had become convinced that there really was something wrong with him in some subtle but fundamental way. But he wasn't alone, it seemed.

Gunshots echoed in the distance.

"I don't understand any of this," Johnsmith said. What sense was there in taking a hard line? He trusted Frankie Lee Wisbar a hell of a lot more than he trusted the Conglom. "I just don't understand."

"Nobody really does," Frankie said. "And there's no time to explain it now."

More gunshots crackled, these sounding a little closer than the last.

"What are you going to do with me?" Johnsmith asked.

"Nothing," the Arkie leader said. "You can go back with Frankie if you like."

Johnsmith was astonished. Were they really going to let him go? He knew that Frankie was one of them now. How could they afford to do such a thing.

"Or you can stay with us," the leader said. "We always need more people."

"Aren't you afraid somebody will overhear what we're saying?" Johnsmith asked.

"Communications are cut off inside this room," the leader said. "This place is pretty well defended. It's one of the places where onees are imprinted."

Johnsmith thought it over. He would be free if he stayed here, as free as anyone on Mars, at least. But it would be a precarious existence. And then there was Felicia. . . .

He owed her something for loving him.

"How do I know you won't shoot me when I turn my back?" Johnsmith asked.

"What's to stop us from shooting you now?" the leader said.

"How do you know I won't turn Frankie in?"

"*They* don't," Frankie said. "But *I* trust you."

He nodded. She was right; he couldn't conceivably have done such a thing to her.

"Maybe you'll work with Frankie," the leader said, "on the inside."

Johnsmith wasn't sure if he would dare, but, then again, he thought he might.

"We'll see."

The Arkie leader gave him back his gun. "You two better get going," he said.

"When we get back outside this room," Frankie said, "we can never talk about this, not a word."

"Okay."

Instead of heading toward one of the escape hatches, Frankie guided him straight back to the gate.

"Now, when this thing opens," she said, "run for it, run as if your life depended on it."

Johnsmith nodded. It occurred to him that he might

get shot by those *outside* the gate; now, that would be truly ironic.

The gate cracked open, showing only darkness on the other side. There were helmet lights bobbing around.

"It's opening," somebody said. It sounded like Sergeant Daiv, but Johnsmith couldn't be sure.

"Don't shoot," Johnsmith said. "It's Biberkopf and Wisbar. We're coming out."

Johnsmith nudged Frankie's back with his palm, and she ran out ahead of him. No sooner were they outside in the lava tube, than the gate shut behind them. It had only opened a meter wide at the most.

Nobody fired a shot.

"How the hell did you do that?" Daiv demanded to know.

"I threatened to shoot their leader, if he didn't let us go," Frankie Lee lied. "It was a stalemate, and when they heard you coming, they chickened out."

"Oh." Sergeant Daiv didn't look as though he was quite ready to believe her story, but there were more important things to worry about at the moment. "The other tubes didn't lead anywhere, so we came after you two," he said. "Good thing we did, looks like."

"Yeah," Johnsmith said, already beginning to wish that he had stayed with the Arkies. Well, it was too late now. He had thrown away his one chance for freedom.

"Let's melt through that door," Sergeant Daiv said.

"I don't know if it will work," Frankie said. "It's a highly reflective surface."

"Then we'll blow the fucking thing open," Sergeant Daiv told her with his customary belligerence.

Johnsmith knew that this was so much hot air, though. Even if they had brought explosives with them, they couldn't have used them. They were deeper under the volcano now, a mountain the size of Missouri. How could they risk bringing tons of rock down on them?

Sergeant Daiv must have realized this, too. He stood

back and fired his .357 magnum point blank at the seam in the center of the gate. The bullets spanged off the slick surface without leaving so much as a dent.

Johnsmith cringed as the bullets ricocheted, but nobody was hurt.

"That's the toughest goddamn plastic I ever saw," Sergeant Daiv said with a mixture of annoyance and admiration. "Did you see that, for Christ's sake?"

"Very dense," Frankie Lee Wisbar said.

"Yeah, I noticed," Sergeant Daiv said, holstering his pistol. "I'm just trying to figure out where these Judases got ahold of it."

"Maybe they built it," Johnsmith said. "Maybe they can do anything we do."

"What?" Daiv turned on him angrily. "They're just a bunch of ragtag anticap radicals, Biberkopf. How the hell could they develop that kind of technology?"

"Well, I saw some of the stuff they've got back there. It looked pretty sophisticated."

From Sergeant Daiv's scowling reaction, it was clear that Johnsmith should say nothing more.

"Well, anyway," Daiv muttered, "we've got them on the run now."

Several of the prisoners voiced their agreement, observing how close to the boiling point Daiv was.

"We better look for a way around this goddamn door," he said after what passed for a thoughtful moment.

As his helmet light swung around, Johnsmith caught a glimpse of Frankie's relieved eyes through her mask. He could have told Daiv the truth, he supposed, but why should he? Besides, wouldn't Torquemada be suspicious of him for walking out of the Arkie plant unharmed?

No, he had better keep his word to Frankie and the five other Arkies. He was on their side now.

They were soon back at the intersecting lava tubes.

As they emerged, the rattle of gunfire shattered their cautious sense of victory.

Sergeant Daiv went down.

"Jesus Christ!" somebody screamed.

Sergeant Daiv was lying at Johnsmith's feet, limbs twitching spasmodically. His face mask was shattered, and blood pooled in his eyes sockets as it gouted from a hole in his forehead.

Johnsmith hit the dirt. He used Daiv's body as cover, cocking the .45 and looking for a target.

Some of the prisoners were firing wildly, and others were backing into the tunnel leading to the Arkie plant. Johnsmith saw that the only way out was the way they had come. They had to make a run for daylight. He couldn't be sure, but he didn't think the Arkies would shoot him or Frankie.

"This way!" he shouted, waving his pistol toward the tube leading outside. "Back to the carrier!"

The prisoners did as he said, some of them bumping into each other, the rest crawling on their hands and knees. Anything to get out of the line of fire. Bullets thundered and screeched off the volcanic rock, and particle beam fire blinded Johnsmith momentarily. But he stood his ground, waving the prisoners into the lava tube that would lead them to safety.

He saw bodies dropping to the tunnel floor all around him, but most of the prisoners were out of gunshot range in a few seconds.

Frankie Lee Wisbar was next to him, firing her pistol at the empty darkness, in case anybody was watching.

"Let's get out of here!" she cried out.

Johnsmith turned to flee, slipping in blood. He stumbled, his right shoulder bouncing off the wall, but he righted himself and kept going. Frankie was right behind him.

They were outside in what seemed a much longer time than it really was, a few seconds that seemed like hours. The Martian afternoon was dazzling, even through the polarized plastic face masks. Dead ahead was the carrier, its back end opening to them like a willing lover.

Particle beam fire rained down on them from somewhere above. A man was cut in half, his choking death cry threatening to burst Johnsmith's skull with its plaintive agony. A woman watched in horror as her legs were burned out from underneath her. She fell onto the cauterized stumps and lurched forward a few paces like a drunken dwarf, before collapsing onto the red sand.

It was a slaughter! The Arkies had allowed them to come inside, and now they were killing the prisoners at their leisure. They were positioned on the rupes of Olympus above, and they were dug in pretty well.

Only eight prisoners made it back to the carrier. Torquemada stood in the front of the personnel compartment, staring straight ahead, looking very grim.

No sooner was the last prisoner through the hatch than the carrier was off, quickly gaining speed. Beam fire scored its armor as it hurled itself across the desert. Its robot controls had responded to the emergency as no human could have, getting them out of range in seconds.

"Oh, my God," somebody wailed. "Oh, my dear God."

Alderdice threw off his helmet. Johnsmith was relieved to see his friend as he removed his own helmet and gloves. In his horror and panic, he had forgotten all about him.

"Are you okay, Alderdice?" he asked.

"Yes, yes, I think so." But Alderdice's face showed that he was anything but all right, though physically unharmed. "It was terrible, monstrous."

"Yeah, but we're alive." It was Frankie Lee Wisbar. "We're all alive, Alderdice."

But Alderdice looked as though he'd just as soon have been dead, at least at that moment.

"They were waiting for us," a guy said. "They let

us walk in, and they picked off a few of us, but they were really waiting for us to come back outside. Jesus.''

Torquemada said nothing.

"If it hadn't been for Biberkopf here," the man said, "we'd all be burnt meat right now. Not only was he the only one who killed any of the bastards, but he saved the few of us who are left."

He had actually led them into the worst part of the slaughter, it seemed to Johnsmith. But what else could he do? He couldn't have let them stay in the lava tubes. At least now they were out, and headed back to Elysium.

If Johnsmith hadn't known better, he would have sworn that Angel Torquemada was in shock. But Torquemada finally made his way down the aisle, and looked down at Johnsmith, who sat wiping sweat off his face.

"I saw what you did through Sergeant Daiv's monitor, Biberkopf," he said. "You showed real courage and brains today."

"Thank you, sir," Johnsmith replied.

"Next time out," Torquemada said, "you'll be team leader."

Johnsmith closed his eyes. He put his hands over his face to hide the tears welling up in his eyes. He felt as if he had died and gone to hell. What kind of world was it where courage and intelligence were rewarded with more suffering and exposure to deadly danger?

Mars was hell, it seemed.

He felt a light touch on his damp right hand. He opened his fingers to see Frankie Lee Wisbar, her expression knowing and yet caring. She saw the tears in his eyes and put her arms around him. He buried his head in the pliable plastic of her pressure suit, and felt her fingers running through his matted hair, as if she were a mother whose child had fallen down and hurt himself.

"It's all right," she said, nearly crooning. "It's all right, Johnsmith."

But Johnsmith knew that it wasn't. That things would never be the same again.

He wept for the dead. He wept for himself. He wept for the living, and for the people on Earth who were so empty that they had allowed this to happen to their fellow human beings. But who was he trying to kid? This kind of thing had always gone on since the beginning of recorded history; his surreptitious reading had taught him that much, at least.

The grim silence of the prisoners was accompanied by the whine of the carrier's engines all the way back to Elysium. They were given water, but no food on the return trip. Nobody could have digested anything after what they'd been through today.

At least, Johnsmith told himself as the desert began to darken, he had not been a coward. If he had betrayed the Conglom, so what? As the Arkies had been quick to point out, the Conglom had not exactly done well by him, so why should he worry about the Conglom? Maybe he wasn't really a hero, as the surviving prisoners seemed to think, but at least he wasn't a disgrace.

The carrier slowed as it approached the compound. Johnsmith was surprised to see that the two other carriers were already docked.

The engines shut down, and the carrier rocked gently as the prisoners got to their feet. Alderdice had been sleeping. He seemed confused as his eyes opened wide and then blinked against the glare.

Once inside the compound, those who were not wounded were permitted to go directly to their barracks. They limped in, exhausted. But no sooner had Johnsmith crossed the threshold than he was beset by a jubilant Felicia. She leaped on him, arms and legs encircling him and almost knocking him down.

"Oh, Johnsmith!" she sobbed. "Thank God you're all right. When the other carriers came back without you, I was so worried. I didn't know which one you were on."

Somehow, he managed to keep his balance, even though Felicia squirmed and covered his face with wet, hot kisses. "I'm okay, Felicia."

"They wouldn't tell me what had happened to your group," she said, her feet finally touching the floor.

"We ran into trouble," Johnsmith said. "There were a lot of casualties."

"Oh, my poor Johnny!" Felicia buried her face in his chest. Though he was tired, Johnsmith didn't mind. He was rather touched by Felicia's unabashed relief to see him alive and well. Ronindella had never been like this, even in the best of times.

As he lay down on his bunk, Felicia still clinging to him passionately, he wondered why he was thinking of Ronindella now. She hadn't entered his mind in weeks, months.

Kissing Felicia deeply, he recalled with grim satisfaction that his wife was in his past. He would never see her again.

FIFTEEN

"MY GOD! " RONINDELLA shrieked in a decidedly un-evangelical fashion. "Your father's a hero!"

Smitty II smiled. He had always known that his Dad was a hero, but he felt good that his Mom finally saw it too.

She was looking at *Pixine,* and the moving images on the page depicted a series of action sequences within the bowels of Mars. Wait until the kids at school saw this, Smitty thought gleefully. Dad was shown wiping out a gang of anticap thugs in these caves under a gigantic volcano. It was just about the neatest thing Smitty had ever seen in his whole life!

"At first I thought this was some kind of mistake," Ronindella was saying. "But there can't be two people named Johnsmith Biberkopf on Mars, can there? And besides, there he is, right there in three dimensions and enhanced color. He never looked so handsome when he was here."

Smitty thought his Dad had always looked pretty good, but he didn't say so. He had seldom seen his Mom so happy. Why rock the boat?

"Look at him in that paper uniform," Ronindella said. "He's so trim and athletic looking."

"Mom . . ." Now was the time to bring up something they hadn't talked about in weeks.

"What is it, honey?"

"Remember that contest I won?"

"Mmm." She obviously wasn't paying attention to what he was saying.

"You know, the one where I won the trip to Mars."

"Mars?" She dropped the copy of *Pixine*. "It was a trip to Mars? I thought it was Luna. . . ."

"Yeah, you remember. You tried to trade it in for cash, or a new car. They said I could only have the trip to Mars, because I'm a minor."

"Oh, yeah." She turned to Smitty with wonder in her eyes. "Well, honey, why don't we just go to Mars, then?"

"Really, Mom?"

"Really." She had that look on her face that only appeared when Dad's money arrived every month. Only this was a lot more intense. "Why should we waste an expensive trip to Mars? After all, only a few thousand civilians get to go every year, right? It's wonderful that you won this contest, isn't it?"

"It sure is."

"And ordinarily people have to pay through the nose for a trip like this, right?"

"Right."

"So let's go and have a good time."

"And see Dad?" Smitty asked. He wasn't sure if she wanted to see him or not.

"We'll visit your father." She smiled at him.

"Great!" Smitty couldn't remember feeling this happy in a long time. A very long time. They were going to be together again, on Mars.

"We'd better start planning this right away." She closed *Pixine* and got up. "The Church will give me a leave of absence, since I'm still legally married to your father. If we can just get some—"

The phone rang. Looking distracted, Ronindella went to answer it.

Ryan Effner's handsome face came into focus. "Hi, hon," he said. "Are you getting ready for our session with Madame Psychosis?"

"No, I'm not," she said with a note of satisfaction.

"You'll be late." Ryan said, evidently oblivious to the change in Ronindella.

"I'm not going to see Madame Psychosis."

"Aren't you feeling well?" Ryan frowned, beginning to see that something was wrong.

"Never better."

"Well, then, would you mind explaining why you're not going today?"

"I'm not going today, Ryan," Ronindella said merrily, "or any other day."

"What?"

"You heard me. You might have tricked me into going to that cybershrink, with her New Age nonsense and that drugged gas, but this is the end of it."

"But I thought . . ."

"I'm going back to my husband, Ryan. Johnsmith needs me."

"What in the name of God are you talking about?" He laughed aloud. "He's on Mars, for Christ's sake. How can you go there?"

"Smitty's won a free trip for two."

"But that was weeks ago. I thought you weren't interested."

"I suggest you pick up the current issue of *Pixine.*"

At that she signed off, leaving a gaping image of Ryan on the screen for a moment before it faded to a dull gray.

"All right, Mom!" Smitty yelled. "I guess you told that scumbag where to get off."

"Smitty . . ." But Ronindella couldn't bring herself to scold him. Smitty had never liked Ryan, and the boy's intuition had turned out to be more accurate than hers. Well, the Lord works in mysterious ways, she told herself.

"We'll be with Dad before you know it," Smitty said. "Right, Mom?"

"Well, it takes quite a while to get there," Ronindella said. "But it'll be interesting, I'm sure."

"It's like those miracles they're always talking about at Church," Smitty said thoughtfully.

Ronindella grinned. "You know, it really is."

"When do we go to Mars?" Smitty asked.

"Oh, I hope the offer is still good."

"Yep, it's good for a whole year."

"Wonderful, honey." She went to Smitty and embraced him. "Our family will be back together again." And Johnny's pension would make them a lot more comfortable than they ever could have been on Ryan's teaching salary. But that wasn't something to discuss with a child.

What the hell was going on? Ryan sat at the phone, completely mystified by the conversation he had just had with Ronindella. He had thought that she was completely wrangled, and now this. . . .

Well, he'd straighten this mess out in a hurry. The first thing to do was contact Madame Psychosis. She'd know what to do. There was a secret code to contact her on the phone. It was to be used only in case of emergency, of course, but it seemed to Ryan that this situation qualified.

"Let's see. . . ." He had written down the code somewhere. He opened his desk drawer to search for it. Duplicates of his credit cards, receipts, bills, but no code. Where the hell had he put that thing?

He got more and more upset, his stomach hurting, as he pored through the drawer. Finally, he became so frustrated that he pulled the drawer out and dumped its contents on the desk top.

A piece of paper fluttered to the floor like a sick

moth, lighting on the pile of cards and notes. He pushed his squeaking office chair back and bent to pick it up. He noticed that his hands were trembling. He hadn't been this angry in years. No, it was more than anger. He was hurt. Badly hurt. How could Ronnie do this to him?

"This will straighten things out in a hurry," he said, certain that the fallen slip of paper was where the code was written.

But it was only a notice about his low job performance. It had been sitting on his desk a couple of mornings ago, but he hadn't bothered to look at it, thinking that it was nothing more than a routine job evaluation.

"Shit!" he said, loud enough for heads to turn in the neighboring cubicles. He crumpled the evaluation slip and tossed it in the wastebasket.

Goddamn it, if he couldn't find the code, he would go to see Madame Psychosis personally. It was probably better to do it that way, anyhow.

He got up and started to go toward the door. His face felt hot and he hardly noticed the people staring at him as he walked. He couldn't have talked to Madame Psychosis here, he realized. His next evaluation would reflect the tortured conversation he had just had with Ronnie, and following that call with another one to his cybershrink would be disastrous for his career. This had to be worked out at the New Age Building, and later in private with Ronnie. She would have to understand that she couldn't go back, only forward. She was denying her karma by going to Mars.

Getting into the elevator, he pressed the button for the roof parking lot. He had forgotten to put on his protective headgear, and cursed his stupidity for it. But he didn't go back inside the building to get it. Instead, he dashed recklessly across the hot concrete roof as soon as the elevator door opened.

The flyby's engine failed to start on the first try. He

cursed it and tried it again. It caught, and he lifted off
the roof, heading downtown.

What had she been talking about, something about
the new *Pixine?* Maybe he should take a look at it before he went running off to Madame Psychosis. Well,
there was a viewstand only a block away from the New
Age Building. He could just park and run over there to
see what she was so excited about.

He brought the flyby down into a slot. He didn't wait
to see if the license plate was scanned correctly. Let
them overcharge him. He had more urgent things on his
mind at the moment.

By the time he got to the viewstand, he was almost
delirious from the raw UV beating down on him. Luck-
ily, there was a sunshield over the stand. Sweating and
gasping, Ryan made his way past a *Fuckbook* dumpbin
display and the flyzines shelf. He stopped for just a
second to glance at the tiny section with text maga-
zines. Johnsmith had always stopped to look at these
little insignificant zines that barely sold enough copies
to keep their publishers in business.

Pixine, the most popular periodical in the solar system, was stacked by the creditier. Ryan grabbed a copy
and ran it over the creditier plate, stuffing his card in
the slot.

"Thank you," said the creditier.

Ryan thumbed through the zine, his eyes smarting
from the brilliance of the imagery. There were the usual
stories about 'gram stars, celebrity affairs and mar-
riages, Kwikkee-Kwizeen ads, and one piece with a
stentorian voice that announced: "Heroic Conglom
Troops Rout Rebels on Olympus."

He was about to pass the article by, and in fact had
turned the page to shut off the obnoxious voice, when
he realized that one of the brave troopers was none
other than Johnsmith Biberkopf.

"Holy Gaia!" he shouted.

Ryan looked around in embarrassment, but nobody

seemed to be paying any attention to him. It was probably customary for people to shout here, especially in the *Fuckbook* section. He flipped back to the offending page.

". . . was the courageous act of team leader Johnsmith Biberkopf, a former University professor who has sought a new life on the Red Planet."

Ryan couldn't believe this bullshit, but he kept listening, and watching the impossibly muscular, idealized figure of Beeb blasting away at unshaved guys with faces like rodents.

". . . singlehandedly killing a dozen of the enemies and rescuing an entire squad of freedom fighters from a batallion of violent malcontents whose goal is the usurpation of the entire social structure of the solar system . . ."

Ryan wondered briefly why he had never heard of such a vicious bunch of cutthroats, if they were so dangerous.

". . . the brilliant Conglom strategy to save our worlds for freedom and . . ."

Ryan slapped the zine shut. He almost bumped into a skinny man reading a copy of *Fuckbook* as he hurried to get to the New Age Building down the block. As soon as he got into the lobby, he headed for the elevator to the thirteenth floor without even stopping at the drinking fountain.

He was already in the elevator when he realized that he had left his credit card in the viewstand slot.

"Jee-zus!" Well, there was nothing to do but go back and claim it. He pressed the lobby button, but the elevator continued to move majestically upward.

When it got to the thirteenth floor, he punched the lobby button repeatedly with his index finger. It seemed to take forever for the door to close, but at last he started down . . . to the twelfth floor, where a thin man wearing vacutites got on. Ryan wanted to strangle him, but there was nothing he could do.

The elevator ride finally came to an end, however, and Ryan sprinted to the door. His mouth was dry and he was sweating horribly, his shirt stuck to his back, but he ran all the way back to the viewstand.

Panting, he stopped at the slot, relieved to see that the same people were standing around looking at zines. His fingers felt around the slot, which he could not see clearly after coming in out of the blazing sunlight.

There was nothing in the slot.

He turned around and shouted: "Did any of you see who took the credit card I left here?"

A couple of *Fuckbook* browsers turned, their head gear obscuring their expressions. None of them replied.

"Somebody must have seen it!" Ryan screamed. "You were all standing here five minutes ago, when I left. Now who was near this goddamn slot?"

The viewstand customers turned away. Ryan had the uncomfortable feeling that they thought he was crazy, or was trying to pull a scam, or was unwound from too many onees.

Furious, he clutched the nearest browser by the shoulder. "Was it you?" he demanded. "Did you steal my fucking credit card?"

The guy shook himself loose and backed away.

"Which one of you took it?" he screamed. "I need that card. I'm gonna call the police if I don't get it back in ten seconds. Do you hear me?"

They all heard him, of course, but most of them just shrugged and turned away. One or two even laughed.

"Fuck you!" he shouted. "Fuck the whole bunch of you!"

He stalked off, thinking about really calling the police. But if he did, he would have to hang around while they filed a report. Fuck it, he would call in the stolen card later. He had other cards, but his credit was overdrawn on all of them. He would pay them off later. Right now, he had to get back up to the New Age Building and see if he could persuade Madame Psychosis to bill him for this visit next time. Surely she would do it. After all, he had been coming here for years; she owed him that much.

He tried to calm himself as he entered the lobby for the second time today. It was hard to do—his breathing was ragged and he felt sticky and itched all over—but he tried.

On the way up to the thirteenth floor, he counted each breath he took, from one to ten, and then he started at one again. It was the ancient Zazen training that he had learned from Madame Psychosis in one of his early visits. It served to calm him very effectively, usually. But not today.

He burst into Madame Psychosis' parlor in a fit of pique that could not be soothed by the cosmic strains of synthesized music. No psychedelic gases could contain his anxiety. No philosophical discourse could soothe his battered spirit.

"What the hell is that woman trying to do to me?" he bellowed.

Madame Psychosis smiled serenely as her credit slot snaked up from nowhere. "Please insert your credit card, in order to begin your session."

"I lost the only card I had with me," Ryan explained. "But I've been coming here for years. Can't you please bill me for this visit later?"

"Your file can't be reached without your credit card number. Can you recite it?"

"Oh, shit. I don't think I can. Isn't there some other way?"

"I'm afraid not." Madame Psychosis looked concerned. "But would it be so difficult for you to get the card? I'll still be here until you return."

"Until five o'clock, right?" Ryan looked at his watch in desperation. It was already four thirty-eight. He would never get home and back in time with a duplicate card. "Look, I can't make it, and my card's been stolen. Can't you help me out just this one time?"

"I'm afraid that there can't be any exceptions." Madame Psychosis made a compassionate gesture with her hands. "We must take responsibility when we are unprepared."

"I wasn't unprepared," Ryan said, from between clenched jaws. "I had a card when I left home. But I bought a *Pixine*, and accidentally left the card in the viewstand slot. I went back to get it, and somebody had stolen it."

"Tsk, tsk," said Madame Psychosis.

"Is that all you can say?" demanded Ryan Effner. "Is that all you can say to me after the years of analysis I've put in here?"

"You're reverting to infantile behavior," Madame Psychosis admonished him. "Your accusatory tone is inappropriate and irresponsible."

"Fuck you!" Ryan cried. "I've spent hundreds of thousands of dollars here. How dare you brush me off with that line of bullshit?"

The celestial music swelled up powerfully, and the psychedelic gas issued forth from its ducts copiously. Ryan inhaled it as he raged against the cybershrink, but it didn't serve to calm him down, as intended.

"Mr. Effner," the cybershrink said calmly. "Please calm yourself."

"Ah, ha! So you do know my name! Pretended you couldn't tell who I was without the card, right?"

"Mr. Effner, please."

Ryan smacked his right fist into his left palm with a resounding crack. "Goddamn you, I want to see some action right now," he said grimly, "or I'll . . ."

"Or you'll what, Mr. Effner?"

Was she challenging him? This fucking fake human piece of shit who had been robbing him blind for years? Who had just messed up his life beyond belief in a single day?

He screamed incoherently. It was a long, full, nasty scream from down deep inside. It felt good. It felt better than anything he'd experienced in days, weeks. He screamed again, with even more passion.

"Mr. Effner, please," Madame Psychosis said sternly. "This is no time for primal scream therapy."

"Oh, yeah?" Ryan looked around for something to strike back with. The only thing he saw besides immaterial images was the credit card slot on its serpentine stand.

Reaching down, he grabbed it. Feeling it sliding out of his grasp, as it retreated back into the floor, he wrenched it with all his strength.

Grunting, he felt it come free in his hands with a crack. And he had though it was metal. Bits of plastic fell, sparks ignited and fell into the gaseous void. He stepped forward into the vertiginous artificial cosmos surrounding Madame Psychosis, and bellowed: "I'm gonna get my money's worth out of you, bitch—one way or another!"

Madame Psychosis went dead. Obviously the threat of violence had bugged her programming.

Ryan laughed. He lunged forward, only to feel a sharp pain in his shin. He fell, clutching at his leg, but not letting go of the credit stand.

He saw what he had run into, now that he was on his hands and knees on the floor. It was a projectogram, sending up 3-D images of whirling galaxies and nebulae. He got up on his knees, and, winding up like a baseball player, he smacked the 'gram as hard as he could.

The Horsehead Nebula winked out of existence as the 'gram crashed to the floor.

"Wow!" Ryan loved it. He had never felt so powerful, so in control of his destiny. He sucked in more of the gas, and went looking for more 'grams. Prodding ahead at ankle level with his makeshift club, he found another one and demolished it with a single clean stroke.

He found six altogether. When he had smashed the

last one, he marveled at what he saw. It was nothing but a dimly lit room, maybe twenty by eight feet, with a weirdly dressed robot sitting in the middle on a chair with cables running from the back. Vents issued the psychedelic gas through louvers, obscuring the carpeted floor. The sensation of floating in space had been nothing but slick New Age talk, drugs, and 'grams. He had always known that, of course, but he had never really *known it*.

There wasn't much left of his splintered, plastic club, but he would use what he had to finish off Madame Psychosis.

"This is a felony," she said, suddenly active again. "Do you realize what you are getting yourself into?"

"Fucking right I do," he said, bringing the credit stand down on Madame Psychosis' head as hard as he could.

The head did not fly off, as he had hoped. Instead, it canted to one side and lolled there, a big patch of pliable pink plastic hanging down, exposing part of a titanium skull.

"This is a felony," Madame Psychosis repeated.

Ryan lifted the credit stand again, but it crumbled in his hands. There was nothing left of it at all.

He looked around for some other weapon. The pew he always sat in was nowhere to be seen. He remembered that it came up from the floor, and looked for some kind of trap door or something. He didn't see it, so he turned back to the cybershrink with the intention of dismantling her with his bare hands, if he had to.

"You'll have to live with the consequences of your actions," said Madame Psychosis, holding a hand out to him commandingly.

Grasping her wrist and forearm, he yanked the arm off. Another spray of sparks illuminated the room for a moment, and then flickered into dying embers. He hefted the arm carefully. Perfect weight for him, if he choked up a little.

He swatted Madame Psychosis in the head again, as if he were one of Beeb's Vikings swinging a broadsword. This time he had the satisfaction of seeing the jaw fly off, while the head moved up and down as if it were pleased with him. Madame Psychosis no longer lectured him on the legal punishments in store for him. In fact, as he continued to flail away at her, she ceased speaking altogether, and soon ceased moving altogether. Nevertheless, he kept on beating the cybershrink until she was nothing but a pile of plastic, metal, memory droplets, and cables scattered on the carpet.

Exhausted, he took one final poke at the pile of mechanical debris at his feet and threw the arm down.

"I could use that pew now," he panted. But the pew still didn't appear. He sat on the floor in the lotus position, just as he had learned it from Madame Psychosis.

The gas was no longer pouring from the vents. Only the acrid smoke and stench of burning plastic and his own perspiration remained. Ryan wiped his dripping face with the back of his hand, and realized that the gas had made him crazy. He had been angry and upset, and the gas had driven him insane. He had just wrecked millions of dollars worth of machinery, and Madame Psychosis had reported him to the police before he did her in.

He was a shoo-in for the Triple-S.

"Kind of funny when you think about it," he said aloud. His voice echoed through the room. He watched a spark fizzle out amid the wreckage of Madame Psychosis, and laughed. "Beeb would have said it's ironic."

Ryan Effner chuckled. He suddenly thought of himself as an asshole, for the first time in his life. A loser. He had thrown his whole life away. That woman had jinxed him, just as she had jinxed his old buddy. Now she would go back to Johnsmith and leave him to rot. He was pretty sure that he wouldn't luck out and get sent to Mars. No, this violent episode would doom him to the harshest duty in the solar system—the lunar pits.

He threw back his head and laughed. He laughed for a long, long time, until the tears came to his eyes. Until his gut ached.

Until they came to get him.

SIXTEEN

JOHNSMITH AND FRANKIE Lee were working together today. They hadn't had an opportunity to talk much recently, not since the incident a few days ago, when an Arkie had been captured. Only when they were outside, separated from the others, with a direct communication helmet-to-helmet channel, could they converse safely. The cold penetrated their supposedly seamless, heated pressure suits, making them uncomfortable enough to keep them working steadily, even though they were unsupervised. As team leader, Johnsmith was nominally in charge.

"Is that Arkie prisoner a plant?" he asked. "I mean, did they want him to get caught?"

"Sure," Frankie said, handling a wieldo. She manipulated it as though it were a marionette, and a thirty-meter long section of prefabricated sheet was delicately picked up by its extensors and set in place on the orange sand. Only a wieldo could hold the sheet steady against the powerful wind. "How do you *think* we communicate? We can't always wait for the Conglom to order an attack, you know."

"I see," Johnsmith said, admiring her dexterity. "So this guy has been sent out to be captured, just so he could be here to give us a message or something?"

"Most likely. We'll get a chance to talk to him sooner or later, I hope."

"Well, it's not as though he could just wander off somewhere, now that they've got him."

"True, but they might use a probe to get information out of him, or they might brain slice him. If that happens, not only does he end up a vegetable, but we're both in a lot of trouble, too."

"You and me, you mean?"

"Do you see anybody else working for the bad guys around here?"

"The bad guys?" Johnsmith was confused—how could she be loyal to the Arkies if she thought they were the bad guys?—until he saw Frankie grinning through her face mask. "Oh, you were joking, huh?"

"Yeah." She grinned even more broadly. "You take everything so seriously, Johnsmith. You're pretty cute, you know."

He tried unsuccessfully to manipulate his own wieldo, watching the sheet thud to the ground. He managed to pick it up again, thinking that he liked Frankie a lot, but that he was a little afraid of her at the same time. She was so worldly . . . and so dedicated, too. She had risked her life twice on the Olympus raid (as it had come to be known), once against the Conglom forces, and once against the Arkies, who easily could have mistaken her for one of their enemies.

He liked Frankie, all right, but he felt that he had a certain duty toward Felicia. Still, his espionage activity might get him in a lot of trouble, so he hadn't told Felicia about what had really happened on the Olympus raid. If she ever escaped, then she would learn the truth.

The wind felt strong enough to push over their wieldos, but they remained seated in them. Johnsmith used the wieldo to reposition the sheet, which served as a windblock, as it conjoined the section Frankie had just put into place. Johnsmith was pleased with himself for getting it right this time.

At that moment it occurred to him that the reason he had come back, rather than staying with the Arkies, was Felicia. He had really been unable to face the prospect of leaving her in misery, allowing her to believe that he was dead. It seemed odd and egomaniacal, but nobody had ever loved him as fully and as selflessly as Felicia. He could hardly believe the intensity of her passion sometimes. And yet she seemed to be completely sincere.

That's what had finally won him over. How could he give up something as sweet as that?

Well, he'd have to if they probed the new prisoner's brain. There was no way he could cover up for them if Torquemada got the okay from the Conglom to brain slice. It was an unpleasant thought, but he had to face the possibility.

"One thing I've been wondering," Johnsmith said, eager to take his mind off probes and brain slicing. "How did you imprint those onees the night of the Arkie raid? I mean, you were outside with the rest of us."

"I programmed one of the robots that was on line that night. Of course, I knew when the raid was coming, so I instructed the robot to slip the archecoded onee into the matrix while Torquemada was busy, and set the machines to imprint every single onee that way until further notice."

Johnsmith thought that was very clever, and his enjoyment of Frankie's story lasted until their break.

They went back inside and removed their pressure suits. Inside the mess hall, Johnsmith joined Felicia and Alderdice. Frankie went to sit with someone else.

"You're with her all the time," Felicia said.

"Who?" Johnsmith dabbed at his vegetable paste and compcarbs with a fork.

"Don't play dumb with me, Johnsmith Biberkopf," said Felicia. "I'm talking about Wisbar."

"But I've been assigned to a work detail with her," Johnsmith protested. "What else could I do?"

"You've been enjoying it a little too much," Felicia said. "I see you smiling and talking with her."

"What do you want me to do? Spit in her eye?"

Alderdice chortled, causing Felicia to glare at him until he sobered. "Sorry," he murmured.

Felicia turned her anger back on Johnsmith. "Well, what do you have to say for yourself? Why have you been so attentive to Wisbar?"

"Honey, you're the only one who thinks there's anything going on between Fr—between Wisbar and me."

"Frankie," Felicia said, making a sneering face. "That's what you were going to say, wasn't it?"

"Well, you're the only one I know who calls her by her last name," Johnsmith said with annoyance.

"Oh, am I?" Felicia stuck out her chin like a prize-fighter, daring him to strike back.

"Yes. Look, Felicia, I'm not going to stop being friends with Frankie or anyone else just because you're jealous."

"I am not jealous!" Her eyes widened dramatically.

"What do you call it, then?" Johnsmith looked down at his tray.

Felicia's angry expression turned sad. She began to cry. "I can't help it if I love you!" she wailed.

"Felicia . . ." But what could he say now? She was upset, and she would blame him for it. If only she knew the truth, about how he and Frankie were working against Torquemada and the Conglom. But he couldn't say a word about it.

"You don't love me!" she sobbed.

The other prisoners were turning to watch. God, how he hated such scenes. He was so embarrassed that he wished he could go crawl into a hole someplace and die.

"Felicia," he said, "please."

She sniffed, tears rolling down her face. Then, just

when he thought she was about to calm down, she swept all three of their trays from the table. Plates and cutlery clattered onto the floor resoundingly.

"Hey!" Alderdice cried, as hot coffee spattered onto his pants.

Felicia paid him no heed, getting up so abruptly that her chair fell over. She stormed out of the mess hall, crying, without saying another word.

A long silence followed. At last Alderdice spoke: "I wish we had robots to clean this up."

But, of course, they had no cleaning robots, which were so common back on Earth. The prisoners did all the cleaning at Elysium. And Johnsmith was pretty sure he knew who would be assigned mess hall duty today. Torquemada had ridden Felicia pretty hard lately. That was part of the reason for her outburst, he was certain of it. But he was tired of her jealousy, just the same.

As he had anticipated, Felicia was assigned to spruce up the mess. Torquemada assigned him to a training detail, however. And when he got to the gymnasium, he found that there was only one prisoner waiting for him.

He had never seen this man before, a stout fellow with a shaved head. There was no doubt that this was the new prisoner, who had been sent from Olympus. "What's your name, soldier?" Johnsmith asked him.

"Jethro Pease."

"I'm the team leader who's been assigned to train you," Johnsmith said.

"I've already been trained," said the sullen Pease, in a thick New England accent.

"Well, then I'll retrain you. My name is Johnsmith Biberkopf. Where were you imprisoned originally?"

"Polar Base Four." Now that he had heard Johnsmith's name, his manner seemed to change subtly. He seemed more cooperative, but it was nothing an observer would have noticed. Johnsmith wasn't sure if it had really happened, in fact. It might have been wishful thinking.

"And how did you escape?"

"It was easy. I could have done it anytime. But this one day, I'd had enough. I just walked out onto the ice to die. I sat there with frost forming on my pressure suit. And I was beginning to feel pretty good. It's true what they say about freezing to death. You start to feel all warm and cozy."

"Oh, yeah?"

"Yeah. Anyway, as soon as I got used to the idea that I'm dead, this dilapidated minicarrier comes drifting out of the snow. I'd never seen anything like it. It had these weird symbols painted on the side of it in bright colors. I thought I was hallucinating, but I wasn't."

"What were the symbols?" Johnsmith asked.

"I didn't know it at the time, but they were runes."

"Runes, as in the ancient form of writing?"

"Runes, that's all I know. That's what they called it."

Well, well, well, Johnsmith thought. The Arkies even used the same writing as Vikings.

"Mr. Biberkopf," Jethro Pease asked, "are you interrogating me?"

That was probably for the benefit of anyone who was listening. Or was it? Johnsmith couldn't tell if this guy knew who he was talking to or not. Maybe he was just a good actor. In any event, Johnsmith hoped that Torquemada saw his questions as an interrogation. As team leader, he had the right to ask any questions he wanted, of course. But he really was searching for a way to get the information Pease had been sent to give Johnsmith and Frankie Lee Wisbar. It would come in due time, he suspected. Just now, it was probably best to start Pease's training.

"You look like you're a bit out of shape," Johnsmith

said. "I think we'd better start with a few laps around the gym."

Pease groaned, but he didn't protest.

They started off jogging easily. After a couple of laps, Johnsmith quickened the pace, actually enjoying himself. He would never have believed this, if he had seen himself at this moment a year ago.

Pease wheezed and fell back. Turning, Johnsmith ran backwards as the Arkie tried in vain to keep up.

"We'll have you fit in no time," Johnsmith shouted back to him. "I'll work with you every day, until you're ready for some martial arts training."

Pease couldn't run any farther. He stopped, putting his hands down on his thighs as he bent over to catch his breath.

Johnsmith, who had barely broken a sweat, slapped him on the back. For the benefit of anyone who was listening, he said: "We believe in discipline around here, unlike the Arkies."

Pease turned his red face and glanced over his shoulder at Johnsmith with something like contempt. It occurred to Johnsmith that the Arkie didn't realize this display was designed to preempt any suspicion, and was nothing personal. Or perhaps Pease was acting, too. Perhaps he understood exactly what Johnsmith was doing, and was playing along for the benefit of their Conglom jailers.

"Okay, you rested long enough," Johnsmith said in his best Sergeant Daiv manner. "Let's do some calisthenics now. Get down and give me twenty pushups."

Pease slowly did as he was told, although he only made it to sixteen.

"All right," Johnsmith said after about thirty seconds. "Let's pick 'em up and go."

As they ran around the gym, Johnsmith wondered why—if the Conglom forces were in such good shape and were so well disciplined—they had been so badly beaten by the Arkies in the Olympus raid. Frankie claimed that she had been unable to warn the Arkies, so how come they had been ready?

Maybe they were just smarter than the government forces. In spite of Torquemada's hawklike appearance, he really wasn't very intelligent, as far as Johnsmith could see. He had led his troops right into a slaughter, and he had never even shown any remorse. What harm would it have done to express a bit of sadness about the people who had died on the raid?

Johnsmith went to the showers without any hint that Jethro even knew he was an Arkie spy. Of course, Pease might have just been waiting for a time when he was certain they wouldn't be overheard, which could take forever. Or maybe he was waiting for Johnsmith to bring it up. . . . Well, the time would come, sooner or later.

Pease was sent to an isolated room underground, where he would be interviewed by Angel Torquemada later. Perhaps the decision to use the mind probe was still pending . . . or perhaps Torquemada already had permission. That was doubtful, though, if he had to hear from a Conglom panel on Earth.

Most likely, there was still a little time to find out what he wanted.

That night, Felicia refused to sleep with Johnsmith. He felt lonely and deprived, but he didn't beg her to come back to his bunk. Let her stay in her own, if she wanted to act like a jealous bitch. He was tired of being manipulated. He couldn't stop Torquemada from doing it, but he could stop Felicia.

If he had been firmer with Ronindella, maybe he would still be on Earth. That was something to think about while his racing mind gradually faded into sleep.

The next morning, he was back on the wieldos with Frankie.

"I was assigned to the Arkie prisoner yesterday afternoon," he said.

"Yeah, I know." Frankie went on manipulating the

wieldo, as she spoke. "Word gets around fast, you know."

Johnsmith nodded. He really didn't know, of course, because he had pretty much confined his circle to the few people he had known since coming to Mars. Those who had attempted to befriend him after the Olympus raid did not interest him.

"I didn't get a chance to talk to him," Johnsmith said. "I mean, to ask him why he was sent to us."

"I don't know what can be done about that," Frankie said, dropping a roofing panel on top of four walls with a sure hand on the wieldo.

"Well, I've got an idea," Johnsmith said. "We'll have him write it down."

"*Write* it down?" Frankie turned to him with a dubious expression. "What makes you think he can write?"

"Most people can write a little," Johnsmith said. "If he can't we'll have to think of something else."

"I guess we can try it," Frankie said, fingering the wieldo once again.

"We better get started," Johnsmith said. "Maybe I can find a way to do it during training this afternoon."

But he didn't.

Torquemada entered the gym just when Johnsmith was getting his courage up to pass a slip of paper to Pease. On it he had written: "Why did they send you?"

He was reaching into his pocket for a pen when the conch shell sounded. He was sure that Torquemada was behind him, so he snatched the note from the startled Pease and bunched it up. Clutching it, he turned to face Torquemada.

"How's the physical training going?" Torquemada asked.

"Fine," Johnsmith said.

"Good, good." Torquemada walked around the two men, sizing up Jethro Pease. "This man is a very special prisoner, you know, Biberkopf."

"He is?"

"Yes, and do you know why?"

"No."

"Because he's the first Arkie to ever come back to us of his own free will."

"You mean, he defected?" Johnsmith gaped. He had never imagined such a thing. It didn't make any sense. He was acutely aware of the balled up piece of paper in his hand. As soon as Torquemada turned his back, Johnsmith stuffed it in his pocket.

"You're probably wondering why we're keeping Mr. Pease in isolation when he's not exercising," Torquemada said. "Well, it's because we don't know if he's really come back to us, or if this is some kind of Arkie trick."

"Oh." This was pretty confusing, Johnsmith thought. How the hell were they going to find out anything? And what if the guy really was an Arkie deserter? What if he told Torquemada about Johnsmith's attempt to slip him a note? Johnsmith had to hope that this was just an Arkie ruse to worm Pease's way into Torquemada's confidence.

"Mr. Pease has already told us some very interesting things about our enemy's encampment." Torquemada favored them with one of his rare smiles. "And I look forward to learning more from him in our next session."

So that was it. Torquemada hadn't been using a probe. He didn't have to brain slice Jethro Pease. Pease was a turncoat.

And now Pease was looking intently at Johnsmith. Was he going to tell Torquemada about the note?

SEVENTEEN

JOHNSMITH FELT THE sweat rolling down his temples, collecting in drops, and hanging from his chin. He was aware of his pulse, and felt strangely off balance. He watched Pease's beady eyes for some sign, but saw nothing there except curiosity.

Torquemada, carrying the conch like a baby, glared at them both. "Carry on," he said. "I'll see Mr. Pease in an hour."

Johnsmith watched him walk off. He wanted to be relieved, but he couldn't quite bring himself to believe that he was off the hook. He turned to Jethro Pease, who stood looking back at him.

"I think we've had enough exercise for today," Johnsmith said. "Let's shower and go to the mess hall."

Pease smiled, revealing a gap-toothed set of almost green teeth. "Sounds good to me," he said.

"Yeah." As they walked out of the gymnasium, Johnsmith's legs trembled almost uncontrollably. He couldn't have forced himself to run another lap. It was all he could do to make it to the showers. He was profoundly frightened by what had almost happened. If Jethro Pease had mentioned that note to Angel Torquemada . . .

He reported his failure to Frankie the next morning.

She looked glum. "I don't know about this," she said. "Maybe it's a fake. If Pease convinces Torquemada that he's a defector, or deserter, or whatever, then he would be able to move around a lot more freely than he can now."

"Yeah, I thought of that."

"And he didn't mention the note to Torquemada, did he?"

"No, he didn't."

"Well, then . . ."

"But maybe he just thought it was part of the treatment," Johnsmith said.

"The treatment?" Frankie stopped working and turned toward him.

"Yeah, interrogation, physical abuse, and all the rest of Torquemada's shit. Maybe he thought it was some kind of trick."

"If so, why wouldn't he report it to his supervisor, who is, after all, Angel Torquemada? That way, he wouldn't be in trouble, would he?"

"Not right away," Johnsmith agreed. "But if it turned out to be nothing, then he'd have me to deal with. And for all he knows, I'm one of these guys with the temperament of the late Sergeant Daiv."

"Well, he didn't know Sergeant Daiv," Frankie said, returning her attention to the wieldo.

"Maybe not, but he knew someone like him at the polar camp. And a guy like that could make life pretty miserable, if you got on his bad side."

"I guess so."

"You know what I think?" Johnsmith said. "I think we'd just better wait. They're not going to probe him or brain slice him, or anything like that, so if we're patient . . ."

"We'll get our chance."

And they did get their chance, but it took several weeks. Eventually, Pease just became another prisoner, once Torquemada had all the information he could squeeze out of him. Johnsmith and Frankie didn't know what he had told Torquemada, but if he was sent by the Arkies, it couldn't have been much. If he wasn't, on the other hand, they could be in a lot of trouble.

One day Jethro Pease was sent out with a construction crew, which included Johnsmith. Frankie wasn't there, but Johnsmith knew that he had better make an attempt to communicate with the guy.

Johnsmith offered to show Pease how to use a wieldo. Apparently, Pease had never been on one before.

"Ever driven a seeder?" Johnsmith asked.

"Yeah, at the pole." Pease seemed to regard him with suspicion.

"Well, it's not that much different using one of these." He pointed to the wieldo, "You sit here, and fit your fingers into those holes. After that, it's mostly just a matter of hand-eye coordination."

"Uh huh."

"You want to give it a try?"

"Why not?"

Pease sat down and stuffed his fingers into the controls. He wiggled them tentatively, and seemed surprised when the extensors mimicked his motions precisely.

"Pretty soft duty," Johnsmith said. "Especially for a guy who was an Arkie a month or so ago."

Pease said nothing, but continued to cautiously manipulate the wieldo.

"Just get used to the controls for now," Johnsmith said. "There's plenty of time."

"Okay."

"So you deserted the Arkies, did you?" Johnsmith asked, trying to sound as though he were making casual conversation. "That's never happened before."

"Oh, yeah?" Pease didn't sound as if he much cared if it ever happened again.

"You're the first," Johnsmith persisted. "And maybe the last, for all I know. But tell me something. . . ."

"What?"

"Is your helmet communicator on short range?" Johnsmith coughed, hoping that if anyone overheard his question, they'd think nothing of it.

"Huh?" Pease glanced at him sidewise through his face mask. "You mean helmet to helmet? I guess so."

"Good, because I have a few things I want to talk to you about in private."

Pease removed his hands from the wieldo. "Such as?"

"Such as, did you really run away from the Arkies?"

"Well, as I keep telling Mr. Torquemada, I left of my own free will. What he didn't seem to understand was that nobody tried to stop me."

"What?"

"People have been leaving Olympus for a while now, and it's not something they try to stop you from doing."

"I don't think I follow you." Pease seemed to be saying that he hadn't defected. Of course, Angel Torquemada would interpret his actions that way, for propaganda purposes.

"There's a day coming," Jethro Pease said simply.

"A day coming? What are you talking about?"

"There's a day coming on Mars. If we can figure out where it's going to happen, we'll be there. I just trusted in fate to take me to the right spot, if I went out wandering."

"So the Arkies didn't send you."

"No."

Johnsmith still didn't know if he believed Pease. But surely the guy must have known that Johnsmith was one of the two Arkie spies . . . unless he was telling the truth, in which case he might not have known anything.

"See, there's going to be a . . ." Pease seemed to be groping for words. ". . . a change."

"A change in what?" This was getting very strange.

Johnsmith began to think that Jethro Pease just might be schizophrenic.

"A change in this planet, in the solar system." Pease's eyes were wide. "Maybe even the whole galaxy."

Was there some bizarre religion starting up here on Mars, affecting even the Arkies? God knew that there had been more than enough of them on Earth in recent years. It reminded him of the ancient Romans, with their myriad mystery cults—one of which had been Christianity.

"What kind of a change is it?" Johnsmith asked gently.

"It's the one predicted by the Sacred Archecode," Pease said. "The sailing Ship with a serpent's head, carrying men with metal heads through the ocean of worlds."

"But it's just a Viking ship," Johnsmith said.

Pease didn't seem to hear him. He was entranced by the vision of the Arkie prophets. Ignorant of history, he neither knew nor cared what a Viking was.

"When it comes sailing into our world, this Ship of time and space and God and the devil, it will change everything," Pease said.

"And you told Angel Torquemada all this?"

"I tried to," Pease said sadly. "But he wasn't interested in anything but the layout of the Olympus hideout."

Johnsmith felt the goosebumps rising underneath his pressure suit. "And did you tell him what he wanted to know?"

"Oh, sure. What difference will it make after the Ship sails into our universe?"

This meant that Angel Torquemada undoubtedly was planning to deliver a crushing blow against the Arkies at this very moment. He had to tell Frankie, and together they had to warn the Arkies. Every last one of them would be killed or captured, or run out onto the desert to perish, and then there would be freedom for nobody on Mars, ever again.

"We'll all go sailing when the Ship comes." Pease's reverential tone suggested that the word "Ship" must be written in upper case, befitting a venerated object. "The deserts of Mars will be transformed, and we'll transcend this miserable existence, once and for all."

Johnsmith listened politely to the man's ranting. As soon as Pease calmed down, Johnsmith said, "Maybe we'd better get back to work, at least until the great day comes. What do you say, Mr. Pease?"

"Okay," said Jethro Pease, who went back to the wieldo in a desultory manner.

This changed everything. Johnsmith had to talk to Frankie right away. But it was so difficult to be alone with her, especially in light of Felicia's jealousy.

The wind died down for a moment, and Johnsmith had an idea. It almost seemed absurd, but it was the only way he could be in intimate circumstances without arousing Angel Torquemada's suspicious mind.

He had to sleep with Frankie.

At mess, he knew that Felicia was waiting for him to sit down next to her and make conciliatory noises. Instead, he sat with Frankie.

"Will you sleep with me from now on?" he asked.

"What?" Frankie said, sucking on a nutrishake.

"I asked you if you'll sleep with me from now on."

Frankie looked a little surprised. "From now on? Don't you think that's quite a lot to ask?"

"Well, just for tonight then. And then we'll see how things work out."

Putting down her glass, Frankie said, "You don't know how often I've hoped you'd ask me this, John-smith Biberkopf."

"Then you accept?" Johnsmith said, feeling his heart beat a little more strongly than he might have expected.

"I don't know." Frankie chewed her bottom lip. "Aren't you afraid this might hurt Felicia?"

"She's been acting too possessive lately," he said, surprised at how accurate this statement was in regard to his feelings, in spite of the element of expediency involved. "Not only that, but I really don't feel the way I used to about her. A lot has happened in recent weeks, and I feel that we've grown apart. I need a change."

"So I'm just a change?"

"I like you a lot, Frankie," Johnsmith said in all honesty. "Are you sleeping with anybody?"

"No, my guy was killed a few months before you arrived here, and I haven't had the appetite for sex since then."

"I'm sorry," Johnsmith said, feeling like a shit. "I didn't know, Frankie."

"Of course you didn't." She reached over with her right hand and squeezed his fingers. "I guess it's about time I started living again."

She was going to do it! He was aroused quite a lot by anticipating sex with her. He had felt betrayed by Felicia deep in some secret place, ever since he returned from the Olympus raid. She couldn't have known that he had come back on account of her, of course. But her jealous rages had finally made him fall out of love with her, once and for all. Maybe Frankie could fill the void left by his disappointment.

But there was the immediate situation to consider now.

That night, he went to Frankie's bunk instead of waiting for her to come to his. He didn't want to chance Felicia's having a change of heart and showing up in his bunk. Judging from the way she had refused to look at him on his way out of the mess hall, he didn't think there was much danger of it, but he had to make sure he talked to Frankie tonight. There was no way of telling how soon Torquemada planned to strike.

"I hope your neighbors down at this end of the barracks don't mind if we make a little noise," he said.

"They often make noises of their own," Frankie said, opening her arms wide as he pulled back the covers to lie down with her. "They won't mind."

She wore nothing, and her skin was smooth and warm. As they began to touch one another, Johnsmith found that he thought of little else besides Frankie's lean, lithe body. He rubbed her and squeezed her, and she stroked him with gentle, loving hands. Their intensity rose slowly, purposefully, until Johnsmith thought he would burst from the sheer force of his desire.

He kissed her from head to toe, unmindful of anything but her lovely body. She ran her fingers through his hair as he descended upon the sweet tasting essence of her femininity. She came to climax rapidly, then. He was wildly aroused by her orgasm, but he would have given her more, had she not pulled him to her.

"I want you now," she said simply, as he nuzzled her neck.

He entered her, and at first they barely moved at all. But the pace gradually quickened, until they were like some beautiful two-backed beast, sharing a single heartbeat, rising to a celestial music all their own. It was as if they would never descend.

They came together.

Afterward, as they lay in each other's arms, their sweat mingling under the blankets, Johnsmith whispered in her ear that Jethro Pease had told Torquemada all about the Arkie's Olympus camp.

Her eyes gave away nothing as she asked him how much Torquemada knew.

"It's hard to say. Pease is crazy, a follower of some weird Arkie cult."

"You mean the Ship?"

"Yeah, I guess you heard about it."

"When I was living at Olympus—that was before I assumed the identity of a woman who had been captured by the Arkies—I went to some of the Ship meetings. There were some people who believed in the Ship as a kind of religion. We all believe that there is some liberating force behind the archecoded onees. Somebody has *seen* that Ship, Johnny."

Johnsmith was silent. Religion made him uncomfortable, but Frankie was not saying anything as irrational as Jethro Pease. It wasn't as if she were an advocate of the Video Church or anything like that. Still, the idea that a certain onee showed the way to the Truth and the Light. Well . . .

"We have to get out of here right away," Frankie said. "Once we've warned them, the Arkies can move their base of operations to some other part of Mars."

"Is that possible?"

"There's been some talk about it in the past. I don't know how complete the evacuation plan is."

"It doesn't matter. They've got to get away from Olympus before Torquemada wipes them out."

Frankie kissed him. "You're a *mensch,* Johnny."

He smiled at her, and kissed her back. "Thanks. You're pretty special yourself."

They slept together every night after that, planning their escape from Elysium after making love. Frankie had spoken with a number of Arkies who had escaped from Elysium; it was part of her training.

"The best and easiest way is to steal a minicarrier while we're outside."

"That won't be so easy," Johnsmith said.

"Well, there are two minicarriers in a hanger, and I knew how to reprogram the sentry."

Johnsmith rolled on his back and sighed. She was right, and he knew it. This was their best chance, and he found himself trembling to think of what they were going to do. "We're both working outside tomorrow," he said.

"Yeah, and that's when we'll do it."

EIGHTEEN

UNFORTUNATELY, SEVERAL OTHER people were working outside in fairly close proximity. These included Felicia and Alderdice. Johnsmith had the crazy idea that they might be able to take his two friends with him, since minicarriers could safely accommodate up to six passengers.

As team leader, he could give them orders to go over to the hangar, and then he would explain things to them. Of course, Felicia might not do as he said, out of spite. There wouldn't be much he could do about it, in that case. And Alderdice might not be able to defy his obedience implants. Well, he would just have to find out for himself if they would come.

Felicia was running a big tractor, digging out a huge rectangle of sand for the foundation of a new, permanent building. Helping her was Alderdice, who calibrated the exact dimensions of the enormous hole in the sand.

"Alderdice," Johnsmith said. "I need to talk to you."

Alderdice rolled up a blueprint and held it like a baton. "Sure."

"Can we talk helmet to helmet?"

"Okay." Alderdice switched onto the appropriate channel with his chin.

"Look, I'm going to need you and Felicia over by that hangar."

Alderdice's brow furrowed. "I don't know if Felicia will go," he said. "She's pretty angry at you."

"That's why I need you to persuade her."

"Oh, I see."

"Maybe if you don't mention me at all, she'll go along without protest."

"Yeah, maybe."

"It's important, Johnsmith said. "Otherwise I wouldn't ask, my friend."

"Okay." Alderdice looked a little confused, but the two of them had been through so much together that Johnsmith knew he could be trusted.

"I'll be over there working with Frankie." Johnsmith gestured toward the hangar.

"I'll talk to her," Alderdice said.

"Thanks." Johnsmith leaned into the wind and walked back to where Frankie was kneeling, absorbed by her covert work on the sentry.

She jumped when he came up beside her. The casing of the spidery robot's thorax was open, and she was busily substituting modules and memory droplets. Johnsmith had no idea where she had gotten the stuff; presumably from the Arkies, but he couldn't be sure.

"How's it going?" he asked.

"Fine, about another ten minutes and we'll be ready to fly out of here."

"Listen, I've asked somebody else to come along," he said.

Frankie had been preparing to slip a module into place, but she stopped cold and looked up at him. "What did you say?"

"Alderdice is coming, and he's bringing Felicia," Johnsmith said nervously.

Frankie nodded. "I see," was all that she said.

"I can't leave them here," Johnsmith said. "They're my friends."

"It's going to be pretty dangerous," Frankie said.

"Felicia's wanted to get out of here since the day we arrived," he said. "And Alderdice . . . well, we'll see."

"Maybe we can use their help," Frankie said. She went back to work.

Just when she was closing the thorax casing, Alderdice and Felicia staggered up under a strong gale. Johnsmith saw the pain and resentment in Felicia's eyes.

"Helmet to helmet," he said.

Felicia stood off to one side while he and Alderdice talked. She did not look at Johnsmith, only at Frankie. Her expression was anything but friendly.

"Alderdice, there isn't much time." Johnsmith watched the robot scuttle off onto the desert, its guidance system askew. "We're getting out of here, and I want you and Felicia to come with us."

Alderdice gaped through his face mask. "What did you say?" he asked.

"We're leaving. We're going to escape. Come with us."

Alderdice shook his head. "You know I can't do that. My implants."

"Fuck your implant," Johnsmith said. "We can get away from this hell hole, but this will be our only chance."

"I can't do it, I tell you," Alderdice said. In spite of the cold seeping through his pressure suit, he was sweating. "It's against the law."

"I'll go," Felicia said to Johnsmith with an icy calm. "You won't have to ask me twice, you two timing son of a bitch."

"Good." Johnsmith was relieved, but he still had Alderdice to deal with. "Just fight it this one time. You've taken onees, and that shook your faith in the rightness of your damn programming implants, Alderdice. Just take it to its logical conclusion. The whole fucking Conglom is rotten to the core. Why should you let it keep you in chains?"

"It's not a matter of letting it," said a desperate Alderdice. "I don't have any choice."

"No, you don't." Frankie was holding a pistol, pointing it right at Alderdice's chest. "You're coming with us, or I shoot you where you stand."

"Frankie . . ." Johnsmith was stunned. "What are you doing with that . . ."

"We can't leave anybody here who knows what we've done," Frankie said.

"They'll find out sooner or later," Alderdice said.

"We'll take every second we can get," Frankie said. "Now, get in this hangar."

Alderdice reluctantly did as he was told. The two minis were resting on runners in the shadows inside. The cockpits were open.

"Get in," Frankie said.

Alderdice, Felicia, and Johnsmith clambered up and inside, taking up three of the six seats. Frankie got in last.

"These seats aren't very comfortable," Alderdice complained.

"Shut up," said Frankie.

"Don't you dare tell him to shut up, you bitch," Felicia snapped.

"Please," Johnsmith said, "all of you." He reached up to close the cockpit.

A shadow appeared, crossing the threshold of the open hangar door.

"Somebody's coming!" Felicia cried. "Torquemada."

Frankie pointed her pistol at the open door. A man entered. He was far too short to be Torquemada.

"It's Jethro Pease," Johnsmith observed.

"Take me with you," Pease said, holding onto the runner supporting the mini. "Please."

Johnsmith looked at Frankie. She shrugged.

They pulled Pease inside the mini, and Johnsmith shut the cockpit. They heard the hiss of oxygen filling the enclosed space.

Frankie turned on the power. Nothing happened for a few seconds, and then there was a piercing whine. The mini shook and its engines roared into action.

"Let's get the hell out of here," Johnsmith said.

Frankie punched a few buttons on the panel in front of her, as if she were making a phone call back on Earth. The mini shuddered violently as if lifted off its runners.

It shot forward with terrific speed, flattening them against their seats.

"Whoo-hoo!" Jethro Pease shouted.

They flew out over the desert a couple of miles, and then banked. The mini passed over the Elysium compound. The prisoners stopped working and stared up at the unexpected sight. Just before they lost sight of the compound altogether, Johnsmith got a glimpse of a solitary figure rushing out of the onee plant. It had to be Angel Torquemada, he realized with great satisfaction.

At that moment, he decided that even if they were caught, this adventure was worth it.

There was a festive atmosphere inside the minicarrier. Even Alderdice wasn't as unhappy as he might have been. They were free of Torquemada and that wretched compound, at least for the moment.

"If only we had some champagne," Johnsmith said. The smaller size of this craft made the sensation of movement much more immediate. Johnsmith felt a little giddy.

"Do you know what you're doing, Wisbar?" Felicia said.

"Olympus is almost exactly due west," Frankie said. "I think I can keep the guidance system going in a straight line until we see a mountain the size of Missouri. If not . . . well, you pays your money and your takes your chances.''

Felicia's brow furrowed. Clearly, she had never heard this archaic expression before, but she was too proud to admit that she didn't understand what Frankie was talking about.

The giddiness soon turned to motion sickness. Alderdice was the first to be affected.

''Can you set this thing down?'' Johnsmith said. ''I think Alderdice is going to be sick.''

''We can't stop,'' Frankie said. ''They're after us now, and they won't even *think* about slowing down, much less stopping.''

Johnsmith knew that she was right. ''I'm sorry, Alderdice, but you'll have to wait until we get to Olympus to be sick.''

Alderdice groaned. He was not having a good time, but he tried to hold it in. Fortunately, it had been just before lunch when they had hijacked the mini, so there was little solid food in his stomach. Somehow, he managed to hold it all in.

''Uh oh,'' Frankie said about half an hour later.

''What's going on?'' Johnsmith demanded.

''They've bollixed the program from Elysium somehow, I think.''

''How did they do that?''

''I don't know, but the damn thing isn't going in the direction I've been telling it to go in. Some kind of bug in the programming, I guess.''

''Shit.''

''So far they've only made it change direction. But pretty soon they'll be able to make the mini turn around and go back to the compound.''

''What can we do to stop it?'' Johnsmith asked.

''Bring the mini down.'' Frankie didn't wait for a consensus. She slowed the mini's velocity, and bumped to a rough landing on the red sand.

''Everybody all right?'' she asked.

Alderdice breathed a sigh of relief as he put on his helmet. As soon as everyone's head was covered, Johnsmith thrust open the cockpit, and they climbed out onto a desolate plain hundreds of kilometers from any human habitat.

"Now what?" Felicia asked.

"Now we search for the Ship," said Jethro Pease. "That's what I was doing when they found me, and that's what I'm going to do now."

"Well, they've been tracking us," Frankie said, "That means it won't be long before they'll be here hunting us down. We better get over into those hills." She pointed to distant crags, barely visible through concentric whorls of orange dust.

Felicia looked as though she might protest for a moment. But then she followed the others meekly.

"I'm sure now that I'm destined to be there when the Ship sails in," Jethro Pease said as they marched across the barren Marscape. "It's what I was put here for."

"You were put here as a nonproductive citizen, who the Conglom found to be no longer useful," Alderdice said.

Pease seemed hurt by this allegation. "That doesn't mean I can't be there when it happens."

"That's right," Frankie said. "Maybe we'll all be there."

"And maybe not," a scowling Felicia said. "You know, I thought the Arkies were a courageous band of visionary revolutionists, and now I'm beginning to think you're just a bunch of religious fanatics."

From the silence that greeted Felicia's remarks, it was clear that nobody was interested in what she thought, least of all Frankie. Still, she continued her cynical and yet naive chatter as they trekked across the desert toward the ragged hills.

The sun set rapidly, as it always does on Mars. They kept walking, and Johnsmith began to worry about how long their oxygen was going to hold out. Surely they had a few days to live. But what then?

He remembered seeing a twentieth century video, originally a celluloid film, about an astronaut lost on Mars. The guy found some rocks that gave off oxygen when he burned them. Wishful thinking; a miracle. Just what they needed now.

The going got pretty rugged as they reached the foothills. Jagged stone plinths protruded from the sand like the rotting teeth of a giant.

"Maybe we can rest here," Alderdice said. He was clearly very tired, and in some ways he still had not accepted the morality of what they had done.

"No, we have to keep moving," Frankie said.

"Why?" Felicia demanded. "We might as well die here as up in those mountains."

"Some revolutionary you are," Johnsmith chided her. "You give up way too easily now that you're really free, Felicia."

He saw her clench her teeth angrily and turn away. But he no longer cared.

"You can stay here if you want, Felicia," Frankie told her. "But going over these mountains is our only chance."

"How so?" Alderdice asked.

"On the other side is the travel route between the pole and Elysium. There are tours of influential people every few days. If we're lucky, one will pass by and we can signal to the carrier. They're programmed to always pick up lost travelers, and some of them even have human pilots."

"Then we can still make it," Alderdice said. "We can still get out of here alive."

"The chances aren't good," Frankie said.

"What choice do we have?"

They started up the mountainside, looking for the less precipitous passes. The pressure suits helped, since they were made of extremely durable polymers. The low gravity and low atmospheric pressure helped, too. Johnsmith had never imagined it could be so easy to climb a mountain.

At last they stood at the summit, gazing down upon an ancient seabed.

"The carriers skim along close to the bottom of the seabed," Frankie said. "That way they don't get buffeted by quite so much wind."

"Oh."

"The Arkies have been planning to waylay a carrier down there." She pointed to a passage between two plateaus, no more than twenty kilometers wide. "There's no way they'll be able to get past without seeing us, and they'll have to stop and pick us up."

"And if they don't?" Felicia asked.

"Then we'll have no choice but to disable the carrier."

"How?"

"I'll shoot the pilot."

"*If* there's a human pilot," Johnsmith said.

"And if there's not, I'll try to blow out its guidance system."

"Christ," said Alderdice. "It sounds as if our chances are *very* slim."

"Very slim indeed," Frankie said.

They began the descent down to the seabed. Tired as they all were, they reached the narrow passage by dawn.

NINETEEN

"IT'S JUST LIKE your father to do this," Ronindella said, staring out through the transparency at the Martian desert. "Especially after we've come all this way just to see him."

Smitty didn't say anything. He was disappointed that his Dad hadn't been at Elysium when the tour got there, but he was pleased about the escape . . . even if the timing wasn't so good.

"It seems as if everything he touches turns bad," Ronindella groused. "See the woman piloting this bus?"

"It's a carrier, Mom."

"Carrier, bus, what's the difference? Anyway, she was the co-pilot on the Interplan ship that brought your father to Mars. And do you know what happened?"

"No."

"The captain was murdered by Arkies, and they sent a complete crew to fly her ship back to Earth. They didn't need Prudy, so she's been stuck here ever since, poor thing. God bless her."

Smitty thought the carrier pilot was mean, but he didn't say so. Besides, what did his Dad have to do with any of this stuff? Just because he was on their Interplan ship, it was supposed to be his fault?

"And what do I have to go back to?" Ronindella went on. "Ryan's been sent to the moon, and your father's income in going to evaporate, now that he's become a deserter. What am I going to do?"

Maybe you could get a job, Smitty thought. But he didn't dare to say it aloud. Someday he would, but not yet.

"I'll have to appeal to the Church," Ronindella said. "That's all there is to it."

Smitty groaned.

"They'll help me. I know they will. If they don't help the victims of men like Johnsmith Biberkopf, the Conglom won't give them so much air time."

Smitty didn't know if he believed that, but his Mom always said this kind of thing. She was pretty sure that the Church was there to help her out, but it seemed to Smitty that she put so much into her Church activities that they were getting more than their money's worth from her. His Dad had said things along those lines once or twice, but she had accused him of being sacrilegious and he had shut up.

"You could stay on Mars," the old man sitting across the aisle said. "They always need people here, volunteers for the hard work that has to be done on the frontier."

"Frontier?" Ronindella said. "Do you really expect me to slave away with a bunch of common criminals for the rest of my life, mister?"

"It would be good for the boy." The old man smiled at Smitty, revealing gleaming white dentures. "A healthy environment, unsullied by the corruption of our tired home planet."

Ronindella eyed the old man suspiciously. "Are you a Connie?"

"I am indeed a member of the Conservation Party, Miz. Perhaps you've heard of me. I am Herbert L. Silver, elected representative from Mid North America."

"Sinner," Ronindella hissed.

"I beg your pardon." Mr. Silver looked indignant.

"You people promote the ways of Satan," Ronindella said. "You've held back progress for far too long."

"Madame, the Conservation Party has tried to preserve what is best about the Earth."

"Now you're trying to stop progress on the other planets and the Belt. I know what you're all about."

"Stuff and nonsense." The old man was looking at her with fire in his eyes.

"I'm not going to let you use your evil influence over my son," Ronindella said, her voice rising.

"I assure you—" The Connie Rep's protests were cut off by the whining of the carrier's motors.

Smitty was sure that they were nowhere near the outpost the tour was supposed to visit next, and yet they were stopping. Something had happened. Maybe there were Martians after all, and the pilot had seen one.

No such luck. He could see five people in pressure suits standing on an outcropping a little to the left up ahead. They were waving their arms wildly, as if they were afraid the carrier would pass on by without stopping to pick them up.

The carrier slowed down and began to descend the few meters to the ground. The passengers were jostled slightly as it landed, and Smitty watched the five people climbing down from the outcropping to get aboard.

The cabin was sealed off, and the pilot got into her pressure suit so the hatch could be opened. They came in one by one, and the last one, a woman, was holding a gun in her right hand.

Through the transparency, the passengers watched in horror as the woman took off her helmet and pointed the gun at the pilot. She was a pretty, thin woman with short, dark hair—and she was hijacking the carrier.

"Oh, my God," his mother and the Connie said in unison.

The other passengers were babbling away, too. They

were all scared shitless. Smitty felt a little scared, but he thought this was kind of neat at the same time.

The cockpit was pressurized again, and the transparent seal was lifted. The alien odor of Mars wafted in as one of the hijackers entered the cabin. He reached up to remove his helmet.

"Please keep calm," he said.

It was only then that Smitty realized what he was seeing.

His Dad saw him at the same time.

"Dad!" Smitty cried.

"Smitty!"

"Johnny!" Ronindella screamed.

"Ronnie!" Johnsmith exclaimed.

The Connie rep glared at Ronindella. "So *I'm* the criminal, am I?"

Smitty was in the aisle, running to his father. Johnsmith stooped to embrace him.

"Son!" Johnsmith said with tears in his eyes. "I can't believe it!"

"What I can't believe, sir," said an indignant Representative Silver, "is that you have hijacked this vehicle, violating the laws of the Conglomerated United Nations of Earth."

"Another few hours, and we would have died out there," Johnsmith said. "And we're not going back to Elysium, now that we're considered criminals."

"Perhaps you should consider giving yourselves up," the Connie said. "It will probably be a lot easier on you in the long run."

"We've been on Mars for years," Johnsmith said, "and none of us have found anything easy here."

Two of the other hijackers were coming into the cabin now, a man and a woman.

"But how do you know?" the woman was saying. "How can you possibly know it's going to happen, that it isn't just an illusion?"

"I know," the man said simply.

The woman had a funny expression on her face, as though she had never run into anybody like this before. Smitty thought that was odd, because the man was very ordinary looking, short with a shaved head.

"Where are you taking us?" a woman in the back of the cab asked.

"To Olympus Mons," the man with the shaved head told her.

"Oh, I was hoping we'd get to see that," the woman said drily.

The engines whined again, and the carrier began to lift off the dry seabed. As soon as it was through the pass, Frankie instructed the pilot to fly to the northwest at top speed. The carrier accelerated, and soon the orange desert was an indistinct blur beneath them.

Ronindella would not speak to Johnsmith. She hadn't forgiven him for becoming an Arkie, and she wanted him to know it. It was amazing to Smitty that they could have been apart all these months and start fighting as soon as they saw each other. His Dad didn't seem to care, though. He seemed happy just to be sitting here talking to Smitty, and that was great. Let her sit there sulking; that would give Smitty all the more time with his Dad.

"How did you get to Mars?" Johnsmith asked, grinning at Smitty.

"I won a contest."

"What? That's incredible!"

"Yeah, it was a Kwikkee-Kwizeen contest, and I—"

Smitty was cut short by one of the Arkies, a sweaty, fat black man, coming down the aisle.

"Johnsmith," the man said. "Something has happened."

"What?" Johnsmith leaned forward in his seat. "What is it, Alderdice?"

"Frankie's punched in a code to talk to Olympus. . . . " Alderdice seemed very worried.

"Yes, and what happened?" Johnsmith said.

"There's no answer."

Johnsmith didn't wait to hear more. He got up and went through the cab, ducking his head to get into the cockpit.

"Alderdice says you can't get through to Olympus," Johnsmith said. "Are you sure you've got the correct code?"

"We're getting through now," Frankie said.

"Well, that's good news." Johnsmith saw that Frankie did not look relieved. "Isn't it?"

"Well, it would be, except that there's nobody home."

"Nobody home? I don't understand."

"We're getting a recorded message." She lifted a tiny earpiece to his face. "Listen."

Johnsmith held it to his ear. He heard a man's ecstatic voice saying, ". . . the Viking Monument." A pause followed. "The signs have been observed . . . the Ship is on its way . . . gather at the Viking Monument . . ."

"It's on a continuous loop," Johnsmith said, after listening to the message twice more. "It says the Ship is on its way to the Viking Monument."

"Yes." Jethro Pease's eyes were glazed with delight and wonder.

"What is the Viking Monument?" Prudy asked.

Johnsmith stared at her blankly, trying to remember if she had ever spoken to him before, except to order him around. "I think it must mean the monument where the first Viking lander set down almost a hundred years ago."

Nobody spoke for a few seconds, giving Johnsmith time to consider the implications of the message. The Viking Lander Monument as the site of a Viking ship's arrival—a ship that existed only as a fantasy on an archecoded oneiric sphere the size of a ball bearing? Insane.

"Why don't we go see for ourselves?" Frankie said. "It should be easy enough to do."

"Yeah," the pilot said. "There's an automatic guidance program that hits all the touristy spots. The Viking Monument is definitely on the agenda, almost due west in Chryse."

"Then punch it in," Johnsmith said.

Alderdice, Pease, Felicia, and Frankie all looked at him curiously. He assumed that they were responding to his commanding tone, which surprised him, too. Johnsmith had never been a believer in destiny or fate, and yet it now seemed that just such an entity was beckoning.

"Do as he says," said Frankie.

"But how do we know . . . ?" Felicia trailed off.

"We don't know anything," Johnsmith said. "But we don't have anyplace else to go."

Felicia looked frightened and confused, like a little girl who had just walked in on her parents having sex.

"The Ship, the Ship," Jethro Pease chanted. "We're going to see the Ship."

The pilot had finished punching in the coordinates. The whine of the engines changed pitch, and the hijackers were thrown against one another as the carrier pointed to the west.

Johnsmith went back and sat down with his son.

"Where are we going, Dad?" Smitty asked eagerly.

"We're going to see something nobody's ever seen before, Smitty."

"Yeah, what is it?"

"I don't know exactly. Let's just call it the Ship, for now."

"The Ship!" Smitty remembered the onee he had touched in his Dad's effapt, on that sad day when they had come to clean the place out. He didn't know if he should tell his Dad about it, though. After all, he wasn't supposed to use onees, not even by accident. Not even one he found among his Dad's belongings. . . .

"Smitty, there's something happening on Mars. I first got a glimpse of it through an onee, the night before I was drafted."

Smitty couldn't believe it. Here was his Dad, confessing that he had used onees, too. In fact, they might even have used the same one.

"It was a ship," Johnsmith said. "A Viking, or Geatish, ship. I saw it, not knowing that the onee had originated in an illegal plant on Mars. I thought it was just a hallucination, but now I'm beginning to think there's more to it."

"Dad," Smitty whispered, not wanting his mother to hear.

Johnsmith leaned closer to his son.

"Dad, I touched one of those onees, too."

A strange look came over Johnsmith Biberkopf's face. His brow furrowed, and he frowned. But his expression gradually changed. He smiled at Smitty. "Then you know all about it, don't you, son?"

Smitty grinned. It was okay, after all. All the bullshit about onees didn't matter. He and his Dad had both taken them, and they were together now, and it was going to bring them even closer together. Smitty felt like yelling at the top of his lungs, telling everybody in the carrier, everybody on Mars, everybody in the whole frigging solar system.

"This is great, Dad," he said.

"Yeah, it sure is."

They both threw back their heads and laughed, two guys who loved each other, and who shared a very special secret.

Ronindella turned and glared at her husband. "Oh, I hope you're having fun, Johnny," she said. "I just hope you're having a wonderful time subverting your own son, because when they catch up with you, they'll lock you up and throw away the key."

"Maybe so, heart of my heart," Johnsmith said, his

voice dripping with sarcasm, "but I will at least have known something you'll never know."

Ronindella sneered, clearly not interested in what he had to say. "Asshole," she said.

"You think I'm a fool," Johnsmith said. "But the truth is, I've loved someone besides myself, and you never have."

Ronindella turned on him in a rage. "I love God," she snarled.

"That's a convenient excuse for acting with almost complete selfishness," he said calmly. "As long as you can convince yourself that you're closer to God than the rest of us, then you can treat us like shit. Well, I'm not buying that anymore."

"Look who's talking about selfishness," Ronindella screamed. "You lost your job and got drafted, leaving your wife and child to shift for themselves."

"You got almost all the money I've earned on Mars," he said. "And as for losing my job . . . well, at least I had one once."

Ronindella pursed her trembling lips. He had never talked to her like this. What had happened to him? Had he gone totally mad here on Mars? "How dare you speak to me like that?" she said, but the fire was no longer in her.

"I dare to talk like that, because it's the truth. You live here as a Conglom slave for a while, honey, and it makes you see a lot of things clearly that you never saw on Earth."

Smitty was looking up at his Dad admiringly. He had dreamed of a moment like this a thousand times, but he had given up on ever actually seeing it. It was so neat to see his Dad fighting back, telling his Mom off, just as she deserved.

"Please," Representative Silver said. "You really ought to try to be a little more amicable, the both of you."

"Shut up!" Ronindella shrieked at the old man.

"I beg your pardon," Silver said with great dignity.

Ronindella didn't answer. Instead, she turned toward the transparency, and watched Chryse Planitia fly by.

Johnsmith was relieved to see her breast rising and falling in sleep a few minutes later. Ronindella always slept soundly, looking angelic, after battling with him. Well, he was glad to see that she could rest. He certainly couldn't. He should have been enervated and exhausted after the past few days, but he wasn't. He was as fresh as a kid on a summer morning.

The day that Jethro Pease had spoken of was almost here.

TWENTY

THEY SAW THE signs of the Ship long before they reached the Viking Monument. The sky over the desert had darkened and taken on a strange, aqueous quality that Johnsmith had never seen on Mars before. It almost looked as if a thunderstorm were brewing; but that, of course, was downright impossible.

Still, something was happening, and whatever it was, it was something new.

"It's a disjunctive node," Jethro Pease said.

Everyone in the carrier turned to look at him. He sat in a window seat near the front, gazing out at the forbidding, dark sky.

"What did you say, sir?" Representative Silver asked.

"I said it's a disjunctive node," Jethro repeated.

"Might I ask what that means?"

"Sure, you can ask all you want, but I can't really explain it to you."

The Connie Representative shook his head.

"I've heard of it," Frankie Lee Wisbar said. "It's kind of like a bubble in the continuum. If you should wander into one, and the bubble bursts, you'll end up in some other time and place."

"And where did you hear about this wonder of nature?'' Representative Silver asked, trying to sound sarcastic, but looking just a trifle nervous.

''In Arkie training sessions. They taught us that the Conglom wants to harness this thing, but it's bigger than any government. It's kind of a . . . philosophical or . . .''

''. . . or religious thing,'' Silver said, glancing sternly at the daydreaming Jethro Pease. ''But that's all misguided twaddle. If it exists at all, it's nothing more than a natural phenomenon. The human race needs it for the virtually unlimited energy it might provide.''

So that was it, Johnsmith realized. A wonder of nature was to be exploited by the Conglom as a kind of interdimensional, extratemporal power plant.

''We've arrived,'' Frankie Lee Wisbar announced.

The carrier settled down onto the surface, as everyone grabbed a pressure suit and got into it as quickly as possible. Two minutes later, the last of them had climbed out onto the surface and was staring at the Viking Monument, no more than fifty meters to the south. Hundreds of Arkies were clustered a little farther to the west. Their voices created a constant roar in Johnsmith's helmet, as if they were an ocean.

Decades earlier, a transparent cube had been erected around the lander, which stood just a few feet from a big boulder on the rock-strewn plain. It looked like a big tin can on struts, parts wrapped in aluminum foil, with a primitive robot arm protruding from it. On it was fastened a plaque, describing the descent of this first Viking lander way back in 1976.

To the west, the disjunctive node boiled. It wasn't getting larger, but it seemed to be taking on definition, becoming more focused. The longer Johnsmith gazed into its watery depths, the more he thought he understood it . . . though of course he did not understand it at all. He was simply awe stricken. And yet there was a feeling of familiarity stirring in him, a feeling that would not go away. Never a believer in fate, he never-

theless thought that perhaps he had been born to witness what was about to happen.

"Look!" Smitty cried.

Something was taking shape inside the disjunctive
node. It was not clear just what it was, but it was *big*.

"I'm scared," Felicia said.

In spite of everything, Johnsmith put his arm around
her shoulder for a moment. They watched the node
come closer, changing as it moved eastward. The crowd
of Arkies moved on the ground below, following it in
a ragged procession through the Martian desert. Some
of them were chanting. Jethro Pease ran to meet them,
to stand under this miracle . . . or phenomenon, depending on one's point of view.

The rest of the carrier's passengers, the pilot, and the
hijackers, stood by, gazing up in wonder. The disjunctive node was slowly moving toward the Viking Monument with the stateliness of a papal procession.

Now Johnsmith understood why there had been so
much violence, both to the body and spirit. He saw
Representative Silver trembling under the shadow of the
disjunctive node, and knew that nobody in the solar
system had quite been prepared for this.

Except for the Arkies. They had figured it out, where
all the technology of Earth had failed. They had accepted it as a religious experience, and their instincts
had led them here, to bear witness to this sight for the
ages.

"It's just a rain cloud," Ronindella said. "You've
come all this way just to see a rain cloud."

As if rain on Mars would not be any big deal, Johnsmith thought.

"That's no thunderstorm," Felicia argued. "It's the
beginning of a revolution that will sweep through the
entire solar system."

Both of them were wrong, Johnsmith realized. Ronindella, with all her talk of miracles, did not recognize
a genuine miracle when she saw one, and Felicia did

not understand that there was not a political solution for everything. He was saddened by the incompleteness of their respective visions, these two women whom he had loved at different times of his life.

Three carriers appeared, coming from the east. They must have been sent from Elysium, Johnsmith thought. The Conglom had figured it out, and they had doubtless sent Angel Torquemada to save the day.

But this was too big for Angel Torquemada, or anybody else.

More carriers arrived from the north, south, and west. Dozens of them whined, sending up swirls of dust as they descended on Chryse Planitia. The carriers landed, almost simultaneously, all around the monument. Ramps shot out and shock troops sprinted down them and out across the desert.

Particle beam fire outlined the disjunctive node's underside in red; it was so close now. The beam seared the procession of Arkie pilgrims, and four figures dropped to the sand, kicking and twitching in their death throes. Gunfire popped in the thin atmosphere like a string of firecrackers.

The Arkies did not try to defend themselves. They were dying by the dozens, as the Conglom prisoners, driven mad by isolation and trained to kill, ran through them like heated knives through oleomargarine.

It was a slaughter, the Conglom's revenge for the disastrous raid on Olympus. And there was Angel Torquemada, standing outside the nearest carrier, officiating over the massacre like some evil god.

Johnsmith wondered why the troopers hadn't attacked him and his friends first. Perhaps Torquemada feared harming Representative Silver and the other tourists. More likely, he was saving the escapees from Elysium for last.

"That son of a bitch," Felicia said.

Johnsmith turned to see her determined face, just as

she wrenched the pistol out of Frankie's hand and squeezed off three shots.

Angel Torquemada tumbled end over end, finally colliding with the landing strut of one of the carriers. Blood soaked his pressure suit, and he did not move again.

"Good lord," Representative Silver said.

Felicia tossed the gun away. Its arc seemed slightly slower than natural, because of the low gravity, and it clanked dully against a rock when it finally came down.

Angel Torquemada was dead, but it didn't seem to matter to the troops. They were consumed by blood-lust, murdering the Arkies at will. Their war cries mingled with the screams of the wounded and the dying, creating a cacophony of fearsome magnitude.

Johnsmith's helmet radio crackled as the disjunctive node came closer. It was no more than thirty meters away, just over the heads of the Arkies.

Its final shape coalesced. The darkness at its bottom became green, its top half gray. A long shadow cut the gray in two. Suddenly it became clear to Johnsmith just what he was seeing.

It was indeed a huge bubble, just as Frankie had described. Inside it was a large volume of sloshing sea water, and a foggy atmosphere swirled just above the waves.

But it was the thing bisecting the fog that made Johnsmith stare, without blinking, while the battle raged around him.

It was a long ship. In fact, it was *the* Ship, the one he had seen while under the influence of onees. Bearded men pulled at oars, and their triskelion shields hung from the gunwales. They were Vikings.

And the entire spectacle floated not fifteen feet overhead!

The surviving Arkies were following the disjunctive node, gazing up at it fervently. That meant that their attackers were coming nearer to Johnsmith and the vulnerable, little group around him. In a few seconds, they would turn their weapons on those gathered by the hijacked carrier. Smitty might be killed!

There was no time to get aboard the carrier and take off, even if Johnsmith had known how to pilot it. Beam fire was already scorching the sand near them. Prudy was hit in the shoulder. She went down screaming in pain.

Johnsmith grabbed Smitty by the wrist, and yanked him toward the Viking Monument. He leaped, and the Martian gravity enabled him to reach the height of the transparent dome housing the antique lander. Knees bent, he landed squarely on top, but Smitty couldn't keep his footing.

"Dad!" Smitty was dangling by one hand, but Johnsmith pulled him up.

A moment later, they stood together on the monument. A piece of the clear plastic flew away, hit by a bullet. They couldn't stand here any longer.

The disjunctive node was directly overhead.

"Jump, Smitty!" Johnsmith shouted. "Now!"

Together, they leaped upward into the water. Colors shifted prismatically as they entered the disjunctive node, the beam fire's glow distorted by its powerful forces. Their pressure suits were as good as diving gear, and they quickly floated toward the rippling shadow of the long ship above.

Johnsmith never let go of his son, and together they bobbed to the surface.

Men were shouting in a strange language, their voices muffled by Johnsmith's helmet. Did they recognize him and Smitty as humans, dressed as they were in their pressure suits?

Apparently they did, because they extended oars into the water to fish them out.

"Grab hold of that oar, son!" Johnsmith shouted.

Smitty did so, and he was drawn through the foam to the long ship and hauled out of the water by two burly men with yellow beards and braided hair.

A few seconds later, Johnsmith felt powerful hands under his arms, lifting him aboard and setting him on deck.

He unfastened his helmet, tossed it onto the rough planks, threw back his head, and laughed more heartily than he ever had in his life. Helping Smitty with the smaller helmet the tour had provided, he continued laughing as the dour Norsemen eyed him warily.

A huge man stepped forward, like some great, golden bear. Johnsmith put an arm around Smitty's shoulders protectively, so intimidating was the man's sheer physical presence.

But the chief, or king, or whatever he was, clapped his hands onto his enormous belly and laughed even more heartily than Johnsmith and his son had laughed. At that, the other Vikings gathered around them, all laughing. One of them slapped Johnsmith on the back, nearly knocking him over.

They all chattered away in a sing-song, ancient Scandinavian tongue. Johnsmith couldn't understand a word of it. He was relieved that they were friendly, though, and that was enough communication for now.

"Johnsmith Biberkopf," a voice said from behind the Vikings.

"Who's that?" Johnsmith said, incredulous to hear someone speaking his name in this of all places.

The crowd parted as a man dressed in a helmetless pressure suit and metal Viking helmet joined them. Johnsmith couldn't believe his eyes.

"Don't you recognize me? It's Hi—Captain Hi Malker, from North Tel Aviv."

And indeed it was. His beard had grown out, and his hair was long and unkempt, but it was Hi, all right. Johnsmith was speechless for a moment, and then managed to sputter: "Hi . . . how did . . . ?"

"It's a heck of of a story," Hi Malker said. "But it all started that night we had the firefight with the Arkies."

"And you fell right into the disjunctive node?"

"Oh, no." Hi laughed. "I was captured."

"But how did you get here?"

"The bunch that captured me got separated from the main attack force. We wandered around out on the desert for days. We were going to die, and then all of a sudden this incredible thing happened. I don't know what became of the Arkies, but I managed to climb up on a rise and jump into the water, and here I am."

"So the Ship *has* been seen before," Johnsmith said. "No wonder the Arkies were so sure it would happen."

"Yeah, it's been popping up on Mars every now and then," Hi said. "There's a rhythm to it, and you can sort of tell when it's going to happen."

"I know. The Arkies and the Conglom both figured it out."

Hi sobered. "So that's what all that fuss was about."

"It was pretty bad," Johnsmith said. "A lot of people were dying down there."

Hi shook his head. "I got to know those Arkies," he said. "They weren't such bad people. Could have shot me or left me to die out on the desert, but they didn't."

Johnsmith suddenly thought of Frankie, and Felicia, and Alderdice, and even Ronindella. He was overcome with grief to think of them all dying at the hands of the Conglom troopers. They were lost forever, as invisible as the surface of Mars was through the mist and sea water filling the inside of the disjunctive node.

"When are we going to be back on Mars?" Smitty II asked, perhaps thinking of his mother for the first time since they had escaped.

"Not for awhile," Hi said. "We'll probably pop up in this other place next."

"What place is that?" Smitty asked.

"The place where all the monsters are."

TWENTY-ONE

SOMETIMES, AS THEY sailed through a sea of time and space, Johnsmith wondered if the chieftain was actually a cousin of Beowulf. The watery disjunctive node certainly could have passed for the lake where Grendel's mother dwelled. Suppose that these really were the Geats, a tribe of Norsemen who had, after all, vanished from the face of the Earth a thousand years ago, give or take a century or two.

As he strained at an oar, he decided that this might indeed have been what became of the Geats, or at least some of them. He said as much to Hi Malker and Smitty. Hi was at the oar across from Johnsmith, and Smitty was standing on the deck between them.

"I wouldn't know about any of that," said Hi. "But I see no reason why it can't be true."

"Yeah," Smitty agreed. "The fantastic part is that we're here at all, Dad."

Johnsmith laughed. He was happier than he'd been in a long time. If only he knew what had become of Frankie and the others. Poor Alderdice was probably dead or in solitary confinement by now, unless he could convince them that he'd been taken as a hostage—which was what had really happened, when you got right down to it.

The Geats (as Johnsmith now thought of them, whether his theory was correct or not) were taciturn most of the time. Every once in a while their chieftain, Hygelac, would bellow orders at his gangers, and they would silently obey. Angel Torquemada had never been nearly so commanding a presence. Even so, Johnsmith suspected that Hygelac had not been born with so prestigious a name, the same as the giant Geatish king who had lived in the time before Beowulf and the nasty business at Hrothgar's mead hall, Heorot. If you wanted to be a leader, a bit of showmanship never hurt. Why not name yourself after a hero?

"When are we gonna see the monsters, Hi?" Smitty asked.

Hi grinned. "Well, I don't know much about them. Just what I've picked up from the guys here."

"You understand what they're saying, don't you?"

"A little bit, after all this time. They talk about the place where the monsters are quite often."

"Well, Hi, maybe they're speaking symbolically," Johnsmith said. "Here there be tigers—that sort of thing."

"I guess they could be," Hi allowed. "But they seem pretty serious about it."

"Do you think we'll ever get back to Mars?" Johnsmith asked.

"Maybe. I know these guys have been there several times."

"How about Earth?"

"They haven't got back there yet. It's as if Earth is a little out of the loop most of the time, and can only be reached rarely, whereas they pop up on Mars fairly often."

Johnsmith nodded. He stared off into the foggy darkness surrounding them on all sides, and remembered Ronindella's preacher talking about Limbo. At the moment, there was nothing beyond the few thousand gallons of water and the canopy of misty oxygen overhead, nothing at all. "I wish that the node would pop into existence somewhere," he said. "Anywhere."

"Yes, it does tend to get on your nerves after awhile," Hi agreed. "It's such a tenuous life."

"Where does the air come from, Dad?" Smitty asked.

"I haven't the faintest idea," Johnsmith admitted. "But it never seems to run out."

"See that scum floating on the water?" Hi said. "Maybe it's photosynthesizing."

"There's no sunlight," Smitty said.

Hi shrugged.

"I think this disjunctive node is in stasis," Johnsmith said. "It never changes in here, a little piece of Earth as it was hundreds and hundreds of years ago."

"It's not part of Earth anymore," Hi said.

The Norseman in front of Johnsmith turned and offered a half-eaten bowl of *lutfisk* to eat. He grinned, revealing his missing front teeth without self-consciousness. Johnsmith still couldn't understand what he was saying, but had figured out that the guy's name was Snorri.

The *lutfisk* wasn't very appetizing. Not only had Snorri eaten half of it, but it didn't smell very fresh, either. Nevertheless, Johnsmith ate some of it. The only food they could get was the flesh of unknown fish that the Geats provided. At least they shared their food.

In fact, the Geats were generous in many respects. They had given Smitty a helmet, which fit awkwardly over his head, obscuring all but his chin and mouth. He looked comical, but he seemed to enjoy wearing it. He thought he was the terror of the seven seas, no doubt. Well, it was a healthy life for a boy here. In spite of the mystery surrounding the atmosphere they breathed, the air seemed clean and fresh.

"Dad," Smitty asked, peering off into the mist, "I've been wondering about something."

"What's that, son?"

"Why do you have to row this boat?"

"Well, from what I can gather, there's a danger we might slip right out of the node if we don't. Fortunately, the node's not moving very fast, but it is *always* moving."

"What would happen if we slipped out?"

"I don't know . . . and I don't think I want to know."

"There's nothing out there," Hi Malker said. "Not even the vacuum of space. I don't see how we could exist outside the node, except when we pop up on some other world that'll support our kind of life."

"Oh." Smitty ran off, down the deck and back again, playing as children will do even in the strangest of circumstances.

When Johnsmith thought about what Hi had just said, he saw a logical flaw. If they didn't know what was outside the bubble, how could they be sure that it wouldn't support human life? Admittedly, he wasn't about to dive down and find out, but it was an intriguing question. Rowing gave him plenty of time for rumination, much more than he had ever managed while sitting in his cubicle at the University. It was good exercise, too, something that he had come to appreciate since he'd been sentenced to Elysium . . . whenever and wherever the disjunctive node existed in relation to that time and place.

"Aoogah!" a startled warning cry sounded. The Geats grabbed their spears and shields, while Hygelac stood near the dragon prow, gazing into the fog with broadsword in hand.

"What is it, Dad?" Smitty said.

There was no time to answer him. The ugliest creature Johnsmith had ever seen in his entire life had emerged from the surf, foam streaming down its squamous neck.

"It's a monster!" Smitty cried, answering his own question.

The Geats were stabbing at the thing with their spears while shouting Nordic oaths, and Hygelac hacked away at it with powerful swipes of his sword. The monster's eyes, which ringed its huge maw in a most unsightly fashion, shifted from one man to another, as if it were trying to decide which one to eat first. As its long neck leaned forward, the head actually slithered aboard the long ship, its dozens of eyes peering about curiously.

With one mighty stroke, Hygelac decapitated it. Or nearly so—the head hung by a thin string of tissue as black fluid gouted out of the neck stump.

The monster's hideous mouth worked, but no sound came forth. Apparently, the vocal chords had been severed. As the neck began to sink back into the water, Hygelac sliced off the string connecting head and body.

The huge head thudded onto the rough planks of the deck. The mouth and eyes quivered for a few seconds, and then were still. Hygelac stood astride his trophy, shouting his war cry to any other monsters who might be about.

"Wow!" Smitty said. "Did you see that?"

Johnsmith nodded, unable to speak. It had all happened so quickly that he wouldn't have believed it, were the monster's head not lying in plain sight, still oozing some foul fluid. It smelled very bad. The Geats impaled the still quivering head with three spears and proudly propped it up near the dragon head.

"Smitty," Hi Malker said, "do you remember what you asked me? About when we'd be getting to the monster place?"

"Yeah."

"We're there now. That's why they're displaying the head, I think. As a kind of challenge to the other monsters."

Through the mist, an alien world appeared. In it were dripping stone warrens, where twisted shapes crawled or pulsated; and bubbling pools with sinuous shapes moved just beneath the surface. The entire spectacle was dimly lit by some pale, wet fire.

The long ship's keel almost skimmed the surface of this strange place, or so it seemed to Johnsmith. He was very frightened of what he saw: the hellish environment went on for as far as the eye could see; hundreds of monsters thrived here, perhaps thousands. They were of every imaginable shape and size, and many of them were lifting misshapen heads to watch the disjunctive node pass over. Some of the larger ones, able to reach the node's watery bottom curve, moved toward the Ship.

"God, I wish I had a weapon," Hi said.

"Maybe there are some in the hold," Smitty said. "Hygelac got my helmet down there."

"Smart," Johnsmith said.

While the Geats leaned over the side and made threatening gestures at the monsters with their spears, Hi and Johnsmith were tugging at the heavy wooden cover of the hold. They threw it aside, and Smitty jumped down to see what was stored there.

After a moment, he hollered something indistinguishable over the Geatish shouts.

"What did you say, son?" Johnsmith could see him faintly, as Smitty bent to uncover something wrapped in furs.

"I said, wait'll you see what's down here, Dad!"

"Can you hand it up to us?"

"I think so."

Smitty struggled with something that looked as if it were made of metal. A harpoon of some kind? Johnsmith reached down to take it, finding it much lighter than he expected.

"Jesus," said Hi Malker. His eyes were open wider than Johnsmith had ever seen them.

There was good reason for Hi's amazement. Johnsmith was cradling a particle beam cannon.

"Where do you suppose they got that?" Hi said. "Come on, let's see if it works."

"It couldn't possibly," Johnsmith said. "Could it? I mean, the power supply has got to be worn down."

"What about these?" Smitty's grinning face appeared in the hold. He was brandishing three power packs.

"Let's slap one of those babies on," Hi said. "And then we'll see if any of those ugly bastards comes near this boat."

It was only a matter of seconds before the power pack was fastened to the cannon. Johnsmith switched it on, and an azure light appeared on the stock, indicating that it was ready for firing.

"All right!" Smitty exulted.

"Clear a path, you Vikings!" Hi shouted.

Johnsmith carried the particle beam cannon toward the bow. He stood next to the puzzled Hygelac, whose leathery face frowned down at him from a lordly seven foot height.

"Maybe I should let him shoot the damn thing," Johnsmith said. "After all, he's the boss around here."

But it was clear that Hygelac didn't think it would work. He must have known what it could do, though, because he pointed to the monsters and shook his head. Perhaps he had used it until the power supply wore down, not understanding why it no longer worked.

Several of the monsters had now swum into the disjunctive node and were surrounding the ship.

"He doesn't understand that you've fired it up," Hi said. "Let one of those monsters out there have it, and then old Hygelac'll get the idea."

Johnsmith carefully balanced the particle beam cannon next to the dragon prow, letting it rest on the curving wood of the gunwale. The creatures in the water were bolder now, many of them circling and showing their hideous, otherworldly selves. Bracing his right foot against a futtock, Johnsmith fired the cannon.

"Neat, Dad!" Smitty said, jumping up and down in his excitement.

The Geats gasped as the crimson, pencil-thin beam cut through the fog, searing a bristling appendage off a creature that looked part insect, part seal. It howled in pain—a sibilant, piercing noise—and dropped back into the water.

Feeling a high degree of excitement, Johnsmith swung the cannon around, burning through the flabby, tentacled body of a cephalopodesque thing with malevolently intelligent eyes. It made no sound, but Johnsmith saw the life go out of its eyes as it sank out of sight.

Hygelac slapped him on the back, knocking the wind out of him. The Geatish chieftain gestured at the cannon with his immense right hand, and Johnsmith reluctantly turned it over to him. Killing the aliens had been a good deal more pleasurable than Johnsmith wanted it to be.

Hygelac fumbled with the firing mechanism for a moment. As soon as Johnsmith pointed it out to him, he remembered how to fire it, grinned, and squeezed the trigger, watching the beam pierce the fog. He swung it almost as wildly as his broadsword, picking it up from the gunwale and firing from the hip while whooping his war cry. The beam left a boiling wake as it swept through the surf.

After a few bursts, he winged a creature that flipped up out of the water and glided toward them on glistening folds of skin, like some nightmare bat. The flying thing went down, screeching as it plummeted into the waves like a World War One biplane. Those on deck were showered with salt spray.

"Way to go, Hygelac!" Smitty clapped his hands with glee.

No other monsters came near the Ship after the amphibious flying creature was killed. Their hoary backs showed as they dived deep, escaping before any more of them were slaughtered.

Hygelac looked disappointed. The bloodlust was clearly upon him, and he didn't like to stop killing—especially with a weapon of such potency in his hands.

The Geats were all admiring him, commenting on the massacre in their ancient language. Their inflections sounded more like Icelandic than Danish, Johnsmith thought, but he really didn't know much about those languages. He didn't even know that much about English. All he could think about was the heady experience of cutting a gooey swath through these monsters.

Hygelac was saying something to him. Johnsmith shrugged to show that he didn't understand. Hygelac turned to his warriors and shouted a few words at them, which Johnsmith recognized as a command to man the oars. He went back to his place on the bench behind Snorri's sweating back, and began to pull with the others. Smitty sat beside him, grasping the end of the oar with his small hands to help his father.

Hygelac barked more orders as he hefted the cannon with his muscular arms. He was making them row faster and faster. But why?

And then Johnsmith saw what the Geatish chieftain was up to. They were rowing the Ship more swiftly than the disjunctive node was moving through this strange world. Soon they would be at the node's edge, and then they would fall off!

Johnsmith stopped rowing, but nobody objected. They all shipped their oars a moment later, and the ornately carved dragon's head prow drifted toward the edge.

This couldn't be happening! Johnsmith thought of Smitty's tender flesh being torn apart by those monsters below, and he charged toward the port end of the Ship.

"Hygelac!" he screamed. "What are you doing?"

But Hygelac waved him away and concentrated on

watching the edge of the disjunctive node. It was a dark, cloudy curve in front of him as the Ship drifted ever closer.

Johnsmith stood on the deck, aware now that it was too late. He knew that if he continued to make a fuss, the gangers would hold him down and cut his lungs out, a common Norse punishment for cowardice. Besides, they would be toppling into the monsters' world any second now. He watched silently as the Ship sailed toward oblivion. But just a few meters from the end, Hygelac grunted something in his guttural tongue, and all of the gangers on the starboard side dipped their oars in the water.

The Ship banked, sending Johnsmith reeling. He fell to his knees painfully as the Ship's port side skirted the very edge of the disjunctive node.

Cackling like a madman, Hygelac pointed the particle beam cannon at the creatures who peered up at him. He cut them down like Thor tossing thunderbolts at his enemies. His gangers cheered him on as he killed monster after monster, alien bodily fluids rushing out as alien skin was burned away in neat slices. Hygelac was having a field day.

"Wow!" Smitty shouted. "He's great. He's the Geat with the heat!"

At that moment, the top of the node opened like an enormous iris.

TWENTY-TWO

"WHAT THE HELL is going on?" Johnsmith asked in a perfectly calm voice.

Nobody answered him. They were all too busy gawking up, as the opening at the top of the disjunctive node widened, to pay attention to questions for which they had no answers.

A gigantic shape loomed in the nothingness beyond the opening. It was bifurcated, like a wishbone—but it would have had to come from a turkey the size of an Interplan ship.

The two pointed ends of the intruding object seized the sides of the Ship. The oarsmen were heaved into one another as the entire vessel was lifted out of the water by the gargantuan tweezers.

"Dad!" Smitty screamed.

Johnsmith put his arms around Smitty to protect him, and they passed through the dome of the disjunctive node into yet another world.

The Ship was set on a vast, perfectly flat plain. It should have listed, but it didn't; the deck was level. They looked around in silence. Other than a few perpendicular shapes decorating the stark landscape, there was nothing much to see. The place was clean and still, its color metallic, its few features decorative rather than natural. The two-pronged device that had plucked them out of the monsters' world was nowhere to be seen.

"Where are we, Hi?" Johnsmith asked.

Hi shrugged. "I've never been here before."

"Maybe Hygelac can tell us," Smitty suggested.

Hi tried to find out what Hygelac knew, gesticulating and using the few Geatish words he had picked up since he had been aboard the Ship.

"He thinks he's gone to Valhalla," Hi said. "He's certain that we must all have died in battle, and now we're about to meet Odin."

"Dad!" Smitty pointed to a tiny dot on the horizon.

Everyone watched as the dot shimmered and grew larger. It took on the shape of a man. When Johnsmith realized just who it was, he jumped over the side and ran across the cushiony ground toward him.

"Dad!" Johnsmith shouted. "Dad! What are you doing here?"

It was indeed his father, dead twenty years and yet alive, who Johnsmith saw. The same thinning hair, the slight paunch, the business vacutites—there could be no doubt that it was Harald Biberkopf.

Johnsmith stopped running just before he reached his father. They did not embrace; that had never been their way. They did, however, smile at each other.

"Dad," Johnsmith said breathlessly, "it's sure good to see you."

"Good to see you, too, Johnny." The voice was just as Johnsmith remembered it, refined but not stuffy. His father had been a man who read books. Real books. He had been considered a crackpot by his neighbors, but that had never bothered him.

"How did you get here?" Johnsmith asked. "I mean . . . "

"I know what you mean. I died when I was only forty-five. As you can see, though, death isn't the end."

"But you were cremated."

"True, but that was only a body, while my essence—

soul, if you like—rattled around out in the cosmos until there was some use for me. It was easy for them to recreate my body.''

"Them?''

"I'm talking about the ones who are really running things," Harald Biberkopf said. "Gods, maybe, or superintelligent aliens. I guess it all depends on how you look at it."

"I see." Then maybe Hygelac was right. Maybe this *was* Valhalla, in a very real sense. And maybe it was heaven for him and Smitty.

"I want you to meet your grandson," Johnsmith said. "He's right over there."

But when he turned around to point at the Ship, it had vanished.

"Where are they?" he asked, beginning to panic.

"Don't worry," his father said, withdrawing a cigar from his breast pocket. "They're safe."

"But Smitty . . ."

"You'll see him again. By the way, do you have a match?"

"No."

Harald looked bemused. He put the cigar away and said: "All this killing is very bad."

"You mean those monsters back there?" Johnsmith said. "But they were attacking."

"What nonsense. They were just curious."

"They surrounded the ship!"

"Well, they're stuck in that place, most of them for the rest of their lives. Any diversion will do. They didn't know how vicious those Vikings are." He looked at Johnsmith sternly. "But son, I'm a little disappointed in you. I never thought you'd turn out to be a killer."

"Dad . . ." But what could he say? He had enjoyed himself, blasting away at them with the particle beam cannon. He felt a deep shame now.

"Well, the Conglom has trained you for violence," his father said. "But it's over now."

"You mean I'll never have to go back to Mars, or that place where the monsters are?"

"That's right. By the way, son, do you know why those so-called monsters are in that place?"

So-called? Johnsmith remembered that the monsters made themselves scarce after the shooting started. "No. Why? What is that place?" he asked.

"It's an asylum. You were killing harmless mental patients."

"Oh, no!" He had been butchering troubled, intelligent beings. How would he ever live it down? But perhaps there was a historical precedent. Had Grendel been a patient who swam through the disjunctive node and ended up in Denmark during the Dark Ages, only to be killed by a savage Geat in a strange, new world?

"Anyhow," Harald went on, "the beings who run things were pretty upset with you and your friends going on a killing spree, especially in a place where the inmates need peace and quiet more than anything."

"Jesus." Johnsmith shook his head "I didn't know. It's a heavy responsibility to bear."

"Yes, it is. Which brings us to your wife. What do you want to do about her?"

"Then she's still alive?"

"In a manner of speaking."

Johnsmith refrained from asking what that comment meant.

"Well," Harald asked again, "have you decided what you want to do with Ronindella?"

"How come it's up to me?" Johnsmith said, temporizing.

"Because this is *your* universe," his Dad said.

"My universe? I don't get it."

"Ontologically speaking, this whole adventure could have started when you were under the influence of an onee. Maybe even your first onee experience."

"Do you mean to tell me that I've just imagined all of this? That it's all one long hallucination?"

"Possibly."

Johnsmith's mind reeled. If he was hallucinating, then all he had to do was disengage the onee from his nervous system by dropping it. He looked down at his hands, seeing that there was nothing in them. In fact, he was still wearing his pressure suit, with its heavy gloves. "But I'm not using an onee," he said.

"How do you know what?" Harald asked. "You could be hallucinating that you're not holding one, while you're actually under the influence."

"Yeah, I guess I could." Johnsmith felt despondent. Out of all the universes he could have created, why did he have to live in one that was so depressing?

"So what about Ronindella," his Dad asked.

"Oh, let her get married to Ryan."

"Ryan's working in a lunar pit. You had him sent there, because you were angry at him."

"Did I?" Come to think of it, he had dreamed about Ryan being sent to Luna. "Well, let them both go back to Earth and get married. They deserve each other."

Harald nodded sagely. "And Felicia?"

"Let her marry Alderdice," Johnsmith said, feeling malicious.

"That's a good idea," Harald said. "Better than you might realize. Of course, one of them will have to get a sex change. I think it would be best if it was Felicia. Her hormonal imbalance will improve."

"Can you get Hi a new Interplan ship?"

"No problem."

"What about the Geats?" Johnsmith asked.

His Dad grinned. "We'll send them to Valhalla."

"Good."

"Anybody else you care about?"

"That leaves only Smitty II and Frankie," Johnsmith said. "I'd like to have them with me."

"Fine. Where do you want to live?"

Johnsmith thought it over. "Not on Earth, because

the planet is too far gone. Not on Mars, either . . . and Luna and the Belt are out of the question.''

"You aren't restricted to the solar system. You can have any world you want.''

"In the whole galaxy?" Johnsmith was incredulous.

"I told you they run the whole thing." Harald shrugged. "Or maybe you do. In either case, you can have any world in any galaxy. You can make up a new one, if you like.''

"Fantastic!" But he couldn't seem to decide what kind of world he wanted.

Harald looked at his watch. It was a purely symbolic gesture, of course, since time no longer had any meaning.

"Okay, Dad," Johnsmith said. "I'll leave it up to you. Surprise me.''

"You're sure you don't want to pick one out?"

"Yeah, I'm sure.''

"All right, then." Harald Biberkopf turned and walked away, receding in size with unnatural rapidity.

"Dad, come back," Johnsmith called after him. Their visit was too short. Way too short.

"Can't, son. I've got to go see your brother." His voice was distant. "So long.''

He was soon a shimmering point on the horizon. And then he vanished.

"Dad . . ." Johnsmith stared at the place where his father had winked out of existence. He felt tears come to his eyes at the thought of his brother existing somewhere in the continuum. He hadn't seen Eddie in twenty-one years. He wanted to see him now, wearing his spit and polish Conglom Marines uniform, but he supposed that he'd have to be patient. All things were possible, so maybe he'd bump into Eddie sooner or later.

But where would he go now? What would he do? He sat down on the soft ground and thought about all he'd been through, and all he had learned.

Unable to keep his eyes open, Johnsmith decided not to fight his exhaustion. As he dozed, the brave new world where he had talked to his dead father faded.

He was awakened by birdsong. Slowly, he opened his eyes. He saw a naked boy playing in the gentle surf of an ocean. Slowly, Johnsmith realized that he wasn't wearing any clothing, either. A mild sun warmed the sand cradling his body. It was not Sol, the sun of Earth, but it was similar. It seemed a little more orange, but its rays felt good, not harmful . . . nurturing.

Sitting up, he looked around. A slender, smiling woman was coming toward him, her hips swaying gently as she passed through the shade of a violet tree. She carried a straw basket full of fish, crustaceans, and berries. He had never seen her naked in the light before, though he knew her lovely body intimately. She came and sat next to him in the sand, and it seemed as though this pleasant life had been going on forever.

"He picked a good world," Johnsmith said.

"Who?" Frankie asked.

Of course, she didn't understand what he was talking about. This was *his* world, and Frankie wouldn't know about his meeting with his father. It was just as well. The memory was already drifting away. "I was just talking to myself, I guess."

Smitty II came running out of the surf. He was carrying a strange mollusk that was indigenous to this world, and he showed it off to Johnsmith and Frankie.

Frankie smiled and tousled the boy's damp hair.

"That's great, son," Johnsmith said. And he meant it, too.

They made a fire at sunset. While they were cooking their sea food, Johnsmith looked out over the sea, where blue and green curved onto a scarlet horizon. For the merest moment, he thought he saw a ship . . . a long ship with an ornately carved dragon prow.

"Is something wrong?" Frankie asked.

"No, I guess not," he said after a moment.

He turned away from the sea and put his arms around his loved ones, kissing them both before they all sat down in the sand to eat.

ARTHUR C. CLARKE'S VENUS PRIME

by Paul Preuss

VOLUME 1: BREAKING STRAIN   75344-8/$3.95 US/$4.95 CAN
Her code name is Sparta. Her beauty veils a mysterious past and
abilities of superhuman dimension, the product of advanced
biotechnology.

VOLUME 2: MAELSTROM   75345-6/$3.95 US/$4.95 CAN
When a team of scientists is trapped in the gaseous inferno of
Venus, Sparta must risk her life to save them.

VOLUME 3: HIDE AND SEEK   75346-4/$3.95 US/$4.95 CAN
When the theft of an alien artifact, evidence of extraterrestrial
life, leads to two murders, Sparta must risk her life and identity
to solve the case.

VOLUME 4: THE MEDUSA ENCOUNTER
75348-0/$3.95 US/$4.95 CAN
Sparta's recovery from her last mission is interrupted as she sets
out on an interplanetary investigation of her host, the Space
Board.

VOLUME 5: THE DIAMOND MOON
75349-9/$3.95 US/$4.95 CAN
Sparta's mission is to monitor the exploration of Jupiter's moon,
Amalthea, by the renowned Professor J.Q.R. Forester.

**Each volume features a special technical infopak,
including blueprints of the structures of *Venus Prime***

PRESENTING THE ADVENTURES OF

BY HARRY HARRISON

BILL, THE GALACTIC HERO
00395-3/$3.95 US/$4.95 Can

He was just an ordinary guy named Bill, a fertilizer operator from a planet of farmers. Then a recruiting robot shanghaied him with knockout drops, and he came to in deep space, aboard the Empire warship *Christine Keeler*

BILL, THE GALACTIC HERO: THE PLANET OF ROBOT SLAVES
75661-7/$3.95 US/$4.95 Can

BILL, THE GALACTIC HERO: ON THE PLANET OF BOTTLED BRAINS
75662-5/$3.95 US/$4.95 Can
(co-authored by Robert Sheckley)

BILL, THE GALACTIC HERO: ON THE PLANET OF TASTELESS PLEASURE
75664-1/$3.95 US/$4.95 Can
(co-authored by David Bischoff)

BILL, THE GALACTIC HERO: ON THE PLANET OF ZOMBIE VAMPIRES
75665-X/$3.95 US/$4.95 Can
(co-authored by Jack C. Haldeman II)

THE CONTINUATION
OF THE FABULOUS
INCARNATIONS OF IMMORTALITY
SERIES

PIERS ANTHONY

FOR LOVE OF EVIL
75285-9/$4.95 US/$5.95 Can

AND ETERNITY
75286-7/$4.95 US/$5.95 Can